All Played Out

Also by Cora Carmack

All Broke Down

All Lined Up

Seeking Her (Novella)

Finding It

Keeping Her (Novella)

Faking It

Losing It

ALL
PLAYED OUT

A RUSK UNIVERSITY NOVEL

Cora Carmack

WILLIAM MORROW
An Imprint of HarperCollins*Publishers*

HarperCollins books may be purchased for educational, business, or sales promotional use. For information please e-mail the Special Markets Department at SPsales@harpercollins.com.

FIRST EDITION

Library of Congress Cataloging-in-Publication Data has been applied for.

ISBN 978-0-06-232624-9

15 16 17 18 19   DIX/RRD   10 9 8 7 6 5 4 3 2 1

For the Make-out Bandit—
You know who you are.
Thanks for all the non-making-out things you do.

All Played Out

Chapter 1

Nell's To-Do List

- Finish studying for adv. biomech.
- Buy more coffee. Lots of coffee.

There's a half-naked man in my kitchen.

Well, honestly, he's more like 90 percent naked with just a pair of black boxer briefs that fit *very* snugly. So snugly in fact that I'm going to round up to 95 percent naked. I make an inelegant squeaking noise, and he starts to turn. Hastily, I try to step back into the shadows of the hallway, but my flip-flop catches funny on the carpet, and I end up dumping all of the books in my arms instead. A big one lands square on my toe, and I grunt while the rest tumble and splay half open at my feet. I close my eyes against the pain in my foot for a few moments, and when I open them again, Naked Man is there in front of me, and he's just so . . . *naked*.

He's got messy, golden brown hair that falls artfully around his face, and in an attempt not to look him in the eye, I drop to my knees to start gathering my books. But then, instead of looking him in the eye, I'm awkwardly looking him in the groin.

"Here, let me help." His voice is deep, and *too close*, as he kneels beside me. I make a mad dash to pick up my things, and I get everything but my notes spiral. That's already in his grip, and he holds it out to me.

"You must be Antonella," he says.

I'm glad he said it because I'm not sure I would have been able to remember in the face of all that skin.

"Yeah, that's me."

A door opens in the hallway, spilling light toward us, and I hear my roommate call out, "Silas?"

I look back, and Dylan is rubbing sleepily at her eyes, a Rusk football shirt falling to the middle of her thighs. She sees me and blinks, then looks past me to her boyfriend.

"Silas! Where are your clothes?"

He smirks at her, and the look he gives her is smoldering and *so* better left in private.

"You're wearing most of them."

Dylan slips around me, and she looks like she's trying to shove Silas back toward her room, but he doesn't budge. She blows out an exasperated breath. "Sorry, Nell. I didn't hear him get up, or I would have made him put on some clothes."

"You could give me my shirt back now." He grins. "If you're really that concerned."

She swats him, and the smack of flesh draws a ridiculous blush to my cheeks.

"Silas, stop it. You're going to embarrass her more than you already have."

"It's six in the morning. I didn't think anyone else would be up."

I shrug, not that either of them is looking at me anymore. "I have a test today in biomech. Gonna cram in a little bit more studying this morning," I say, giving the explanation for which neither of them asked.

She shoves Silas back toward her door, and this time he moves, catching her wrists and pulling her with him.

"Silas." She drags his name out like she's complaining, but she doesn't put up much of a fight when he wraps her in his arms.

Over her shoulder, she calls out, "He'll be gone in two minutes. I promise."

"Fifteen," Silas counters.

"Five."

"Twenty."

"*Five*, Silas."

He groans, and then Dylan's bedroom door closes with a quiet *snick*.

I breathe out slowly, and press my warm cheek against my shoulder since my hands are full. I can only hope that I just turned a subtle pink instead of my usual glaring red.

Doubtful.

I cross to the living room sofa, and dump my books down on

the coffee table. The pages of a few are bent and folded from the fall, and I spend a few moments righting them. When you find yourself wanting to apologize and soothe a book, that's when you *know* you're a nerd.

Back in her room, I hear Dylan squeal and shout, "Silas, don't!"

Judging by the few thumps and then silence that follows, I'm betting Dylan didn't win that particular battle.

I open my notes spiral and pick up the course textbook for my test this morning. The pages of the book are marked with sticky notes (because writing in books is pretty much my definition of evil). The notes have my thoughts and questions crammed into the smallest handwriting I could manage. I flip to where I left off studying last night, and then search for the corresponding chapter in the textbook, but even when I find it, I can't seem to focus on the words in front of me.

My head is back in that bedroom that's not even mine. Not in a creepy way, but just . . . curious. I've known Dylan for over two years now, lived with her half that time, and I saw her on plenty of occasions with her long-term boyfriend before Silas, but now . . . things are different. With her ex, I'd never really felt like I was intruding on intimate moments. But now there's a hallway and a door between us, and I still feel like I'm too close.

I should have known based on how little I've seen Dylan so far this semester and the way she talks about him that this new guy is different, but even so, I never would have been able to predict the palpable chemistry between them. I think back to the moment when he pulled her into his arms. I'm not really one for emotional displays, and I don't think I'm prone to jealousy, but looking at them was like flying too close to the sun. Like their gravitational pull is strong enough to disrupt everything around them, including my ability to concentrate.

I didn't know that there actually were relationships like that. I'd thought it all some gross overexaggeration by writers and movie studios and marketing executives looking to cash in on people's gullible need for affection. I live in a world of facts and figures and equations, but Silas and Dylan . . . as hard as it is to admit, something about them goes beyond logic. Together, they're greater than the sum of their parts.

I suppose it's a good thing that I'm graduating early, in about two months, to be precise. Because my instincts tell me I'd be looking for a new roommate soon if I weren't.

It's twenty-one minutes before Dylan's bedroom door opens, and the two of them return, fully dressed with hair damp from what I'm guessing was a shared shower. My roommate looks sheepish, and the wicked look on her boyfriend's face makes me think of my nonna's lectures about the tempting beauty of Lucifer.

Somehow I don't think Dylan would appreciate me comparing Silas to Satan, even if the strict Catholic upbringing I received in my family didn't quite take with me.

I keep my head down and focused on my books as the two of them say good-bye at the door. There are some definite kissing noises, a few giggles, and a low murmur of words I'm glad I can't hear. I should be able to ignore them, but for a reason I can't quite identify, I'm hyperaware of the two of them wrapped up together in my peripheral vision.

Even when the door closes and Silas is long gone, there's still a strange otherness in the room, like their relationship leaves behind specters to taunt single people with their glowing happiness. It doesn't help that Dylan is still leaning against the door, her eyes sort of glazed over and her lips lifted in a smile. Huh. That must be what really good sex looks like. *Note to self.*

"So . . ." I say. "That seems . . . serious."

She floats over to the couch so serenely, I actually check to make sure her feet are on the ground. She sits next to me and pulls her legs up onto the couch to wrap her arms around her knees.

"It is. It *really* is."

"And you don't think that's fast?" I ask. They'd only known each other for a few months, and they had been kind of together but kind of not. Then they had some kind of split at the beginning of the school year before they worked things out. As far as I can tell, they've only officially been together for around two weeks.

She laughs. "Oh, it's incredibly fast. But it was never going to be any other way with him. He's an all-or-nothing kind of guy."

"And you're good with . . . *all?*"

Dylan's eyes meet mine, and something twists in my stomach. Maybe I am a little bit envious. But not of the guy or even the relationship . . . more of the ability to have such a relationship. After a few completely bland liaisons over the years, I've decided that I just don't have that thing in me that lets people fall in love.

Nonna says I'm picky. Dad says I'm stubborn. Mom thinks I just need someone who's as smart as I am.

I say I'm better equipped for ideas than emotions.

I can't picture myself in a satisfying relationship, period, let alone one that forms and flourishes in a matter of weeks. If I were Dylan, the prospect of *all* would freak me out.

"I can't really put it into words," she says. "At least not ones that don't sound cliché, but I'm okay with choosing it all with Silas because not to do so feels like I'm wasting time. I don't know, being with him just feels . . . inevitable. In the best way. And to slow things down or box them in just doesn't feel natural, you know?"

I nod my head even though I do not, in fact, *know*.

"I am sorry, though," she continues, "about not giving you a heads-up before bringing him over. You stayed so late at the library, and there were a bunch of people at his house, so we came over here for some privacy. We both meant for him to leave, but we fell asleep. I promise I'm not going to turn into one of those roommates who practically moves in their significant other."

I nod again, and I believe her. Dylan is a fantastic roommate, and she has a tendency to put all others above herself . . . to a fault.

"How about I make you breakfast as an apology? Brain food and all that jazz."

"You don't have to do that."

"It's not a big deal. I was going to make something for me anyway. I'll just make extra."

She stands and lopes off to the kitchen. I should leave it at that and get back to my studying, but there's something bugging me, and I can't resist the urge to dig a little. Curiosity and cats and all that jazz. Following Dylan, I lean on the wall just outside the kitchen and watch as she pulls out pans, bacon, eggs, and utensils.

"You seem different," I say. "Happier. Not that you seemed sad before, but . . ." I trail off, not exactly sure *what* she was before. She'd always appeared perfectly content, intelligent, outgoing even. From the outside, her life had looked damn near perfect. So either there was something I didn't know, or this Silas guy is the superhero version of a boyfriend.

Or again . . . maybe the sex really is *that good*. Perhaps she's just drowning in an overabundance of endorphins.

"I am happy. Happier." She grins to herself as she sets about cooking breakfast. "Have you ever been certain you knew something only to be proven completely wrong?"

I think for a moment. "Not in recent memory, no. I don't usually think in terms of certainties until I've tested a theory multiple times."

"I'm not talking about science or math, Nell. I mean . . . about yourself. Have you ever thought one thing about your life only to change your mind?"

"There was a period in middle school where I thought white eyeliner was flattering."

She laughs. And I'm glad for it because her words don't sit right in my stomach. Because there *is* something I've been questioning lately. Or more accurately, stubbornly refusing to allow myself to question even when I want to.

"Suffice it to say," she continues, "I thought I could be happy living just with my head as a guide. That if I made other people happy and accomplished my goals, that would fulfill me. But I never dreamed how much I was missing out until my heart got involved. It's the little things . . . like going to Silas's games and attending parties and meeting new people and acting spontaneously. I feel like I wasted the last two years of college trying to grow up too fast, and now I'm playing catch-up."

I frown. "If you've wasted the last two years, what does that say about me?"

I'd put my time to good use. Not many people our age can say they're going to graduate college after only two and a half years. Granted, I came in with a ton of hours from AP tests and summer courses and the like, but no one could say I squandered my time here.

I'd meant the question rhetorically, but when she remains silent with her gaze carefully directed away, I reconsider my words.

"You think I *am* wasting my time?"

Her reply is slow and careful. "I think that you and I were a lot alike."

"Were?"

"Are. You and I, we both have a tendency to focus on achievements, on checking items and goals off a list. And what I'm realizing is that living isn't about what you achieve, but how you achieve it. We've both moved full speed ahead toward the things we want, but I know I hadn't lived enough to really know what I wanted. In fact, I was spectacularly wrong about most of it."

"And you think I'm wrong, too?"

Damn. Those questions I'm not allowing myself to formulate? It's a lot harder not to ask them when someone is basically asking them for you.

"No, I'm not saying that. I can't know that. Only you can." She pauses, and her gaze is speculative. "All I'm saying is college is a time to experiment. If you were trying to solve some equation or test a theory, you wouldn't only look at it one way. You would evaluate all possibilities, explore different methods, study every variable. So maybe you should look at your time here as an opportunity to explore. Trial and error. Especially since you're graduating early. Because once you finish here and move on to grad school, I don't know how many opportunities you'll have left."

I have to admit . . . she has a point. If I am anything, it is meticulously thorough. But I haven't done that here. I picked biomedical engineering, I put my head down, and I got to work. There's been no exploring or experimenting of any kind. In my classes and labs, I would never choose a predetermined outcome and railroad my study to meet that expected end. That's not reasonable. It's not . . . *smart*.

"So, what?" I say. "I should get drunk and dance with a lampshade on my head?" That's certainly not any smarter than how I've behaved so far.

She pauses in her cooking to laugh, and then laugh some more. "That is . . . not something I ever thought I'd picture. No, you don't have to do a drunken lampshade dance. Unless you feel like it, then have at it. I just think you should step outside your routine, do some of the normal college things."

What does that even mean?

I frown for a moment, and then point back into the living room. "I'm going to study."

Except I don't.

Instead, I sit down on the couch, and I think about what I'm not supposed to be thinking about. Two months until graduation. Two months until I'm done with college.

Granted, I have a research job lined up for the spring semester, and I'm applying for grad schools for next fall, but even knowing I've got a lot of education still ahead of me, there's something so *final* about it.

College is this one big transitional period, and when it's over you're supposed to have transitioned. You're not just an adult in age, but in experience. But the thing is . . .

I don't feel any different.

I don't feel like someone about to embark on the first steps of her career.

I don't feel any different than I did the first day I set foot on campus.

I've learned a lot certainly. My high school science and math teachers can't hold a candle to the kind of stuff I've been exposed to here. But me—the me that is not what I've read in books or memorized for class or learned in a lab—that girl has hardly changed at all in my two-plus years here.

And in my quiet moments, when my brain is not occupied with some problem or study, I wonder if I'm ready. And what happens if I'm not?

Thinking of Dylan's words, I flip to a new page in my spiral, grab a pen, and write.

NORMAL COLLEGE THINGS

I stare at the letters scrawled across the top of the page and think about how Dylan has changed in the past few months, about the "normal" that she found. Then I write down the first item on my list.

Hook up with a jock.

I stare at those three words, and I laugh. They're just so far outside the realm of my existence that I can't even picture it. Besides . . . it's not as if athletes have this magic ability to turn girls' worlds upside down.

And it's not as if a guy is the thing solely responsible for making Dylan happier. It was her choices, whatever weird enlightenment she experienced. The guy was just the catalyst.

Maybe that's all I need, too. I could try some new things, step out of the realms of my knowledge and comfort. Maybe it will rocket me forward into some previously unknown future.

Or more likely it will show me that I was right all along. That I know who I am and what I want, and all these doubts are just my brain balking at change.

With that in mind, I do what comes naturally to my overly organized brain.

I make a list.

Chapter 2

Nell's To-Do List

- *Check off Normal College Thing #2:*
  Make New Friends.
- *Do some laundry, you bum.*

You know," Dylan says, "when I invited you to go play Ultimate Frisbee with Silas's friends, I never expected you to accept."

I wince. "Did you not want me to come?" I tug at the too-tight sports bra that has my boobs pushed so high that I feel like they might rebel and rip the fabric right down the middle. I borrowed the stupid thing from Dylan because I've never had much of an occasion to own a sports bra myself. But she's at least two cup sizes smaller than me, and now I'm afraid I might suffocate in my own cleavage. "I don't have to. Really."

I make a mental note to put "buy a sports bra" on my to-do list.

"No! No. I'm excited for you to meet them all. I just . . . I was surprised, that's all."

I shrug. "I've been thinking about what you said last week. About exploring all that college has to offer." Dylan smiles at me, and I'm fairly certain that look I'm seeing on her face qualifies as smug. I add, "Plus I have no tests coming up, and I'm caught up on all assigned work through the next week and a half."

She shakes her head and leans forward to fiddle with the air-conditioning in her car.

"Of course you are."

She turns the air up, and I'm grateful for the cool blast. Only in Texas is it still this warm in October. I pull my hair up off my neck, glad at least that I always have a hair band on my wrist. The air feels good across the newly liberated and sweaty skin of my neck.

"So, tell me what I need to know about these people."

Dylan drums her fingers thoughtfully on the steering wheel and says, "Well, you've met Silas. Sort of. He is . . . he's . . . well, he's hard to describe, but he'll be nice to you. So you don't have to worry about that. They're all really nice. Both of his roommates will be there. Isaiah Brookes—the guys call him either by his last name or Zay—I think you'll probably like him. He can be a little hard to pin down sometimes, but he's very . . . thoughtful. Smart. Straightforward. The two of you have that in common. His other roommate is Torres."

"Another last name?" I ask.

"Mateo Torres. But everyone calls everyone by their last names. It's a sports thing. Or a guy thing. I'm not really sure. But you get used to it."

"I don't want people calling me De Luca. That's just weird. I'll have to become accustomed to answering to a different name, and while learning a sport I've never played. That seems stressful."

"They don't do it as much with the girls. And really, Ultimate Frisbee isn't complicated. You'll be fine. I promise."

"Fine. Back to the people. You were talking about someone named Torres."

Dylan makes a face and cagily replies, "Maybe it would be better if you didn't spend too much time with Torres."

"Why? Is he dangerous?"

"God, no. He's just shameless. I know how you don't like being embarrassed, and with Torres around . . . well, that kind of thing is inevitable. He'll either say something or do something or take off his clothes."

More naked guys? Seriously?

"Steer clear of Torres. Got it. Check. Next."

"Then there's Carson and Dallas. They've been dating for about a year now. They're sort of the calm center of the group. Carson is the quarterback, so he's the team leader, and he tends to take on that same role off the field."

I purse my lips. "Interesting. Is that common? Do they all display their athletic tendencies and strengths off the field?"

Dylan considers that for a moment. "Maybe. Yeah, I guess. I hadn't really thought of it that way, but yes. Carson is the one who controls the team, who reads them all. Silas is the strength on the field. He makes the short, hard runs through tough defense. He's like that in real life, too. He can weather just about anything.

Torres is flashy on the field and off. Brookes plays the same position as Torres, but he tends to be the more reliable one. He's the one they go to for the simpler throws, whereas Torres makes the bigger, riskier plays."

I think about that for the moment, but it's too much information to digest about people I've never even met. So I file it away for later, when I can put faces to the names.

"Okay. Who else?"

"Well, there's also Ryan. He's not on the team, but he's the manager. He's funny, Easygoing. I mentioned Dallas. She's fun. Spunky. Honest. I'm not sure if Stella will be there or not. She's Dallas's roommate. She's cool, but . . ."

"But what?"

"Nothing. She's just been a little unpredictable lately."

"Unpredictable how?"

"It just depends on the day. Normally, she's vibrant and outgoing and the center of the crowd. But she's just . . . she's dealing with some stuff right now, and so there are some moments when she's . . . different."

"Different how?"

Dylan sighs, and I'm pretty sure I'm asking too many questions. A fault of mine. Or an advantage, depending on the situation.

"I don't know, Nell. It varies. Just be understanding with her, and I'm sure everything will be fine."

I decide not to ask any more questions for a while, and she

doesn't continue, so I'm guessing that's the group in its entirety. It's Sunday, so when she pulls into the parking lot near the open fields by the science building, it's fairly empty.

"You ready?" she asks, and I nod. "Don't be nervous."

"I'm not."

There's not much point in being nervous yet when I don't know what I'm up against. And really, how hard can the game be?

WITHIN TEN SECONDS of stepping onto the field, a Frisbee from a nearby game in progress comes sailing toward me, and in its wake is a large sprinting, sweaty guy heading straight toward me. I yelp, throw my hands over my head, and crouch down low. There's a burst of air over my head, something heavy knocks into my forearms, forcing me onto my knees, and then there's a loud thump a few feet away from me.

When I lift my arms enough to peek out, I see the guy who'd been running toward me, now flat on his stomach on the other side of my body.

He jumped over me.

Suddenly the uncomplicated and unintimidating game of Frisbee that I'd been picturing gets much more stressful. The guy rolls over onto his back and then hops to his feet. Dylan grabs my arm and tugs me up and away from the game that I'm still in the middle of. As soon as we're clear, they start up again at full speed. When we approach a group of people seated around a picnic table, I hear a loud voice say, "I vote that one is on Brookes's team."

The guy that goes with the voice is tall with broad shoulders. His skin is a warm bronze, and his dark hair is shorn close to his head. His teeth are a brilliant white when he directs his smile at me. And I'm fairly certain he's just insulted me, despite that grin.

Dylan's boyfriend punches him in the arm. "Don't be a dick."

"I'm not being a dick. I'm just teasing the girl to make her feel like part of the group. It's part of my welcome strategy. What do you say, beautiful? Do you feel welcome?"

His tone is playful and light, but there's an intensity to his gaze that unnerves me. I freeze and study him, and I know immediately. "You're Torres."

Everyone laughs, and a girl with fiery red hair says, "Somehow she made just your name sound like an insult, Teo. I think she's going to fit right in."

Teo. I think back, trying to remember what first name Dylan had mentioned. Mateo?

He lifts a hand to his chest, the left side where his heart is, and shoots me a wounded expression that is like puppy-dog eyes to the tenth power. I'm not sure whether it makes me want to step closer or run in the other direction.

"At least she knows who I am," he says. "None of you suckers are that important."

I survey the rest of the group, and slowly try to guess which person goes with which description. The girl with red hair is the most obvious. There's a tall, attractive guy with an arm looped over her shoulders, and they're clearly the nucleus of the group.

I point at them. "Dallas and Carson." The guy I deemed to be Carson raises his eyebrows in surprise. There's only one other girl present, a petite Asian with dark hair cut and shaped around a pretty face. "You must be Stella." She smiles and points a finger at the curly-haired guy close to her. She mouths, "Ryan." I nod and take her hint, pointing him out, too. Next up is the guy I saw naked in my kitchen just a few days ago. That's one face I'm not going to forget anytime soon. "That's Silas, which means . . ." I face the last unidentified guy. He's a large black guy with sculpted muscles and a symmetrical face. I get what Dylan said about him being the hardest to pin down. But he's looking at me with a calculating expression that reminds me of myself, and I smile. "And you've got to be Isaiah Brookes."

Torres whistles and draws my attention back to him, "How come you know his full name?"

I shrug.

He hops down from where he's sitting on top of the picnic table and meets me in a few long strides. He loops an arm around my shoulders as if he's known me for years instead of minutes, and suddenly I'm pressed up close and personal to the hardest body I've ever touched in real life. In fact, the closest I've ever come to someone this defined is one of those CPR dummies that are made of metal and rubber and plastic.

Torres says, "Forget having her on my team. I want her on my homework. She's a genius or something."

"Or she saw a picture of us," Brookes says, his gaze still assessing.

Torres asks Dylan, "Did you show her our pictures, Captain Planet? I hope you got a good one of me."

"Actually, I told her you were flashy and shameless. She put together who you were all on her own."

The laughter that follows Dylan's announcement is even louder than before, and it lasts for several long seconds. My eyes flit around the group as they laugh, and I try to take in all the dynamics at work, but my thoughts unravel completely when I feel hot breath against my ear, and then what must be lips brushing my skin as Torres asks, "What's your name?"

It has to be autopilot that has me answering because all my conscious thoughts are too wrapped up in this body that's crowded too close to mine, and how warm he is, and the faint scent of something citrus-y and woodsy that comes from his skin.

"Nell."

"Nell what?"

I pause. I still don't want to be called by my last name.

"Just Nell."

"Well, just Nell. I'm Mateo."

His lips keep barely brushing against the shell of my ear, and the heat of his breath tickles, and I can already feel my face flushing hot. And who gets this close to a complete stranger?

Boundaries. Seriously.

I shrug his arm from my shoulders and say the first thing that comes to my mind. "I'm supposed to stay away from you."

I sound crazy. And like a child frightened of a stranger trying to offer me candy, but as nonsensical as it seems, that's how I feel.

All my senses are on high alert, and the hairs on my forearms are raised, and my breaths are coming faster than they should be considering all I'm doing is standing still.

I feel like prey.

And all he's doing is smiling at me. And it's a smile that tells me he has exactly zero intentions of putting any distance between us.

Just then a slim, shorter black guy comes jogging up and says, "Hey. Sorry I'm late, McClain." When he's standing a few feet away, I amend my description to *less tall*. He might not be as towering as the boundary-defying guy beside me, but he's still big.

Carson, the one Dylan called the leader of the group and the apparent owner of the last name *McClain*, steps up and says, "No worries. We didn't give you much notice." He introduces the new guy as Keyon, and then introduces me and Dylan in turn. I guess Keyon must know everyone else. Then Carson adds, "And that puts us at an even ten. So we can pick teams and get going."

Torres raises his hand. "I'll be team captain."

His proclamation makes my stomach tumble with nerves, and I'm not sure why.

Carson pauses for a moment and then shrugs. "Fine. You and Brookes are probably the fastest. So you can be captains."

They flip a coin, and Brookes gets first pick. I expect him to pick one of the guys. They're the obvious choice. As football players, they're in shape and more naturally athletic. But he fixes his eyes on me for the briefest moment before turning to Torres, his gaze narrowed. He looks at me again.

"Your name is Nell?" he asks.

There's something about him that feels simultaneously commanding and trustworthy, almost soothing. If he looks at me like that too much longer, I might just tell him my full name, birth date, Social Security number, and anything else he wants to know.

Instead, I nod.

He raises an eyebrow at Torres and says, "I'll take Nell."

Chapter 3

Mateo

Ah, damn it all to hell. It's like Zay lives to ruin all my fun. I narrow my eyes at him, wondering what exactly his deal is. I survey Nell as she leaves me. She's pretty. No denying that. Short with curves that could kill. Long dark hair and smooth olive skin. And she's shy.

Don't ask me why, but I've always had a thing for the shy ones. I like being the one to break them out of their shell.

Does Brookes want her, too? Is that what this is about? Or does he just not want me to have her? Probably the second one. I can imagine his lecture already.

No hitting on Dylan's friends. When you inevitably piss them off or break their heart, you'll piss off the whole group.

I'm not an idiot. I'm not gonna fuck with Dylan's friend because then I'll have Dylan's boyfriend on my ass. And Silas Moore is not a pleasant person to live with when his girlfriend is unhappy. But that doesn't mean I can't flirt with her. I *do* know how to draw the line, contrary to popular opinion.

Well, just because Brookes has a chivalrous stick up his ass doesn't mean I have to play stupid. I'm not gonna pick another girl just to make things fair.

"Silas," I say.

"Dylan," Brookes chooses.

She blinks a few times before crossing to stand by Brookes and her friend. She says, "I do believe that's the first time I've ever not been picked last for this kind of thing."

I look at him, wondering exactly what he's playing at.

I choose McClain. He chooses Dallas.

And then I get it.

He's going to use the girls to distract my guys.

Sneaky little fucker.

Well, two can play at that game.

"Stella," I say.

She sighs and gives me a look. "Wrong move, Torres. Wrong move."

Brookes picks Keyon next, which is what I should have done. He's not part of our regular crowd. He's not going to get distracted by anyone. Damn it. That leaves me with Ryan. He says, "Sure. Pick the manager last. I get it."

Stella shrugs. "You're not a college athlete. Nor do you have boobs. You were always going to be last. Suck it up."

My team gathers behind me, and I take a moment to survey

our opponents. Brookes, Keyon, and three gorgeous girls, two of whom are dating my two best picks.

Fuck.

As soon as we huddle up to talk strategy, Silas says, "I'm guarding Dylan."

I barely have time to open my mouth before Carson adds, "And I've got Dallas."

"Aw, come on, guys. You're doing exactly what Brookes wants you to do."

Silas shrugs. "No one else is getting close enough to my girl to play one-on-one defense. Sorry."

"What he said," Carson adds.

I sigh. "Unbelievable. Is this some kind of disease? Like you tap one girl long enough, and it somehow warps your brain? We're *athletes.* You're supposed to care about being competitive."

Silas says, "I care about seeing Dylan in a pair of tiny shorts. Those are my priorities at the moment."

Unfuckingbelievable.

"Fine. I'll cover Brookes. Ryan, you cover Keyon. And Stell, you get girl genius."

That's the best we're going to do.

We have to wait while Brookes explains the rules to Nell, and I take a moment to talk strategy with my team. I look at McClain and Moore and say, "You two. No taking it easy on your girlfriends. Don't let them get past you just because you think you won't get laid tonight if you don't."

That only gets me a sarcastic reply of "Sure, Coach."

Brookes got first choice, so my team takes the disc first. Predictably, Brookes's team is playing man-to-man defense, and he's got the girls matched up with their boyfriends. It's clear within seconds that those girls are willing to play dirty. Technically, Ultimate is a no-contact sport, and you can call foul if things go too far.

McClain and Moore certainly aren't calling foul when their girls make contact. I make a short pass to Ryan, who just barely manages to catch it before Keyon goes sailing past him trying to knock the disc to the ground. I take off running, but Brookes is hot on my heels. I pivot and change directions a few times, trying to shake him off, but he stays too close. The rules of the game dictate that you can't run with the disc, so Ryan's stuck where he is until someone from our team gets open enough for him to make a throw.

He flicks his wrist, sending the disc sailing toward McClain, and I watch with dawning horror as Dallas slips in front of him and intercepts the disc.

The game continues in that vein for the next five minutes, and we're down three to zero when Stella calls a time-out.

"Hey," I say. "I'm the captain. I call the time-outs."

"Yeah, well, we're getting our asses kicked, Captain."

No arguing with that.

Stella stands with her hands on her hips, and even sweaty, she looks pretty. How do girls always do that?

"Let me guard Keyon," she says.

"Why? No offense, gorgeous, but he's a lot faster than you."

"He's faster than Ryan, too. And like I said . . . only one person on this team has boobs."

"Absolutely not," Ryan cuts in.

Stella rolls her eyes. "Come on. He's a freshman. I'll do a little flirting. Maybe a little pouting about how hard the game is. He'll be an easy mark."

Ryan glares. "You don't have to throw yourself at him for some stupid game."

She ignores him and looks at me. "What do you say, Captain?"

Ryan crosses his arms over his chest and directs his angry stare at me. I'm not sure whether his pissy mood is just because he's got a thing for Stella and doesn't want her flirting with another guy, or if his protectiveness has more to do with what happened at that frat party a few weeks ago. I don't know the specifics. Stella certainly doesn't talk about what happened, and I know Silas and Dylan are the ones who found her passed out in a room after she was left there by one of the guys on the team. Silas fought with the guy, Jake Carter, and I got to the scene around the same time as the cops. Carter has since been kicked off the team, but he hasn't been arrested, and he's still enrolled in classes. I've heard a lot of speculation about what happened in that room and afterward and what will happen next from people on campus, but no one here has said a word about it. Not to me anyway.

No one ever comes to me for serious conversations. I shake off the slight sting that thought causes. It's not like I *want* serious. I spend most of my time making it abundantly clear to everyone that my name doesn't even belong in the same sentence as that word.

But for a moment I wish that people trusted me a little more. Then I'd know if letting Stella flirt with Keyon is a bad idea. From the way everyone else tiptoes around her, I assume that some serious shit went down. But at the same time . . . Stella acts like nothing has changed. I might not be trusted with everyone's secrets, but I do know Stella well enough to know that she doesn't take well to other people telling her what to do. If she wants to guard Keyon, who am I to tell her no? Silas and Carson are staying silent on the matter, so I'm guessing they don't want to get in the middle of it either.

I meet her determined gaze and nod. Ryan curses, and I say, "It can't hurt to try. If it doesn't work or you want to switch back, Stella, all you have to do is say so."

She smiles sweetly in return and says, "You guys can thank me now."

A few minutes of flirting later, and suddenly Keyon decides he'd rather guard Stella than Ryan. While Nell is scrambling trying to figure out who she's supposed to be on, Ryan scores our first point of the game.

Next time around, Brookes tries to help her pick up the slack, but he can't help her with Ryan and successfully cover me at the same time. Carson puts his flirting on pause long enough to zip one high and long in my direction. I sprint under it, crossing into the end zone. Brookes is a few feet back, and I make a diving catch to put us within one.

Brookes calls a time-out, and while they talk I fold Stella into a sweaty hug.

"Have I told you how awesome you are?"

She shrugs. "I can always stand to hear it a few more times a day."

"Well, you're awesome." Her smile looks easy, genuine. Until, that is, I spend a few seconds too long staring and assessing it, then her posture goes rigid, and I step back and avert my eyes before I do something to piss her off.

When we come out of the huddle, I'm too confident.

A habit of mine.

Dallas and Dylan toss the disc back and forth a few times, and I groan when Carson and Silas make no effort to intercept or knock down the pass. I'm pretty sure it's a distraction, so I stick tight to Brookes, and I notice Ryan edging closer to me, too. He must have the same idea.

Next thing I know, Dallas has sent the disc soaring over our heads, and when I look, Nell is standing alone, completely unguarded in the end zone.

She's holding her hands out and staring at the disc like it's a missile instead of a piece of plastic. I take off toward her in case she misses it. I want to grab the disc and get it back into play as soon as I can.

As I sprint, the disc slips right through her grasping fingers and nails her in the chest. She gasps; no doubt the air was knocked out of her. The disc ricochets, and if I dive I might can manage to catch it, but I can't quite drag my eyes away from her chest. Her tits are practically spilling out of the top of the tiny tank she's wearing. I'd had a front-row seat earlier with my arm around her. Now she's clutching at herself in pain, but all I can see are her smooth, delicate arms pressed against the curve of her breasts, pushing them even higher.

I should look away before something very unfortunate occurs in my baggy gym shorts, but now I'm picturing that shy girl loosening up beneath me. It's too easy to take those wide eyes she gave me when I draped my arm around her and imagine them in the low light of my room, her head on my pillow and her legs spread wide.

She makes a soft whimpering noise, and now the rest of my senses join the fantasy, and I think of how she would feel, taste, sound. I wonder just how low I could get her inhibitions. Enough to say my name? To scream it?

"Damn," I groan, and try to clear my head. "You all right?"

She looks up at me, still clutching at her chest, and pink spreads over her cheeks. She doesn't say anything.

"Okay," I say. "There is honestly no way to ask this without sounding like a pig, so I'm not even gonna try. And really, in these situations, I find you might as well go balls to the wall and throw it all out there. So . . . at the risk of getting slapped, how are your tits?" I think about offering to check them out for her, but I figure that's probably taking it a step too far.

Her mouth presses into a firm straight line. "It wasn't my . . ." She trails off.

"Tits," I finish for her. "You have them. You can say the word."

"It hit me in the collarbone, not the breasts."

Breasts. I raise an eyebrow, and she rolls her eyes.

I take a step forward and say, "Let me see."

"Absolutely not."

I take another step, until my shadow falls over her, and take hold of one wrist. "As you pointed out, you weren't hit in the *breasts.* Just let me have a look. With the right strength and good wind, a disc can go as fast as twenty miles per hour. I've seen them break fingers and noses."

"Dude, Torres!" Silas shouts behind me. "What are you waiting for? Grab the disc and let's go!"

Hesitating, I ask, "You wanna take a break? Catch your breath and let me see it?"

She shakes her head stubbornly. "I don't want the game to stop because of me."

I turn around and shout back to Silas, "Nell and I are taking a break. You guys keep playing with eight."

Taking her elbow, I pull her off the field toward the picnic tables. She protests, but only mildly, and she still has one hand pressed just above her cleavage. And looking down at her, I can see moisture clinging to long lashes at the corner of her eye.

I sit her down so that her back is to the field, and go down on one knee in front of her. She's so small that it puts us eye level, and I say softly, "Move your hand."

"It's fine," she says. "Just give me a couple seconds, and I'll be fine."

You don't grow up with five sisters without learning that sometimes with women, words are pointless. I reach out and move her hand myself, pulling it away from her chest. The skin just below her collarbone is an angry red, and the disc scraped through a couple layers of skin. Not enough to bleed, but I bet it hurts. "Tell me how it feels. Still a sharp pain? Or more of an ache?"

Her eyebrows slant over her pretty brown eyes. "The pain was sharp and steady for approximately thirty seconds, but now it kind of stings."

"Like a slap," I say.

She gives a short laugh, her shoulders bouncing once before she stills in what I'm guessing is pain. "I can't say I know what that feels like. Though I'm not surprised it's a sensation you're familiar with."

I shrug. "I don't believe in censoring my thoughts. Some people just aren't as fond of freedom of speech as I am."

She shakes her head, and I think she's trying not to smile.

I reach up my left hand and as lightly as possible run my thumb over the red mark. She sucks in a breath and I ask, "Hurts to the touch?"

"Um." She swallows and blinks a few times.

"Does it hurt a lot?"

I brush my thumb over her skin again, even lighter this time, wondering if the Frisbee could have hit hard enough to crack something. There's already a purpling around the center that tells me it's going to bruise pretty good.

She swallows, and my eyes are drawn to the graceful slope of her neck, up to a small chin and full lips. And it hits me then . . .

why this girl caught my eye from the moment she walked toward our group, why I can't drag my eyes or my hand away from her now.

She reminds me of Lina.

And the memory of the only girl I've ever loved packs a punch so hard that it's my turn to raise a hand to my chest to soothe an all-too-familiar ache.

Chapter 4

Nell's To-Do List

- Check off Normal College Thing #2: Make New Friends (in a way that doesn't require physical activity).
- But still maybe get that sports bra just in case.

W hy are you looking at me like that?" I ask.

He shakes his head, but doesn't stop staring at me.

"Uh. Sorry. You just reminded me of someone for a second there."

I wait for him to move away, but he doesn't. His gaze is still fixed on my mouth, and it's strange how just that look provokes a physical reaction in my body, one sensation compounding into the next until my skin feels too tight and my blood too warm.

I wish I could pause this moment, unroll time so that I can examine his expression and his body language, and so I can catalog my own body's abnormal response. But time never stops for my overactive brain, certainly not when his fingers slip up from my collarbone, over my frantic pulse, and grip my chin. The seconds disintegrate into impossibly shorter intervals, and his thumb treks upward to catch at my bottom lip.

I break away then, gasping and holding my chest like I've just been pelted by another Frisbee, by a dozen of them.

This . . . the way my heart is beating unreasonably fast . . . it doesn't make any sense. And I *don't like* when things don't make sense.

It's not like I've never seen an attractive guy before. I've even gone on dates with a few. But I've never had this kind of physical reaction to anyone. It's unsettling not to understand why.

I put several feet between us and glare at him. "I told you to stay away from me."

He hums and frowns and says, "No. No, I distinctly recall you saying you were *supposed* to stay away from me."

"Same thing."

"Oh, gorgeous. If what you're supposed to do and what you actually do are always the same thing, I think I need to stage an intervention."

A tide of thoughts rolls in, and I try to keep them at bay, but there's no stopping it.

Normal college thing #1:
Hook up with a jock.

When I'd written those words, they'd been innocuous. An item on a list. It had been solely about exploration, about making sure I was being educated in every way, not just in the classroom. But even then, the words had been somewhere between a joke and a proposition so outlandish that I felt relatively confident I'd never be in a position to complete it. But now there's a sensuality to those thoughts that didn't exist before.

Before I'd stood face-to-face with just such a jock.

Before he'd touched me.

Before I'd wanted to touch him back.

It doesn't feel like a joke anymore.

On the heels of that sensuality, anxiety swoops in, filling all the leftover nooks and crannies. Because, though I'm familiar with the term "hook up" in all its slang meanings, I'm not familiar with it in the physical sense.

I've never had sex.

I've always meant to. It's something that I've tended to view rather clinically, a normal biological occurrence that shouldn't intimidate me. But there was never anyone with whom I'd felt enough compatibility, and I'd always felt that if you're going to do something, you should do it right. When I started making that list last week, it only made sense that I should check off that particular event while I did the rest of my experimenting.

"Clinical" is not the word that comes to mind when I look at Mateo Torres.

"I was joking about the intervention," he says.

"I know," I snap, defensive.

"Well, you looked a little terrified, so I thought I should put you at ease."

"I'm *not* terrified."

It's silly to be scared of him. He tilts his head to the side, and before I can react, he's eliminated all the precious space I put between us.

"You don't have to disagree with everything I say."

I step back a foot, but he follows.

"I'm not." He only grins, and why is my pulse increasing like that? "I'm not disagreeing with you only to disagree. You're just wrong."

He laughs.

"And I bet you love being right."

I frown, unsure what that has to do with him refusing to give me any personal space. I move again, and when he tries to follow, I press a hand into his chest, holding him back.

"Well, I *am* right a majority of the time, which is why I feel confident in my initial assessment of you."

He leans into me, and I can feel the warmth of his skin through the thin shirt that separates us. My hand is just over his heart, and its steady, strong thrum somehow feels like a chisel, chipping away at my defenses through that simple, innocent touch. I pull my hand away quickly, and he takes it as an opportunity to move even closer. He grins, and I can say positively that I have never met a man this confident. And my family is Italian, so that's saying something.

"And what was your initial assessment?" he asks.

"That you are only concerned with yourself. With how you look. How people see you. And I am the complete opposite. I am concerned with facts. With ideas. With knowledge. I want to be the puppet master, while you are content to be the puppet that doesn't realize he's letting other people pull his strings."

A muscle in his cheek spasms. His eyes widen in surprise, maybe even alarm. Then his jaw clenches, settling his whole expression into stone. But even that lasts only a moment before the tension leaves him, and he pins me with a lazy half smile.

"I do like a girl who's feisty."

He's baiting me. Or more likely deflecting. And I'm not sure if I want to allow it so that this conversation can be over, and I can get some much-needed space. Or . . . if I want to call his bluff, peel back another layer, and take a longer look at what he's hiding.

Or if I want to examine exactly what he means by "like."

I don't get a chance to make a decision before both of us are distracted by a commotion behind us.

My team has just scored, but Mateo's team doesn't seem to be paying the slightest attention. The guy with blond, unruly hair, Ryan, is standing nose to nose with Keyon on my team. I can't hear what's being said, but the tension is plain as day in their body language. And though I can't hear the guys, I can easily hear what Stella is yelling at Ryan's back.

"Jesus, Ryan. Would you chill out? It was nothing!"

When that doesn't work, she takes hold of his arm and tries to pull him away. He doesn't budge. Until she screams, "You're not my fucking boyfriend, okay? So BACK OFF!" Ryan stumbles back then, like her pull on his arm suddenly doubled in strength. He faces her, all tensed up, and she continues, "And I am not a porcelain doll. I don't break easily, and I sure as hell will not be treated as if I already have."

She turns around and storms off, and after a few seconds, Dallas, the redhead, jogs after her. Ryan stares off blankly, clenching and unclenching his hands as if she just barely slipped from his grasp and he hasn't quite figured out how it happened. His expression is a mix of anxiety and alarm and pain, and for a moment it reminds me of the look on Torres's face that he'd hidden so quickly after I accused him of being a puppet.

Sometimes I can be too brash in my observations. I don't always think ahead to the emotions that could follow, and my heart does something akin to a shiver when I think of how I would feel if someone called me out on my own insecurities.

What if someone I barely knew looked into my eyes and said the very thing that I'd thought in my most unguarded moments, the thing that scares me most? What if someone could tell that the reason I concentrate so much on details and data is that they're the only things that keep me from feeling inferior? I disregard emotions because they don't come easily to me, because when other people talk about love or happiness, I feel only a cloying sense of confusion and fear that I'm not capable of those things. Not that I don't experience happiness or love my family, but those are nurtured emotions that have grown slowly and steadily over time, and they exist at comfortable levels. But deeper than that? The kind of happiness that fills a person up? Or love that can overwhelm a person and rearrange the very essence of who they are? I don't believe I have that kind of thing in me. It's just not in my nature.

Which is why focusing on my career has always made the most sense. That's something I understand. Something I'm good at.

But now even that feels off-kilter.

I turn then, intending to apologize, to admit that I'd judged him too harshly, but Torres is no longer behind me. I whip around and see that he's slipped around the other side of the picnic table and is heading back to the field, where what's left of his friends are gathered together talking.

Dylan is there too, Silas's arm draped over her shoulder and holding her tight to his side. They all wear looks of concern as they talk, and I swallow, feeling as if the distance between us is much greater than the length of a table and a dozen yards of playing field.

I'm on the outside here. And what hurts more than the fact that no one seems to notice me as I turn and head for Dylan's car is the fact that I'm comfortable on the outside. It's what I know. It's who I am.

Is that something that can be changed through will alone?

DYLAN DROPS ME off at home, but doesn't come inside. She offers to, sure. She's been looking at me funny ever since she found me waiting at her car alone, but I just told her I'd walked off to think. Which is the truth. Besides, she had plans to go over to Silas's house, and I didn't want to ruin that. I flip on the lamp beside the couch, leaving the overhead light off, and take a seat in my dim living room.

My roommate has been seeing Silas only since the start of the semester, and I can already acutely feel her absence. When she stays at his house, and I'm left alone in our two-bedroom apartment, I should be happy. The place is by no means big, and I should relish the extra space, the alone time.

Instead, the loneliness creeps into the shadowed corners, and I find myself turning on every light in the place just so that I don't feel so alone.

This could be my future.

It's not as if I can keep a roommate forever. When I'm thirty-five, I'll be hard-pressed to find a friend to live with me just so I don't have to come home to an empty house. But I suppose I'll spend most of my time in a lab then anyway. I'm not afraid to be married to my job, or at least I didn't used to be.

But this feeling is just a phase. It has to be. I will love the challenge of working in biomedical engineering. I'll be on the cutting edge of medicine and technology. My time and focus could change innumerable lives. That will make up for any loneliness I might feel in the few short hours a day I'll spend in my empty apartment. Better than getting myself into a relationship that will only be half real. No, I don't want or need to have another person mucking up my life. There is too much I want to do, too much I want to accomplish. And though my relationship experience is limited to a few simple high school dates, I know enough to see that relationships take work. You can't just consider your own needs anymore, and that weighs people down.

No. I'm happy as I am. Especially when it's the only way I *can* be.

Despite those determined thoughts, I find myself pulling out the spiral where I'd jotted down my list a few days ago. I'd added a handful of things that had seemed obvious at the time.

NORMAL COLLEGE THINGS

1. Hook up with a jock.
2. Make New friends.
3. Go to a party (and actually stay more than half an hour).
4. Do something Wild.
5. Lose my virginity.

They're things I associate with college, even though they're out of my own personal wheelhouse. And they're all far enough out of my comfort zone to function as the kind of catalyst I'm seeking in my little experiment.

I reconsider the list for a moment, feeling simultaneously stupid, naive, terrified, and thrilled. It might be silly, but I love this kind of thing. I can't magically make myself a different person. I can't force myself to be better with emotions or at talking to people. I can't snap my fingers and become normal, but I can observe normal people and follow their behaviors. I can check items off a list. Figures that the only way social life would become interesting to me is by making it an experiment.

And even though I'm not expecting any major life changes like Dylan experienced, who knows, maybe with a little practice, things will start to come more easily to me. It wouldn't hurt for me to be a little more comfortable outside of a classroom. It's kind of like the age-old debate between nature and nurture. Just because I'm not predisposed to be like everyone else doesn't mean I can't become that way as a result of my environment.

And then in the future, when my family or my friends or anyone tries to urge me to be different, to focus less on my career, to be normal—I'll know with certainty what that kind of life feels like, and I'll know it's not for me. And I can be done questioning myself once and for all.

With that thought in mind, I jot down a few more tasks for my list. Then I pull over my laptop from where it sits on the coffee table and open it up. With my pulse beating at a frenzied staccato, I type into Google:

College Bucket List.

Then I dive into my research, pen at the ready to add to my list.

Chapter 5

Nell's To-Do List

- *Normal College Thing #3: Go to a party (and actually stay more than half an hour).*

Just shy of a week later, I tug at my horrendously short skirt for the seventeenth time (maybe eighteenth . . . I can't be trusted to count when I'm this nervous).

"I don't see why I can't wear jeans and a regular shirt," I grumble. Clothes have never really been my forte. Give me jeans and a plain V-neck tee any day.

Dylan doesn't look away from the bathroom mirror, where she's brushing another coat of mascara onto her already too-pretty eyes.

"We're going to a Halloween party. Trust me, you'll feel more awkward if you're *not* dressed up. When we get there, you'll see. This is no big deal."

I don't look down at the white button-up shirt that's gaping open over my boobs. I've looked at the awful naughty-schoolgirl costume enough times to imprint the thing on my memory.

"If this costume weren't so . . . so . . ."

"Sexy?" she prompts.

"*Atrocious.*"

"Well, that's what you get for buying a costume the day before Halloween. Everything is picked over by then. You didn't want to go as Jasmine and have your stomach showing, so this is what you got. Besides, it kind of fits you."

I gesture to the button over my chest that's threatening to pop with any sudden movement. "It does *not* kind of fit me."

"I mean, the schoolgirl vibe. It's like the amplified version of you. That's perfect for Halloween."

"There is absolutely no universe where the amplified version of me would not be wearing yoga pants and glasses."

"Fine. It's the bold and wild version of you. Nothing wrong with trying bold and wild for a change."

I groan and throw myself down on the toilet seat beside her. "I've changed my mind. I don't think I should go to this party after all. All those people, and costumes, and decorations. I think Halloween is way too overwhelming for my first foray into the college party scene."

Dylan tosses her mascara into her makeup bag and faces me, her look now complete. She manages to appear both classy and sexy in a homemade Statue of Liberty costume. Only Dylan could make Lady Liberty look hot.

"Just take a deep breath, Nell. This isn't nearly as scary as you're making it out to be in your head. I promise."

"Maybe not for you. But the idea of being in some frat house with a bunch of people I don't know—"

She cuts me off. "We're not going to one of the frat parties. Everyone has been avoiding that scene since . . . well, it doesn't matter. The group decided it would be better to have something smaller, more manageable. It's at Silas's house. And it's only people they know and trust. You'll be fine. I know it."

Apparently "people they know and trust" translates into about thirty people on the lawn, fifteen on the porch, and more people than I can count on the inside. Dylan's hand is wrapped tight around my elbow as we step through the entryway to Silas's house. She's on her tiptoes, searching for him, and all I can think about is making a break for it and getting out of there as soon as possible.

I'm so concentrated on keeping my short skirt down and the too-tight white shirt buttoned up that I don't even realize she's found her boyfriend until she lets go of my arm. At the loss of her touch, I look up, panicked. Silas is dressed as a fireman, and he drops his helmet to circle his arms around Dylan. His fist clutches at the material on the back of her dress, just above her bottom, and I immediately look away, only to lock eyes with the one person I want to see even less than a very public display of affection.

Mateo Torres.

He has a beer lifted halfway to his mouth, but his jaw is slack, and he's staring at me. No, "stare" does not quite do justice to the look he's giving me. His eyes *raze* me, and when I lift my hand to touch my neck, subconsciously covering my all-too-visible cleavage, I'm surprised my skin doesn't flake away into ashes from the fire in his gaze.

Adrenaline surges through me, and for a moment it feels like a fight-or-flight impulse, and I wonder why my brain still reads his presence as dangerous. But then I stop and think. It's not quite the same sensation. Fight or flight generally makes me either panic or freeze up. It's about fear. This is different. When seconds pass and he still hasn't taken his eyes off of me, I recognize the extra sensation riding on the adrenaline's heels.

Power.

He makes me feel powerful.

I drop my eyes, overwhelmed by the rush of pleasure I feel at that idea, and am faced instead with his costume, which I hadn't noticed before. Or more correctly, his near lack of a costume. His chest is bare, and I can't help but measure him with my eyes. His chest is broad, hewn in muscles that couldn't be more defined if an artist sculpted them. His skin is a warm bronze, and it looks so smooth to the touch. Everywhere. Except for the small line of dark hair disappearing beneath a strange, leatherlike cloth.

God. A loincloth. He's wearing nothing but a *loincloth.*

Oh, mercy.

Then he's moving toward me, and I don't know where to look. His dangerous gaze. His naked chest. That cloth that hides only . . . *oh, mercy.*

"Girl genius," he says, and I can hear the smirk in his voice without even looking away from the suddenly interesting spot on the floor. Then he shifts, and something changes in his voice when he says, "Nell."

A part of me likes hearing him say my name entirely too much. And that part . . . is a fool.

"Still ignoring my request that you stay away?" I ask stiffly.

"If you wanted me to stay away, you definitely shouldn't have worn *that*."

A furious blush steals across my cheeks and down my neck. "Dylan insisted I wear a costume, and this was all that was left at the store."

"Thank God for Dylan, then. And for procrastination. Can you do me a favor and say, 'Hit me, baby, one more time?' Pretty please?"

Rather than answering, I actually hit him. But when my palm makes contact with the hard muscle of his shoulder, I wish I hadn't. Because now that I know what his bare skin feels like, I'm not sure I'll be able to forget the sensation. My brain is already cataloging the feel, comparing it to all the other people I've touched, and coming up empty for comparison. Is it normal for him to feel so *warm*?

It's the alcohol, I decide. It must be. I read something once about it dilating blood vessels and bringing warmer blood closer to the surface of the skin.

Yes, that's absolutely it.

Dylan comes back to me then, and I'm so grateful I latch on to her arm like she's my port in a storm. And frankly, "storm" seems too tame a word for the overwhelming atmosphere of this place and the guy standing across from me.

Silas joins her, and then I notice a few more familiar faces in the group. Stella, dressed in a stunning Greek goddess costume. Ryan stands just behind her shoulder in a suit with a martini glass in his hand. I'm guessing he's the dude from that "shaken, not stirred" movie that I can't seem to remember the name of.

"Here's my question, Teo," Stella says, stepping up beside Torres to close off our little circle. "Your normal tendency at parties is to lose articles of clothing as the night wears on. Dare I hope that you're working backward tonight and will put clothes *on* as you drink?"

"Maybe tonight I'll focus on helping other people lose their clothes, for a change. We can call it Strip Halloween. It will be a huge hit. I promise. Take this little Grecian sheet dress of yours. One good pull, and you could start the game."

Ryan shoulders his way into the circle then, and Stella stiffens beside him. It's Torres who says something: "For God's sake, man. I was joking. Loosen up. This is a party."

Those words don't seem to assure his friend. "*I know.*"

Stella rolls her eyes and walks away, over toward the kitchen counter. "And on that note, I'm getting a drink. Anyone else need one?"

Several of the college bucket lists I consulted online had "do a keg stand" listed among the tasks. Along with "play beer pong" and other alcohol-related festivities. After a little more Internet research, I learned what exactly a keg stand and beer pong were. And considering the only alcohol I've ever had was the wine during Communion at church, I figure I need to start small. Which is why "drink alcohol" is number six on my list.

"I do," I say, leaving the group to follow her. Standing at the counter, I survey all the options, and even without looking in the ice chests by my feet, I'm overwhelmed. Stella opens one of the chests and grabs a bottle of beer. I decide my safest bet is to copy her, so I grab one, too.

After she opens hers, she reaches out a hand for mine and opens it for me using a complicated-looking little gadget that reminds me of an oversize Swiss Army knife.

"Thanks." How horrifying would it have been for a girl who prides herself on her intelligence above all else to have been stumped over how to open a bottle of beer?

"No problem. I have a feeling I'm going to need a lot of these tonight."

I want to ask her about Ryan, about the obvious tension, not just between them, but among the whole group where Stella is concerned. But I remember Dylan's warning to be understanding with her. And I know myself well enough to know that sometimes I inadvertently put my foot in my mouth, and whatever is going on, I don't want to cause trouble by prying where I shouldn't. So, I follow her lead and take a big gulp of the beer in my hand.

Then I proceed to gag so violently that I have to turn around and spit the vile liquid out into the sink behind us. My reaction draws the attention of several people in the room, including Torres, who starts toward me.

I panic and turn away from him, only to meet Stella's amused smile.

"First time drinking beer?" she asks.

I nod. "It's awful. Why would *anyone* drink it?"

"It's an acquired taste," Torres says as he steps up beside me. "You get used to it."

"Why would I *want* to get used to it? That would be akin to punching myself just to get *used* to pain."

He shrugs. "That might make sense for fight club or something like that."

Stella smacks his arm with the back of her hand. "Dude. First rule."

He laughs, and they both drink their beer, and I have absolutely *no clue* what they're talking about. *This.* This is why I don't do parties. Reflexively, I take another sip of my drink, and immediately regret it. Groaning, I force myself to swallow.

Proud of myself, I say, "Hey, I didn't gag that time."

It's Stella who spits her drink out into the sink this time. She gasps, "Oh my God."

"What? What did I say?"

I look at Torres, and that same blazing look is back in his eyes, and I swear I can feel my blood heating. Surely one sip of beer isn't enough to heat my skin like his was heated earlier . . . is it? It shouldn't be possible to actually feel the warm blood rising to the surface, should it? Curious, I lift the long-neck bottle back to my lips for another drink. I make a face, but force myself to take a few swallows. As soon as I pull the bottle away from my lips, Torres snatches the beer right out of my hand.

"Let's get you something else to drink. Before you kill me."

"Kill you? How on earth would I kill you?"

"One swallow at a time."

"Oh God, Torres." Stella groans, pushing at his shoulder. "You're terrible."

"What? It's the truth!"

He moves past me to the counter, where he grabs a cup and a few bottles. Stella's eyes meet mine, and she points at Torres's broad back. "Watch out for that one."

But despite her warning, she walks away, leaving me alone with him. I stare after her as she heads out of the kitchen. Ryan makes a move to follow her, but she glares, and moves to stand with Brookes by the front door. My eyes search for Dylan and Silas, but they're no longer in the kitchen.

I gulp, suddenly wishing I had that beer back just so I'd have something to do with my hands. The chaotic atmosphere of the party is even more stressful than Torres's presence, so I turn and settle for watching him as he mixes. He starts with lemonade, and then adds liquor from a glass bottle that I don't recognize. He tips in some cranberry juice and two more kinds of liquor.

"What is that?" I ask.

"A Bad Decision."

"Then why are you making it for me?"

He shoots me a lopsided smile, and I'm forced to acknowledge that maybe the warmth creeping up my neck has far less to do with alcohol than I wish it did. "No, sweetheart. It's called a Bad Decision. The drink. It's my own special invention."

He hands me the cup and I stare at it warily. He moves closer to me, nudging the cup closer to my mouth with his finger.

"Why should I trust you?"

He seems to enjoy my suspicion.

"Always gotta fight me. Just try it. It's sweet. I guarantee you'll like it much better than the beer."

I take a deep breath, think of my list, and then lift the cup to my mouth. The flavor curls over my tongue, tangy and sweet. "I can't even taste the alcohol," I say.

He smiles. "That's why it's called *Bad Decision*. Because too many of those will sneak up on you."

I take another sip, simultaneously watching him lift a beer, *my old beer*, to his lips. If you'd described the scene to me two weeks ago, my first thought would have been *ew, germs*. Now . . . it makes my mouth go dry, and I find myself watching his mouth long after he lowers the bottle. I clear my throat and take another sip to wet my inexplicably parched throat. I don't know why anyone would choose beer over something like this. I tell him, "It's really good. Thank you."

He's looking away from me and out at the party as he says, "For you, Nell, I'll make as many bad decisions as you want."

Then his gaze tracks back to mine, and he winks, and I know if I touched my skin now, it would be burning.

Chapter 6

Mateo

Nell blushes, and my throat constricts because she reminds me so damn much of Lina. If I were already buzzing, I might even believe that I was dreaming or hallucinating or something. It's just so fucking unreal.

From the minute I'd met Lina in sixth grade, I'd been half in love with her. She was smart—smart enough to be the best in every class and to give a thorough tongue-lashing to anyone who tried to mess with her. She had more confidence and control than any pubescent teenager should have, and it was hard not to put her on a pedestal, because she shined so damn bright.

And I was just another Mexican kid. Nothing special. I wasn't that smart. We didn't have much money. I was scrawny and entirely uninteresting.

As we got older, she grew into her strong features, started dressing more femininely, and her body filled out in all the right places to match those new clothes. And *bam*. Just like that, she was the smartest *and* prettiest girl no matter what room she walked into.

Or she was to me, anyway.

In my head, I'd been courting her since middle school, but in reality, I didn't make a move until late sophomore year. I'd bulked up for football, and I'd learned how to talk to people, how to be *interesting*. I didn't fade into the background anymore. We sat next to each other in a class. One of her friends was dating one of mine, so we got thrown together a lot. We started talking. Flirting. And then somehow, miraculously, she was mine.

This girl that I'd wanted for so long. We were together, and it was fucking special.

Until I fucked it all up.

And a girl like that doesn't give an idiot like me a second chance. She's way too smart for that.

And Nell . . . she has the same kind of strong features, same figure, same dark hair. From the side, I might even believe she *was* Lina. And I can't help but feel like she's a second chance of a different kind.

When I come back into focus, I realize I must have been blatantly staring at her. She's determinedly not looking at me and gulping at her drink so fast that she's nearly polished it off already.

"Hey. Easy," I say, taking hold of her wrist. "It may not taste much like alcohol, but trust me, it packs a punch."

"Right." She nods. "Of course."

"So . . . you and Dylan are roommates?"

"Yes. Since the beginning of last year."

"Are you part of her hippy group?"

"Hippy group?"

"You know, all her activism stuff. Is that how you two met?"

"Oh. No. We had a class together freshman year. We both have an interest in making the world a better place, but Dylan does that by working with people. I . . . don't."

"Then what do you do?"

"Well, nothing much yet. But I'm studying for a career in bio-medical engineering."

"Biomedical engineering, huh? What is that? Like . . . designing medical equipment?"

Her eyebrows lift, and she turns so that she's facing me, lean-ing her hip against the counter. She cocks her head to the side, and I'm pretty sure that's a good thing, but I'm suddenly far too distracted by the perfect view I have down her shirt, and those damn pigtails that make my blood rush south.

It's a good thing I'm wearing a snug pair of compression shorts beneath this damn loincloth.

"It can be, yes." She sounds impressed, and I'm grateful that all those years spent chasing after Lina made me take more interest in studying. "It's a growing field, but it can encompass everything from inventing or operating medical equipment to prosthetic de-sign to research. It covers basically anything where the study of machines and technology meets the study of the human body."

"So, what you're telling me is that you're a genius."

She pushes a loose strand of hair behind her ear and answers, "I'm not a *genius*."

"Look around the room, sweetheart." I pause to let her view some of the alcohol-induced stupidity going on around us. "In this place, I think Darwin would definitely deem you among the fittest to survive."

A brilliant smile blooms across her face, and I send up a silent thanks to Mrs. Ehrhardt, my high school biology teacher, for being such a hard-ass and never letting me get away with sleeping in her class.

"I think it's safe to say that you would also be considered in that top tier." She fidgets with her cup, but doesn't lift her eyes to mine.

"Oho." I grin. "A compliment. Softening to me already." She rolls her eyes and sighs. I lean down until my mouth is close to her ear and ask, "You think I'm fit, girl genius?" All I can think about is how well I think *she'll* fit against me. What I wouldn't give to fill my hands with her perfect curves.

"Don't be absurd. It's perfectly clear that you know you're . . ." She trails off and gestures primly in the direction of my bare chest.

"It's perfectly clear that I'm what?"

"You're an athlete. So, of course you're in very good physical shape."

"Personally, I prefer your physical shape, but thank you all the same."

"How do you manage to make *everything* dirty?"

"It's the curse I bear. I just can't help myself."

"Yes, well . . . I'm going to help myself to some fresh air. I think that"—she pauses to fan at her face a few times—"the alcohol has made me too warm."

I want to tell her it's not the alcohol. Or I want to believe it's not anyway. Surely with all the blushing and her nerves, she must be feeling the same connection to me that I'm feeling to her. Or is it only that I've teased her too much? Did I take it too far? Damn it. I just can't help it. I like the fire in her eyes when she's flustered. It's almost as much of a turn-on as that damn outfit.

I finish off the last of my beer, *her* beer actually, and say, "I'll go with you."

"Oh, thanks. But . . . I wanted to make a phone call. I'll come back in a little bit."

I frown. I'm almost positive she has no intention of making a phone call, which means I was right. I'm screwing this all up. *Again.*

With Lina . . . I had years to get to know her, to figure out how to talk to her. We were at ease with each other. Nell is most certainly not at ease with me. And I can already tell she's a complex girl, and I'm going to have to do a hell of a lot better if I want to get to know her.

"Okay," I say. "Just be careful. It's dark out, and there are a lot of people around. If you need anything, come find me or one of the guys."

She nods, takes two steps away from me, and hesitates. Then she turns and says, "Thanks for the drink."

As if watching her walk away weren't frustrating enough, the bounce of that short skirt just below her delectable ass is enough to give a healthy man heart failure. If I don't find a way to get my hands on her tonight, I'm likely to go insane before morning.

TIME DRAGS AFTER Nell leaves, and no matter how many conversations I get pulled into, nothing holds my interest. Partying is what I do. Interacting with people is my strong point. And that makes Halloween pretty much my favorite day of the year. And yet . . . all I want to do is kick everyone out, put some gory movie on Netflix, and be alone with my thoughts.

God, this girl is messing with my head.

Maybe it's because for the first time since Lina and I broke up, I'm not looking at the world in terms of distractions. All the things that used to entertain me, the things that helped me get over her . . . now they're just annoying the hell out of me, and I wish I could drown them all out.

I'm half tuned into a conversation with Brookes and Ryan and a few more people about next week's game when I spy Silas across the room. He gives Dylan a peck on the cheek and then takes her cup and heads for the kitchen, presumably to get her a refill.

I walk away from our group without making an excuse. Zay calls after me, but I wave him off. I dodge around people as quick as I can, and snag Dylan's wrist before anyone else can pull her into a conversation. She freezes up, whirling around to face me, and I immediately let go of her arm.

"Sorry. I . . . Sorry."

She shakes her head. "It's fine. You just caught me by surprise. What's up?"

"I need you to tell me about Nell."

Her brows furrow, and for a few silent seconds I think she might actually help me. Then she bursts into laughter.

"I'm sorry, Torres. But you've got to be out of your mind. There is absolutely zero chance that I'm going to help you hook up with my roommate."

"Come on. I'm not that bad."

"I didn't say you were bad. You are charming and funny and incredibly loyal. But you're also a flirt. And you're easily distracted by new, shiny, scantily clad things. And Nell is . . . she's different. She may not seem fragile, but she is. And I would like to continue hanging out with all of you *and* keep my roommate. I'm not sure that would be possible if I let you anywhere near her."

My spine locks up, and the tension starts creeping up around my shoulders, down my arms, all the way to my clenched fists.

"I'm not going to hurt her."

"Listen, I respect that you're up front with girls about your nonrelationship style. But Nell hasn't dated much. I don't know how she'd handle being with someone like you, so I think it's better if it just didn't happen."

"You can't stop me from pursuing her."

And that was the dumbest thing I could have said. Dylan straightens, squaring her shoulders and giving me an intimidating stare. I can see the protective fire in her eyes, and combined with her Statue of Liberty costume, she definitely doesn't look like anyone you'd want to mess with unless you'd like to get clobbered with a fake torch.

"What I meant to say is . . . I like her. If this were just about getting into her pants, I'd turn around and leave with my tail tucked between my legs. Honest. But I think she's . . . interesting. I don't know how to talk to her, though. Every time I think I'm gaining ground, she locks up tight or runs away. I just need to know what I'm doing wrong."

Dylan sighs and stares at me.

"You promise me that you're serious about this?"

"I am. I just want to get to know her better. And I promise I won't let things go too far until I'm certain I'm in it."

Dylan rubs at her eyes and groans. "Tell me something. The only time I've ever seen you pursue a girl longer than one night is when she's not interested. Is this some kind of subconscious thing you do because you don't really want to be in a relationship?"

"Maybe I just don't see the point in going after someone I'm not willing to fight for."

She purses her lips and begrudgingly replies, "Good answer." She examines me a moment longer and sighs. "I'm so going to regret this."

"Ah. Captain Planet. You're the best."

"Just tell me what you want to know."

"What kind of guys does she like?"

Dylan blinks at me. "You know . . . I don't have the slightest clue. She's never seemed all that interested in guys."

"Are you saying she's—"

"No. I don't know. Nell's life doesn't revolve around social things like parties or dating. She's all about school. She's focused and driven, and she puts her everything into her classes. I think it's because she was the first person in her family to go to college. She feels like she has to prove herself, so she's never really made any time for anything else."

Well, damn. I certainly know what that's like . . . feeling like you have to prove that you're worth people's attention.

"Then why is she all of a sudden coming to parties?"

She bites her lip, worrying it before she answers. "That would be my doing. I told her that she wasn't getting the full experience out of college by just focusing on classes. Now I think she's trying to broaden her horizons a bit."

I smile, and Dylan immediately pokes a finger into my sternum. "Whatever you're thinking, not *that* broad."

"Chill out. I was just thinking that explains why it seemed like she'd never tasted alcohol before. She's trying new things. That's cool."

"And that's exactly why she needs to take baby steps. And you like to jump in the deep end."

"Sometimes that's the best way to learn how to swim."

"Mateo Torres. I *will* kill you if you hurt her."

I tuck an arm around her and pull her close in a half hug.

"Jeez, I thought you were a pacifist." When she bristles, I continue: "Relax. There will be no harm or deaths of any kind."

Silas shows up then with new drinks for both him and Dylan and says, "Dude. Hands off."

I back away, my hands raised, still grinning.

"You snooze, you lose, man. I'm going to steal her from you one of these days."

Dylan shoots me a warning glance, but I'm pretty positive that it's not a reaction to that comment. I take a few steps back and she says, "I mean it, Torres."

"Gosh, Captain Planet. Careful or Moore here might find out about the sweet nothings you've been whispering in my ear."

I leave before Dylan can frown at me again or before Silas can glare.

Couples, man.

Then I forget about them and set off in search of Nell.

Chapter 7

Nell's To-Do List

- *Normal College Thing #6: Drink alcohol (and not at church).*
- *Survive Halloween (preferably without popping a button on this shirt).*

It takes me a long while to find any semblance of calm at this raging party. For a moment I'd thought of leaving, but then I fished my phone out of my bag to discover it was only half an hour since I'd arrived. I decided it probably wouldn't be honoring the spirit of my bucket list if I were to let myself leave after thirty-one minutes.

Finally, I settle myself down beside a mesquite tree on the side of the house and pull my bag into my lap. The only reason Dylan let me get away with bringing it was that I insisted it added to my schoolgirl persona. If she knew I'd also brought along a few spirals and the latest issue of *Scientific American*, she likely wouldn't have been so accepting.

But it's not the magazine I reach for when I open my bag but the familiar spiral, the contents of which have been plaguing my thoughts nonstop for days.

I'm a list kind of girl. I make a lot of them. I make them in the morning, in spare moments throughout the day, during classes when the professors move slower than my thoughts. I make them in notebooks, on my phone, on sticky notes, and just in my head. But now I flip forward to *that* list and start scanning through it. With a smile, I retrieve a pen and draw a line through

6. ~~Drink Alcohol (and not at church).~~

The rush of satisfaction that tears through me at the simple action is astonishing. It's not as if I'd accomplished any great feat or had a brilliant intellectual breakthrough. I'd had a rather yummy cup of Torres's signature concoction, and most of the people here had probably been doing something similar for years now.

The thought of Mateo—no, *Torres*—pinches something in my belly, and I glance back at the very first item on my list. I run my finger over the words, and it is terrifyingly easy to imagine completing that task with the handsome athlete. Then my eyes dip down to item number five on the list.

5. *Lose my virginity.*

The pinch in my belly progresses to a twist, and I cannot decide if it's a good feeling or a bad one. And for a moment . . . I seriously consider the idea.

What if I lost my virginity to Mateo Torres?

It would knock off two items on my list in one go, and I'm nothing if not efficient. But I'm not silly enough to think I should let some list cobbled together from my own imaginings and the offerings of the Internet decide my first sexual experience.

But I have to admit . . . the idea has appeal. He's attractive, that's for certain. Perhaps not as conventionally handsome as Dylan's boyfriend, whose looks just scream a career in film or modeling if football doesn't work out. No, Torres isn't quite that pretty. His forehead is large, and his nose rather blunt. But when he smiles, which he does nearly all the time, it softens his edges and makes him plenty appealing. My own features aren't exactly perfectly formed either. My nose has always been just a tad too large for my face. Well, in my younger years there was no *tad* about it. And while my hair is long, it's never been all that soft or shiny. It's a tangled mess most days, which is why it's most often piled and knotted atop my head.

Beyond that, though, I'm fairly confident that he's attracted to me, which should make the experience enjoyable for both of us. And if his blatant sexuality is any clue, he would be no novice.

I'm partly scared by that. Would he be disappointed that I don't know what I'm doing? Would it make it less . . . well, just *less* for him? What if after all this buildup between us, I bore him?

It wouldn't be the first (or last time) someone found me boring. It's something I've come to terms with in the rest of my life, and I'm happy enough with how I am not to care. But doing something like this . . . for the first time, well, I'm not sure my self-assurance could withstand that kind of blow.

The part of me that isn't scared is intrigued by his confidence and probable experience. Why start completely from scratch when I can use a trusted source of knowledge to further my education at a much faster rate? Maybe he'll understand, and he'll guide me through it with as little turmoil as possible.

Or maybe he won't. Maybe he won't like that I'm a virgin, and he'll find the whole thing bland and a waste of his time.

UGH.

I groan, and flip the page in my spiral so I won't have to look at the words anymore. Starting small with the alcohol had been a wise decision. Perhaps I should do the same with other big items on my list. But how did one get smaller than sex and hooking up? I couldn't just put "kiss." I'd done that before, and a few more kisses weren't going to make any difference in my confidence when it came to sex.

Really, it's the unknown that bothers me. Not just on this list, but in everything. So maybe that's what I need to get used to.

I skip to the bottom of my list and add . . .

17. Kiss a stranger

I tap my pen against the page, surveying the words, and decide that kissing a stranger is a good stepping-stone. Then a voice comes from over my shoulder, making me jump up and drop my spiral in shock.

"Do I count as a stranger?"

I press my hand over my thundering heart and turn to face the subject of my rumination.

"You scared me."

"My bad." Contrary to his words, Torres doesn't look the least bit sorry.

He bends to pick up the spiral, and I lunge forward to stop him. "Wait! Stop!"

It's too late. He already has ahold of it, and lifts it up above his head, completely out of my reach. He's got nearly a foot on me in height, and when I try to jump, I barely get my unathletic self a few inches off the ground.

"Give that back."

"Hold up, sweetheart. I just want to take a little peek."

"Don't you dare! It's private."

Frantically, I try to recall what was written on that page as he holds it above his head in an attempt to read.

"'Go skinny-dipping'?" he says, his eyes dancing suggestively. "Whatever this is . . . I like it."

I step toward him, and he angles his body to the side so that the spiral is farther away, but we're still close.

"'Pull an all-nighter.' 'Sing karaoke.' 'Flash someone.' Oh, sweetheart, tell me this is a list of things you want to do. Please, God."

"It's none of your business. That's what it is."

"Unlucky for you, I'm a nosy person."

He starts to turn the page back, and my heart tumbles in fear. He *cannot* see the first page. Not ever. I hurl myself at him, practically climbing up his body in an attempt to retrieve my list. And all he does is laugh, and stand there as if there isn't a whole person hanging on to him.

"Asshole!" I say, pushing at his chest.

"Come on, you can do better than that."

"Nosy bastard."

He rolls his eyes. "Well, if that's all you've got . . ." He starts to turn the page again, and there's thunder in my ears, and my lungs feel all twisted up inside my chest.

"Fuck you," I say once, quietly. Then I repeat it, louder, my voice raspy from fear and exertion. "Fuck you, Mateo Torres."

And I resign myself to the fact that I'm not going to get my spiral back until he's had his fill of humiliating me. But to my shock, he bends and picks up my pen from where I'd dropped it when he surprised me. Then he draws a line through something on the paper.

"Congratulations. You've officially completed number sixteen. 'Cuss someone out and mean it.'"

He hands me the spiral, then the pen, before folding his arms over his chest and meeting my eyes with a carefully blank expression. I glance down at the item on the list that he's crossed out, and I don't know whether I want to laugh or stab him with my pen. Maybe both.

"You . . ." I begin, and then trail off. I take a deep breath and speak the truth: "You are the strangest person I've ever known."

The things that are the most off-putting about him are also what make him undeniably interesting. He has no respect for personal space. He says whatever pops into his head with no attempt at polite censorship. But he does it all with such ease and confidence that there isn't a drop of malice in it.

He laughs at my calling him strange, and the sound is raucous and light and completely uninhibited. I don't think I've *ever* laughed like that. He reaches out and tugs on one of my pigtails, then says, "I'll take that as a compliment."

It might actually have been one. In the aftermath of our little scene, I'm feeling oddly . . . exhilarated.

"Come on," he says, picking up my bag and slinging it over his shoulder. "Walk with me."

I should ask him where, ask questions of any kind really, but I don't. Instead, when he holds a hand out to me, I take it. I do it without thinking or evaluating or planning a single thing. And having his large hand curl around mine . . . I don't have any words for it. I search for them, for a description of the way it makes me feel, but it's a muddle of emotions, and those have never been one of my strong points. I cannot separate all the things his touch makes me feel, let alone identify them. But whatever it is . . . it's not bad. So I don't resist when he pulls me toward the back of the house.

There are a few people hanging out smoking, and I tense thinking maybe he means for us to join them, but he pulls me farther along toward the back of the yard. They've got an old, dilapidated privacy fence, and there's a whole section of it that looks as if it had been knocked down in a storm. Or perhaps a more man-made disaster, knowing the residents of this house. When he steps onto the broken pieces of the fence, I hesitate.

"Trust me, girl genius. This will be worth it."

I swallow, and step up onto the board and follow him out of the yard into a wooded no-man's-land between the houses. We turn right and walk past a neighbor's house, and then another before stopping. There's a metal fence, with a gate on one side, and he lifts the latch and walks through.

"What are you doing?" I hiss, pulling my hand away.

"What?" He smirks. "Trespassing isn't on your list?"

I shake my head sternly, and he reaches for my hand again, and this time his hold is too firm for me to pull away. "It should be. Add it."

When I still resist, he steps back through the gate to stand directly in front of me, mere inches away. With the hand not holding mine, he reaches up and pushes a lock of hair off my forehead.

"Relax. I know the family who lives here. They're out of town all this week."

This is crazy. And ridiculous.

"Why are we here?"

"That's up to you, sweetheart."

I let him lead me through the fence, and around a wooden shed to the central open area of the backyard.

"I thought," he says, "we could just hang out. Talk. Away from all the noise." He pulls me up beside a quaint tire swing, and gestures for me to sit down on it. It takes some finagling, what with my short skirt, but I manage to lift myself up on it without making too much of a scene. He crosses behind me, takes hold of the ropes on each side, and I hold on tight, preparing for him to push me forward. But before he does, he leans down close, his lips brushing the shell of my ear. He points a finger to the far side of the yard and says, "Then I thought, if you were up for a little more adventure, we could check skinny-dipping off your list."

Chapter 8

Mateo

Nell's eyes take in the swimming pool, surrounded by a mesh fence because the Del Vecchios, the people who live here, have a toddler. A little boy. Her mouth drops open, then closes, and opens again.

She's been remarkably agreeable for the last few minutes, letting me drag her over here, and I don't want to screw that up by pushing her too fast, so I add, "Or you can stay here on this swing and tell me all your deepest, darkest secrets."

Okay . . . so maybe I don't know how to not push her at least a *little* bit.

She gives what might actually be a laugh and says, "What a choice."

"Well, I do like to be fair."

She looks at the pool one more time, her gaze lingering just long enough to make me think she might say yes. I imagine her flicking open the buttons on her white shirt, shedding that cock-teasing costume, and I'm hard in seconds.

Damn. I just can't keep my cool around her.

It's got to be her similarity to Lina. Has to be. I cut myself off from thinking about Lina in that way a long time ago because every time I let myself remember her . . . it would fuck me up for weeks. Messed with my head. With my game on the field. And considering the game is why I lost her, I refused to let myself screw that up, too. That would mean I'd lost her for nothing. So, ruthlessly, I burned away the memory of her in my bed. I replaced it with new memories. Not just in my bed either. My truck, too. Anywhere that made me think of Lina. And not just places either. It sounds psycho, but I did my best to blot out memories of actions, too. There'd been this time with Lina when she wouldn't let me kiss her the whole time we had sex. She held her mouth half an inch away from mine, but anytime I lifted up to seek out her lips, she'd pull away. Only after we both came would she kiss me, and it was the best goddamn kiss of my life.

Last year, three months into my first semester here, I re-created that night with one of the girls on the cheerleading team. It wasn't quite the same. I'd had to hold her face to control her movements, but I held her just close enough, teased us both until we were desperate, only kissing her at the very last moment.

It wasn't the best kiss of my life. It wasn't even particularly good.

But it served its purpose. It had taken the edge off that memory, dulling it with this new one, until the grip of the past eased.

I'd done that so well and so often last year that I rarely thought of Lina these days.

Until Nell.

Because it isn't sex that raised the memories this time, but the cute indentation in her brow when she's thinking. It's the way she talks. Using words that I've only ever read in textbooks, rather than heard out of a person's mouth. The arrogant tilt of her chin when she knows she's right. Those are the things I've never been able to burn away about Lina, and I see them all in Nell.

And I've starved myself from the memory of her so much that I'm too damn hungry now to separate the past from the present. That's the only explanation for why Nell can practically bring me to my knees with a tilt of her head or a long look.

I can't decide whether that means that I should stay far, far away from her, or take this one last opportunity to demolish the remains of my broken heart. I can't help but think that after a few weeks with Nell, I could break Lina's hold on me once and for all.

"Well?" Nell asks, pulling me out of my thoughts. "Are you going to push me or not?"

I smile. "Your wish is my command."

The tire is laid flat so that you can sit with your ass in the opening, but Nell is sitting primly on the other end in a way that's sure to throw the whole thing off balance when it's moving. I reach forward, hooking my hands under her arms and tugging her backward. She falls back, squealing, her body cradled by the tire. After a few seconds, she realizes that she's not going to slip through, and she tilts her head back, looking at me from below.

My mouth goes dry at the sight of her.

Quickly, before I can do something stupid like lean down and devour that plump mouth of hers, I pull back on the ropes and send her swinging. When she comes back my way, I push on the tire, sending her higher, faster. I do this a few times before I allow myself to say, "So tell me about this list."

Her tone blunt, she says, "No."

I notice then that she's still got ahold of the spiral, pressing it tight against her chest.

"Fine. I don't need you to tell me what it is. It's a list obviously, and judging by the contents, it's a bucket list of things you want to do. What I don't get is why. Most people's bucket lists are about seeing the world and following their dreams and seeking adventures. Yours is about cursing and kissing strangers, which leads to the obvious conclusion that you've never done those kinds of things. Keep swinging if I'm right."

I punctuate that last sentence with another push, and I think I see a faint smile across her lips as she flies away from me.

"I knew it." Her eyes meet mine when she returns, and I grin down at her. "So I'm going to guess you've been pretty sheltered. Maybe your parents were strict. Religious probably. If you were a freshman, I'd say you were sowing your wild oats now that you're out of your parents' house, but I'm pretty sure Dylan said once that you two are the same age. So that can't be it. You've been out from under your parents for a while. You are a puzzle, sweetheart."

"It's not that complicated," she says, and I tamp down my wide smile at having won this little battle.

"Enlighten me."

"I've just been really focused on school, and I've not had that much of a social life since I got here. I thought it was time for that to change."

I ease back on my pushes so that her swinging slows to a lazy glide. "So you've been busy with school. Studying biomechanical engineering."

She sits up on her elbows as she swings, looking back at me with raised eyebrows. "You remembered."

"It might not seem like it, but I do listen. When I'm interested."

"And you're interested in engineering?"

"It's a related interest."

She frowns. "Meaning?"

"Meaning it's connected to something else I'm interested in, so I'm interested by association."

"You mean me?"

God, she's direct. Just like . . .

I cut off that thought and focus on Nell.

"Yes, I mean you. I'm interested in you."

"I gathered that."

"So, let me ask again? Do I count as a stranger?"

She sits up in the swing, upsetting the balance, and I have to grab on to the ropes and pull back to bring the thing to a stop. Before she can wiggle out of the tire, I circle around her. I stand

and grip the ropes, just as she gets herself to the edge, ready to jump off.

"Torres . . ." she says, stretching my name out uncertainly. It's not how I'd like her to say my name, but it's not quite an admonishment either. It's just . . . hesitant.

"This list is obviously something that matters to you, or you wouldn't carry it with you. You wouldn't have brought it to a party, of all places." Something occurs to me then. "That's why Dylan is suddenly bringing you around. She's helping you with this list. That's why she warned you away from me. She's probably the one who made you make the list in the first place. I like the girl, but Christ, does she like to tell other people what to do, how to behave—"

Nell pushes to her feet, her chest grazing mine before she jolts back. "Dylan doesn't know about the list. And I would appreciate it if you wouldn't tell her."

I frown. Now, *that* is not what I expected.

"Why doesn't she know?"

Nell worries her bottom lip between her teeth, and God, her lips are already full enough without being swollen from her nibbling. If I didn't know better, I'd think she was doing this on purpose, trying to distract me from prodding further.

"Because this is something private, and you're right. Dylan can be very opinionated. She means well, but these things . . . well, it's more of an experiment for me, and experiments aren't for an audience. They're for discovery."

"I promise I won't tell Dylan." Her shoulders slump in relief just before I add, "If you'll let me help."

"*What?* But I just told you this was private. You'd be just as much of an audience as her. These are things I need to do alone."

"As I recall, there's at least one thing on that list that *can't* be done alone."

Her cheeks flush, and I'm suddenly bursting with curiosity to know what else is on the list. What else might require two people.

And there goes my body's traitorous reaction again. Even if she doesn't want to go skinny-dipping, I might need my own dunk in the pool just to cool down before I go back to the party.

She holds the spiral tighter to her chest and says, "It's not just that I want to do this alone. I want to be through my list before the semester ends in a month and a half. It's easier and faster to do this on my own."

A month and a half. Sounds like a good amount of time to accomplish what I'm looking to do, too.

"For you, I would make time."

"Some of the items on the list are . . . they're of a personal nature, okay? And I don't know you."

"You don't know me? Does that mean you'd go so far as to call me a *stranger?*"

She lets out an exasperated sigh, but I can tell by the frantic clutching of her fingers around the spiral that she's not just frustrated. She's downright terrified.

"Listen." I take hold of her shoulders, stilling her nervous movements and forcing her to look at me. "You don't have to tell me anything you don't want to. And I promise I won't look at your list again. I swear, okay? And I won't tell Dylan or anyone else about it. But I want you to swear that whenever it's something you don't have to do alone or something you shouldn't do alone . . . you'll call me. I sing a mean karaoke, and I pull all-nighters all the time, and I—"

"Okay."

I pause, letting my arms trail down from her shoulders to her elbows.

"Okay?"

I lean a little closer, pitching my mouth closer to hers. "Does that mean I can be your strange—"

She covers my lips with her hand, cutting off my words, and with that familiar proud tilt of her chin she says, "The list says to *kiss* a stranger. Not *be kissed* by one."

And with that she pulls out of my arms and starts toward the pool, her hips swaying to the heavy pounding of my heart.

Chapter 9

Nell's To-Do List

- *Normal College Thing #12: Go skinny-dipping.*

keep my head held high and my back straight the whole way over to the pool.

But inside?

I am an equation with too many missing variables. My heart is doing things that biologically it should not be able to do. Or at least it feels that way. And my nerves begin to bleed through as I try with shaky hands to undo the childproof lock on the fence around the pool.

The pool where I am trespassing.

Where I am breaking the law.

And where I will presumably be wearing far less clothing in a matter of minutes if I do actually go through this.

Just breathe, Antonella. The more you breathe, the less panicked you'll feel.

It's all biology. Hormones and neurons and impulses. This is a biological response to an intimidating situation. I have nothing to fear here. My brain just thinks I do.

While I'm still struggling with the lock, Torres's hands settle over the top of mine, halting my movements. He's directly behind me, one arm on either side, effectively surrounding me with his skin and heat and scent.

"Relax," he says in my ear, but if anything that just shatters the smidgen of control I'd managed to wrangle back from my panic. My shoulders tense, rising up closer to my ears, and I squeeze my eyes shut.

"I can't," I admit, my voice quiet. "You . . . intimidate me."

"Why?"

"Because . . ."

"Because you like me. Even though I'm flashy and shameless. Even though I'm too concerned with how other people see me, and I'm like a puppet who doesn't realize his strings are being pulled?"

I flinch at the reminder of what I said at that Frisbee game. He'd been so close and so appealing, and I'd lashed out with my most ruthless honesty so that he'd give me some space to breathe, to think.

I twist, looking over my shoulder at him, and my back comes into contact with his chest.

"I'm sorry. I shouldn't have said that."

He doesn't look angry. His face is relaxed and easy, but he's so good at putting on a show that could just be what he wants me to see.

"Don't be. I'm just reminding you why you have no need to be embarrassed in front of me. You said we were complete opposites. That you don't care what people think. So don't start now. But if you're too nervous, just say the word, and I'll take us back to the party. Or I'll go back to the party and leave you here to check this item off your list alone."

I swallow. I don't want to be alone. But I'm not sure I'm brave enough to do this with him either.

"Will you go first?" I ask.

He stills behind me, and his jaw clenches. I watch his neck work as he swallows, and I wonder what he's thinking. His voice is deeper, almost hoarse, when he says, "Sure. I can do that."

He pries my hands off the lock, and in a move that sends shock waves across my skin, he places a casual kiss on my fingers before releasing them.

All of a sudden I feel that same suffocating sensation that made me lash out at him with harsh words, but this time it makes me want to lash out in a different way. I want to place my hand on the sharp edge of his jaw and turn his face toward me. I want to bring my mouth to his and find out just how hot the heat between us can get.

But this time I control the impulse. I push it down, try to temper it with logic, but for every reason I think of why I shouldn't kiss him, I think of another why I should.

With a victorious "Got it," he undoes the latch and pulls the metal rod that the canvas fencing is attached to out of a divot in the ground. He folds the heavy fabric back, letting it rest on another part of the fence, and gestures at the pool.

"After you, my lady."

There are only a few feet of concrete between the fencing and the water, so I step in and to the left, and he follows. The water is clear and still, glowing from the reflection of the moon.

"Me first?" Torres asks.

He's already almost naked. All he has to do is slip off that loincloth and anything he has underneath it, and he's done. Before I even give him an answer, he hooks his thumb under the band of his costume, and begins pushing it down his hips.

I gulp in air, and order myself to look away, but I can't. I just can't. Luckily, he's wearing a pair of tight, black shorts beneath, and I'm able to finally pull my gaze away while he's still covered. I hear him lay the loincloth over the fence in front of him, and I turn farther away, lest I be tempted to look back again.

I realize I'm still clutching the spiral to my chest, terrified to let it out of my hands. So while he removes his last article of clothing, I lean over the fence and drop the spiral onto the grass.

I keep my back determinedly to Torres, but even so, I know the minute he moves away from me. I can feel it.

Which is absolutely absurd. It's impossible to feel a person's presence. *Feeling* directly implies touch.

And yet . . .

There's a splash behind me, and no longer able to contain myself, I turn. I watch his head break the surface of the water, rivulets running over his face and shoulders. He reaches up and wipes his eyes, and then he's grinning at me. Wild and carefree and so, so handsome it's hard to breathe.

It's easy to understand why Dylan warned me away from him. There is something impossible to resist about his charm and when he focuses it all on one person? I can imagine he gets just about any girl he wants.

And improbably . . . that girl is now me.

I can't really see anything beneath the water. To my eyes, he's no more naked now than he's been all night. But even so, an illicit thrill runs through because I *know*. Even if I can't see.

Before I can ask him to turn around, he does, wading over to the side of the pool and leaning his arms against the edge with his back to me.

He doesn't say anything to prompt me into action. Nor does he seem impatient. He behaves almost as if I'm not even here.

And that is the thing I don't understand about Dylan's warning. Sure, he's been blatantly flirtatious. And shameless was a very apt description. But he's never been pushy or rude, except for the moment when he stole my spiral, but even that had been oddly . . . thoughtful. And it makes me wonder . . . is he different with me than he is with his friends? Or just different with girls he's interested in? Maybe the thoughtfulness is an act to put me at ease.

Well, if it is . . . it's working.

With a deep breath, I reach for the buttons on my shirt and begin to undo them. The first brush of air against my bare skin makes me shiver. It's not cold outside, despite it being the end of October. Texas doesn't have a traditional winter so much as it has one long summer with occasional cold fronts to break up the relentless heat.

When I get the shirt all the way unbuttoned, I shrug it off and lay it over the fence beside Torres's loincloth. I blush furiously at the sight of the dark shorts on top of his costume. They're longer than boxer briefs, but they're still constructed like them. And I can just imagine how snugly they would fit over his muscled thighs . . . over all of him. I look back over my shoulder, but he's still exactly as I left him, his wet, muscled shoulders glinting in the moonlight.

Quickly, I shove the plaid schoolgirl skirt over my hips, and it pools at my feet. I step out of the garment and pick it up, tossing it on top of my shirt, and then I pause. I could just jump in like this. Admittedly, I'm not a skinny-dipping expert, but I've seen enough movies to know one doesn't have to be completely naked for it to count.

But then my bra and underwear will be wet when I go back to the party. And since my shirt is white, there'd be no hiding it. I'd either have to wait for my undergarments to dry or just say screw it and go back anyway. It would take a long while for my things to dry. Dylan would no doubt wonder where I am. She's probably already wondering.

No. Bra and underwear need to go, too.

With one last glance at Torres, I reach behind me to unclasp my bra, shimmy off my underwear, and throw them both on the pile of clothes.

Then I turn to face the pool.

I look at Torres's back and wonder if he can feel me the way I thought I could feel him earlier. Does he know I'm standing here facing him, completely on display? One peek over his shoulder is all it would take to know all my secrets. But he doesn't peek. Not once.

I bend, sitting on the edge of the pool and slipping my legs in the water. The cool water prickles at my skin, and before I can change my mind, I slide all the way in.

I squeak at the cold sting of the water against my bare skin and hold my arms up. They and my head are the only things that didn't go underwater, and I suck in a hissing breath.

"You should have just jumped all the way in."

I look up to see that Torres has now turned. He's still leaning against the pool's edge, but he has his arms stretched out beside him. I marvel for a moment at just how big he is. His arms, especially, are long and undoubtedly strong.

"Everyone always says that," I say, trying not to shiver. "But I still prefer to ease myself in, rather than plunge all at once."

"And this list of yours? That's not plunging in all at once?"

"I suppose some things might be, but the bigger things, those I'm easing myself into."

"Like?"

Like sex. Possibly with you.

I grit my teeth, and slowly lower my arms into the water, wrapping them around myself both to cover my breasts and recover a little bit of warmth.

"Like tonight I had my first real drink of alcohol. That was the first step. Later, I'll actually get drunk. Even do a keg stand."

He laughs and drops his hands into the water. He begins moving toward me, and the goose bumps already dotting my skin seem to tighten and multiply.

"*You're* going to do a keg stand? Now, that is not something I ever thought you would have on your list."

Too embarrassed to admit that I'd Googled *college bucket list* in an attempt to learn what normal people my age do, I shrug and say, "It seems like fun." Actually, it seems like a disaster waiting to happen, but what do I know?

He laughs, still moving toward me, and comes to a stop about three feet away.

It's just far enough that I don't feel crowded, but still close enough to speed my heartbeat to a frantic pace.

"You just keep surprising me, girl genius."

"That's a good thing?"

"Very."

His eyes are dark, pupils expanded wide in the night, and the look he gives me isn't one I can classify. It's sexual, for sure, but most of the looks he gives me are at least partly sexual. And yet they're all so different. Before meeting him, I hadn't imagined how varied the reactions of attraction could be. It's fascinating, and without realizing it, I've moved a foot closer to him. Close enough now that I could reach out and touch him, if I were willing to un-wrap my arms from my chest.

"I'm not always surprising," I say, feeling an irrational need to quash his attraction to me, to make him somehow less potent. "Generally, I'm quite boring."

"Oh, sweetheart, I don't think you could ever be boring."

And suddenly my eyes are watering, and I need to swallow and swallow again. I hadn't realized until he'd said it just how badly I've always needed to hear those words. Confidence is a camou-flage that does nothing to fill the gaps it covers.

Before he can see my reaction, and before I can think too far ahead, I lift my arms to touch his shoulders and pull myself up enough to press my mouth to his.

To kiss my stranger.

Chapter 10

Mateo

Her lips are so tentative at first that I barely react, wondering if there's a chance that this is her first kiss. And if it is, the last thing I want to do is scare her off.

But then I realize that the brush of her lips was soft and short, not because she was hesitating, but because she's so much shorter than me that she had to pull up on my shoulders, lifting her toes off the pool bottom, to reach me. Her grip shifts and this time her arms go around my shoulders, holding on to me to keep her up, and the change brings her so close that her bare chest brushes mine.

Fuck.

She gasps, and the second kiss she'd been about to give me is forgotten as she closes her eyes and dips her head. She arches her back, as if she wants to draw her chest away from mine, but her arms stay tight around my shoulders, and her tits drag against my skin, wet and hot and . . . *fuck*. That slow glide of skin is enough to snap the last of my resolve.

I wind my arms around her waist, pulling her tight against me, and the soft curve of her stomach presses against my rock-hard cock, and it's a fucking miracle that I don't come right then and there.

She feels so damn good in my arms. Soft and warm and smooth, and I know I'm not going to be able to keep my promise to Dylan. I told her that I would take things slow with Nell. That I wouldn't let things go too far.

But all I want now is to go further, be closer.

But I force myself to ask, "Can I kiss you? Is it okay to *be kissed* by me now?"

Her eyes are wide and dark, and in the scant few seconds that she pauses, my heart feels like it's twisted all the way around in my chest. Then she nods, and I crush my mouth to hers, feeling dizzy with just how much I want her.

She opens to me immediately, pushing her tongue against mine in a way that soothes my earlier fear that she hadn't done this before. One of her hands slides from my shoulder to my neck, and it presses her chest flush against mine. Her nipples are beads of heat against my skin, and her breasts are full and heavy, and I can't wait to feel them, to hold them, to taste them.

But for the moment I'm too busy being undone by the thorough exploration of her tongue in my mouth. She tastes sweet, like the drink I'd given her earlier, and her movements are confident. In control.

Oh no. My girl might be a genius, but she could not learn *that* from books. But what I really want to see is Nell *out* of control. I want to know what it's like to have this proud, intelligent miracle of a girl yield under my hands.

I slip a hand up from her waist, coasting over the outside of her breast and up to her neck. She has to drop her arm from my shoulder to make room for me, but I've got a tight hold on her waist so she won't fall. I spread my palm over the side of her neck, reaching up to grip her jaw and chin with my fingers and thumb.

And then it's my turn. I slant her head back, switching the angle of our kiss, and then I devour that pretty mouth that's been plaguing me all night. Her fingernails tighten against my neck, urging me on, and I search her mouth furiously, as if I might find the origin of her sweet taste that drives me crazy.

I suck her bottom lip into my mouth, and she whimpers. I glory in that sound, determined to coax even more from her.

With her still pressed tight against me, I step forward, toward the wall a few feet behind her. The water flows and shifts around us, and she breaks our kiss to moan.

I can't resist. I ask, "What, sweetheart? Why'd you make that sound?"

I'm pleased to find she can still blush, even when we're naked and molded against each other. I take another step and her eyes flutter closed.

"It's . . ."—she shakes her head, struggling for the words—"the water."

I try not to frown. "The water?"

"It's cold, and you're hot, and the contrast . . . oh—" She breaks off as I press her back against the side of the pool.

"You like the contrast, do you?" She nods, her eyes hazy and her lips swollen.

With one hand still on her neck, I reach the other up to coax her to release her grip on me. She does, letting her arm drop so that both of them hang at her sides in the water. Then slowly, I peel my chest back from hers. Water slides in between us, and just like I'd hoped, she gasps at the change. Now that there's space between us, I lift my hand to her chest, finding one pebbled nipple and worrying it between my fingers. She throws her head back and groans, louder than any other sounds she's made before, and I want her to do it again. I cup her in my hand, and Christ, her rack is amazing. Full and heavy with slick, soft skin, and I've got to taste her. I can't wait.

"Put your legs around my waist," I tell her.

She hesitates, pulling her head up to meet my gaze, and her nerves have returned. Shit. That was the last thing I wanted.

This would be easier with her legs around me, so I could lift her up and out of the water, but if that's going to make her start thinking, make her end this . . . I sure as hell don't have to do it the easy way. I bend, lowering my head and lifting her breast so that her nipple is right at the water's surface. I pull it into my mouth, sucking at the hard tip, and I feel her go completely slack in my arms.

The taste of chlorine only lasts for a few seconds, and then it's just her skin, salty and a little sweet. Her hands grip the back of my head, scrambling for purchase in my short hair. When her left leg wraps around my thigh, I reach down for the other and help her lock them around me. The move pulls her a little farther out of the water, and when I lean into her and the wall, my cock presses tight against the slick heat of her.

Damn. *Damn.*

Her fingers clutch at my head, nails scraping against my scalp in a way that sets me on fucking fire. I switch to the other breast, molding it in my hand while my mouth drops to her neck. I alternate pressing my tongue and my teeth against her skin, and when I hit a particularly sensitive spot, she bucks against me and my erection slides deliciously against her. And I'm so close to where I want to be, and I'm aching for her.

"Torres," she gasps.

I stick with where I'm at, playing my tongue over that spot, dying for her to rock her hips against mine again. Dying to be inside her. I pause to say, "Not my name."

"M-Mateo," she says, trembling as I pull at her taut nipple, and I reward her with a hard suck. She bucks against me again, and I have to pause because just that was enough to bring me close to the edge. The closer I get her to losing control, the closer I get myself.

She mumbles, "This is . . . that is to say . . . I . . ."

After a few more sentences that go nowhere, I slow my assault on her neck and lift my head to look at her.

And God, she's fucking glorious. The ends of her hair are

damp from sloshing water and sticking to her neck. And her skin . . . it's the palest shade of brown and there are no lines, no flaws, just miles of smooth perfection that I can't wait to taste. Her eyes are hooded, and I can see her battle to keep them open, especially when I slide a hand down her ass to pull her tighter against me. She presses her lips together, holding in a sound that I'm desperate to hear.

Slamming my lips down on hers, I nip at her mouth before driving my tongue inside once and then again. I pull back just enough to say, "No more holding your breath. I want to hear you. I want to hear what I do to you. Got that?"

She doesn't answer, and I rock against her again, making sure the head of my cock passes over her clit. Her lips form a circle, and she makes a sound somewhere between a gasp and an "oh."

"Like that," I tell her. "I need to hear you so I know that you feel just as good as I do. 'Cause Jesus, Nell, you're fucking perfect. You taste perfect. You feel perfect. I'm dying to be inside you."

"Inside . . ."

"I bet you're tight, so tight. Perfect there, too." Damn. I could come just thinking about it.

"Torres," she says again, and I fight the urge to spank her ass in response.

"Told you, sweetheart, that's not my name. You know what I want to hear. Let me hear it."

"Mateo, I—"

"That's the one."

I kiss her again, drinking the sweetness from her lips and rocking our hips together again. She tears her mouth away, gasping, and says, "Mateo, we need to stop."

No. *Shit*. That's the last thing I want to do. I want to hold her like this for hours, until we can't stay in the water a moment longer. By then the party should be over, and I can sneak her back to the house and into my room. Then I'll lay her out on my bed, where I can look my fill and taste all the places that I can't reach right now. But she says my name again, and with every second that I'm not kissing her, the image of her in my bed starts to fade.

"Okay," I say, swallowing hard, trying to get myself under control. "Okay."

I slide my hand up from her ass to the small of her back. That should be safer territory, but every part of her makes me hot. Her legs drop from around my hips, and I'm already mourning the loss of her around me. She slides down until her feet touch the pool floor again.

"I'm sorry," she says, still not looking at me.

I take her chin and turn her head toward me. I lean down and kiss her just once. Any more and I'll press her back against the wall again and try to change her mind. "No need to be sorry, girl genius. After all, your list only said kiss. I think we marked that one out a couple dozen times."

And then I step away from her because my hard-on sure as hell isn't going to go away while I'm pressed up against her. I float back a few feet in the water and nod my chin toward her clothes. "Why don't you go ahead and get dressed, and I'll take you back to the party."

Then I turn my back to her even though all I want to do is see those luscious curves that I've just had my hands all over. And while she dresses I put my head down and do a few laps across the pool, willing myself to focus on swimming instead of the release that won't be coming anytime soon.

Chapter 11

Nell's To-Do List

- *Normal College Thing #1: Hook up with a jock*
- *Learn some freaking self-control, woman.*

For a few moments I just stand there naked and dripping beside my clothes. I should be frantically dressing or finding some way to blot the water off my body. Instead I'm watching Mateo's sleek naked body cut through the water in the moonlight. *Torres*, I correct. He needs to stay Torres.

I have never been struck dumb by the naked male form. All the statues in museums of sculpted muscles and curves never really seemed that art-worthy to me. My interest in the body has always been clinical, not aesthetic.

Now I realize that was because I'd never seen it in person. Never seen the powerful way muscles move in action. It goes so far beyond medical. I shake my head before I can start waxing poetic about Torres's magical muscles. God, it's like that guy makes me forget I have a brain.

If he hadn't started talking, there's no telling what I would have let him do. What if he'd just . . . I don't know . . . stuck it in, no warning or whatever. Like . . . SURPRISE! Here's a penis. I picture the scene now. Losing my virginity by sneak attack in the pool, and the vision in my head goes from painful to awkward then back to painful. I can't even think about the fact that he didn't have a condom with him in the pool, and I doubt there are pockets in his loincloth.

"You done yet?" he calls from behind me, and I spin around, covering my intimate places with my hands, but he's got his back to me at the far end of the pool.

"Um, not yet!"

He sets off swimming again and I grab my skirt first. It's dark and plaid, and can withstand a little water. So I use it to get off as much water as I can, then I go ahead and slip it on. Then I pull up my underwear beneath it and proceed to throw on the rest of my clothes as fast as I can. The fabric catches and sticks on my skin, and uncomfortable doesn't even begin to describe how I feel.

I slip on my shoes and call out to Torres, "I'm done."

I guess he doesn't hear me, so I walk around to the end of the pool he's approaching and stand in front of him so that maybe he'll see. He has his head down in the water, but when he touches the wall, he doesn't turn around and head in the other direction. He rises out of the water, shaking his head to clear his eyes, and looks up at me.

I swallow. Bad idea. *Bad, bad idea.*

His eyes travel from my ankles at his eye level, up my legs, lingering at the edge of my skirt, and I wonder just how much he can see from his position below me. But then he continues up, pausing at my white shirt, which clings in places to my damp skin, before he finally meets my eyes.

There's such hunger in his gaze that my knees actually feel a little weak.

Furious that I have so little control of my body, I turn away and say, "I'll meet you by the swing."

Then I dart out of the pool area, grab my spiral, and flee.

Well, there's two more things marked off my list. "Kiss a stranger" and "Hook up with a jock." I feel fairly confident that what we'd just done qualifies as a hookup, and since this is my list, it's my judgment call. And now . . . there's absolutely no reason why I should continue to hang out with Torres. I needed a jock, and I got one, and now everything else can be done without him. I know he said that thing about helping me with the list, but really . . . I doubt he meant it.

That's just his persona, all smooth moves and exactly the right words. And really, he's the last person I want to see me do some of the things on this list. Tonight was embarrassing enough.

I wanted a catalyst. He's more like an atom bomb.

I see him righting the pool fence, struggling to get it latched the way it was, and I panic. What am I going to say to him? Will he expect to know why I stopped us? Or will he want to make god-awful small talk? I'm bad enough at small talk with people I *haven't* been naked with.

Deciding to make my way back to the party alone, I grab my bag from where he'd left it by the swing and move as briskly as I can toward the gate, tucking my spiral away as I go. I hear him call my name a second after I've closed the gate, and I quicken my pace. Within thirty seconds, I'm back at the downed fence at his house, and I slink back in their yard just in time to come face-to-face with my roommate.

When Dylan sees me, she has this harried look in her eye, and she drops her costume torch to throw herself into my arms.

"Thank God," she breathes in my ear. "You disappeared, and I couldn't find you, and you weren't answering your phone, and we were afraid . . ." She trails off, and pulls away to face me. "We were afraid."

I see Silas jog up behind her then, and he releases a heavy exhale. "You found her. Good. Where was she?"

I don't know if it's the bizarreness of the night up until this point, but their worry makes my throat clog, and it aches when I swallow.

"Good question." Dylan's hands are still on my shoulders, and she asks firmly, "Where have you been? And why are you wet?"

I panic, knowing that any second now, Torres is going to enter that gap in the fence that I just came through, and I'll have a lot more questions to answer. So I pull away and walk past Dylan and Silas toward the house, forcing them to turn and follow me.

"Oh, I just went for a walk. The sprinklers came on in one of the neighbors' yards as I was passing, and I didn't react fast enough to avoid getting wet." I look behind me just in time to see Torres step through the hole in the fence. He freezes when he sees his friends, and I ask Dylan, loud enough for him to hear, "Would you care if I went home? This just really isn't my scene."

She frowns. "Sure, of course."

Silas says, "We were about to kick most everyone out anyway. We've got a game tomorrow night, so McClain put a strict curfew on this thing."

Dylan looks up at him, and I realize she doesn't want to leave. Can't really blame her for that.

"You could stay," I say. "If you don't mind me taking your car. I can come pick you up tomorrow morning."

She leans into Silas's side, and he places his hand on her hip. I try not to stare, try not to think about what that must feel like. Comforting? Possessive?

"If it's okay with you," Dylan says, "that would be great. You don't even have to pick me up. I've already got plans to go to the game tomorrow with Dallas, and I've got some clothes here I could wear. Unless you want to go to the game with us?"

"Uh, no. No, I've got some homework to do."

Lie. I'm all caught up, and the professors didn't really assign anything since it's Halloween weekend. But given all the Saturday nights I've spent studying, it doesn't occur to Dylan to question me.

"Okay. Well, let me go grab my keys from inside, and you can go."

I let her and Silas pass me, and even though I shouldn't, I glance back at Torres. He's leaning on the fence, and he should look ridiculous in that costume, but he doesn't. He looks good. And not at all happy.

WHEN I WAKE to an empty apartment the next morning, it doesn't seem to matter that the sun coming through the window lights up every corner. I thought I'd felt lonely last week when this whole list business started, but no . . .

No, *this* is loneliness.

This experiment was supposed to make me realize how good I had it. It was supposed to get rid of my doubts. Well, as experiments are wont to do, it has no care for what I'd wanted the outcome to be.

I make myself a huge breakfast that I couldn't possibly eat alone, like if I just go about my business as if I'm cooking for two, it could make it so. I eat in the kitchen, leaning against the counter because that's what I usually do when I'm busy, when I'm moving so fast and have so much to do that there's no time to feel alone.

But I'm not busy.

I don't have any homework. And for the first time ever, I wish I had a job. Just a normal, boring job like working retail or in an office or anywhere. It would give me something to do, somewhere to be, people to know who have nothing to do with my classes or my family or a group of friends I couldn't possibly fit into. I would maybe even be willing to work in a restaurant . . . something I swore I would never, ever do.

My grandparents started their own restaurant. My parents run it now with occasional help from Nonna, and my brother started working for them full-time as a manager right after high school. It's this huge family affair with aunts and uncles and cousins, and they're so good at putting their hearts into that place, into the food, into every bit of it.

But my heart? My heart never wanted any part of it.

The restaurant is easy for them. Comfortable. I can remember my brother, Leo, hanging out in the kitchen, talking to the employees, stealing food. We'd head to that place every day after school, and he couldn't wait to get there. I dragged my feet. When we both started working as waiters in high school, Leo thrived. I . . . didn't. I didn't fit in with the employees. Everyone was nice enough, sure. It wasn't like school, where I had to worry about how my differences from the other students could cause me problems. But I still didn't . . . fit. And I didn't know how to talk to customers. Leo always earned twice as much as me in tips. It was exhausting to be so different. And it was exhausting to pretend that I wasn't exhausted by it. The only place I didn't feel that was the classroom.

That's where I belonged. Where I thrived. The only place where there was no one to live up to, no one to fall behind, because it was *my* domain. No one in my entire extended family had ever been to college. My grandparents emigrated to the States from Italy a few years after they married. They groomed my mother to take over the restaurant. Dad was a waiter at the restaurant, and she fell for him even though he was older and Nonna didn't approve. My aunt worked in the restaurant, too. By the time I was in high school, things were going so well that they were thinking about opening a second location.

They wanted Leo and me to help run it. I know they did. But I couldn't go my entire life trying to belong in the restaurant when there was another place where it felt so natural for me to be. I wanted to go to college. I wanted to learn more, *be* more. Beyond that, I wanted to go to graduate school, probably get my doctorate. Other kids balked at the idea of more school. I craved it.

All I've ever wanted for my future was to live in a world that's bigger than the one I grew up in. But now I'm realizing that all I did was trade one small, stifled world for another. It's not right that last night was more interesting than every other night in my life so far combined. I'm torn between wanting more nights like it and going back to my normal routine of class, sleep, and more class just because it's safer. Easier. Far less terrifying.

But how long can I live with just safe and easy before my life becomes completely devoid of meaning? I'll have work, sure, but what if I end up not liking it as much as I think I will? For so long, I've thought that the most important thing in my life was my career, getting to where I want to be. Finding a place where I fit. But what if it's not as satisfying as I always thought? What if I got it wrong, and I didn't like class because I fit there, but because

I *thrived* there? Because it challenged me and pushed me in a way that my childhood in the restaurant never had?

And then the big question is . . . am I thriving here? I'm excelling, certainly. My grades are good. I'm making plans. But I don't know if that's the same as thriving. I just don't know.

I used to think about the future in terms of goals and achievements, and now all I can think of is all the things I might end up regretting. And it's all this stupid list's fault. And Dylan's. And *Mateo's*. I was perfectly fine ignoring my doubts until Dylan pointed out how blindly I was pursuing my future, without even exploring any other options.

Does that make me any different from Leo? He stepped right into his position at the restaurant, no hesitation, no thought to any other future because it's what he's good at. I'd thought him so naive.

If he was, I guess I am, too.

I rinse off my plate and load it in the dishwasher, and then dial my parents. My mother answers on the fourth ring, and just by the chaos I can hear in the background, I can tell she's at the restaurant. Probably in the kitchen prepping for the day.

"Antonella?" she says loudly. "Are you there?"

"Yeah, Mammina. I'm here."

She says something in Italian to someone on her end, something about preparing the bread, and after a few seconds I hear a door shut and the din disappears.

"How are you, *passarotta mia*? It's nice to have you call me for a change."

My little sparrow. She took to calling me that sometime during high school. She said all I ever talked about was leaving the nest. And even though I've heard the endearment a thousand times, this time it has tears filling my eyes, and no matter how hard I press my fingers against them, I can't get the tears to stop.

"Mamma," I choke out, my voice surprising me as it cracks. And even though it's just one word, she knows. In that way that all mothers seem to be able to tell what their kids are feeling with just a tiny sound.

"Oh, Nell. What happened?"

I don't have words for all the things I'm feeling. It's all too big. Too frightening to admit out loud.

"I'm doing everything wrong," I tell her, because that's what it feels like. I have this one chance to get things right, and I thought I was doing it it. I thought I knew what I wanted to do and who I was, and now all I can see is a future that terrifies me. A future where I turn out to have made all the wrong decisions.

"Impossible," she says. "You're too smart for that."

That only makes me cry harder. Because that's all I've got. I'm smart. But what does it really matter in the long run? What if I graduate in the spring, and then I go to grad school, and then I get my doctorate, and then I start working only to discover that I've spent years of my life pushing blindly toward a future that doesn't make me happy? My brain has never been the problem. But my heart is an equation I don't know how to solve.

"Tell me what you're thinking," she says. "Whatever it is, we'll deal with it."

She's a good mom. My parents are *good* parents. And I've always felt guilty that my only goal is to not be like them. It's because of them that I don't have to work. Because even though they were sad that I wanted to leave, they wanted me to have every opportunity, to take every chance that was offered to me. They wanted more than anything for me to be happy, and *I'm screwing it all up*.

I suck in a breath, trying not to let on just how freaked out I am. "I just . . . I'm lonely, Mamma. And tired. And I'm worried about the future, and I don't know. It kind of all overwhelmed me this morning."

Understatement of the century. But I hate making her worry.

"Why are you worried about the future? Are classes not going well?"

"No, classes are great. I'm doing really, really well. Still on track to graduate early, and I've been researching and talking to my professors about grad programs." Grad programs that I should already have researched enough to know my top choices so I can start thinking about the application process. But for some reason, I just can't get myself to make a decision. "But, Mamma, what if I'm wrong? I picked biomedical engineering based on an aptitude test and an article I read in a science magazine when I was seventeen. And I know we got my tuition covered here at Rusk, but grad school won't be that easy. It will be expensive. And . . . and I'm just worried that I'm going to spend all this time and money on something I arbitrarily chose as a teenager. Something that I could have gotten wrong."

"If you got it wrong, so what? You think you have to get everything right on your first try?"

"With something like this? Yes. I do."

"Oh, psssh. You are twenty years old. And you are brilliant and beautiful and driven, but you are not perfect, despite how often it seems so." I do a weird, gurgly, sobbing laugh, and I can't help but think about Torres last night. He called me perfect. Several times. But that was an entirely different kind of compliment, and one that has no business sneaking in around thoughts of my mom. She continues, "You are allowed to make mistakes, Nell. And even though it might seem right now like one mistake is enough to derail your entire future, it's not."

"You don't understand, Mom."

"Don't I? I might not have gone to college or picked some high-tech career, but we all make choices. You don't think I agonized over whether or not to marry your father? You don't think both of us had doubts about taking over the restaurant? You don't think it's terrifying to raise children? To know that every choice you make not only determines your future, but theirs, too? The future is never just one choice. It's a thousand. And they never stop. You will choose your future every day of your life. And should you wake up one day to find that you regret the choice you made the day before, then you make a new one. Don't worry about whether you might be wrong *someday*. Worry about whether you're right *now*. Tomorrow can wait."

"Tomorrow can wait," I repeat. The tears are still flowing, but I no longer feel like I'm choking on some invisible ache in my throat. I no longer have to gasp for breath.

"It can," she promises. "No point worrying about what happens at the end of the road when there's a hundred steps to take before you get there. You worry about today's step. Because I promise you, *passerotta*, there will come a day when you stop obsessing over what lies ahead and begin to look backward instead. And when that day comes, it won't matter so much whether every step was in the right direction because life is not a straight line. It will only matter that you took them. That you never let yourself stand still."

"I don't know why people always call me the smart one," I say. "You definitely have me beat."

She laughs, and the sound lifts me in a way that even her words didn't quite manage to do. "I am firmly in the looking-backward stage," she says. "And things are much easier to understand on this side."

"Thanks, Mamma."

"You're welcome. And I'm glad you called. Do it more often."

I agree, and we say our good-byes, and when we hang up, I know exactly what I want to do today. It's officially November now, and I graduate in mid-December. If that's all I have left, I'm going to use every day I have. Maybe I *am* wrong. But short of tacking on another major, it's too late to change my plans completely. I want to check another item off my list, but I can't do it alone.

Chapter 12

Mateo

There's no feeling quite as miserable as returning to a locker room after losing a game. A home game, too, which makes it twice as bad. We went into this game 6–1 on the season, and this was supposed to be the game where we officially surpassed last season's 6–6 record. And even though 6–2 isn't bad, there's this air of uncertainty in the locker room. This deep unspoken fear that everything is going to go downhill moving forward, that maybe we'll fall short again and again until we end up right back at 6–6 for the second year in a row.

I shed my uniform, and Brookes lets out a low whistle beside me. There's a massive purple-black bruise already forming on my left hip and up onto my side.

"That hit at the top of the half?" he asks, and I nod. He shakes his head. "I knew it. That one looked brutal."

I shrug. "Could have been worse. A few inches over and that

second dude's knee could have landed in a much more vulnerable place."

It had been my best catch of the game. I'd had to jump high to get it, and I had two guys trying to block it. We all collided in the air, and we ended up hitting the ground in a tangle of limbs with me on the bottom.

The coaches infiltrate the room then, and Coach Cole steps up into his usual place beside the whiteboard.

"You all know what I'm going to say," he begins, "but I've got to say it anyway. We played a sloppy first half. I'm sure we could blame it on the fact that we had last week off, and that some of you, no doubt, overindulged last night on Halloween. Whatever the reason, it was not up to par with what this team is capable of."

There's one reason he doesn't name, but I have no doubt that most of the team is thinking of it.

Jake Carter.

Formerly one of our team leaders, a senior lineman, and one of our defense's biggest assets. He's the dude that assaulted Stella at a party back in September. He hasn't been suspended by the university, nor has the district attorney brought him up on charges, but Coach got the athletic director to permanently suspend him from the team. Our defense is a hell of a lot weaker without him, but the majority of the team doesn't give a fuck.

There is the minority, though. Guys I've heard grumbling about Coach's decision. None of them have dared to outright mention Stella's name yet. They're not that stupid, but you can tell they talk about it when those of us that know Stella are not around. It doesn't help that she refuses to talk about it, to set the record straight. Hell, I don't even really know exactly what happened, I just know it was bad. But without the facts, I hear people making up their own, and I don't like it. Not at all.

Doesn't help that the dick is still on campus. I'm sure he's spreading his own version of the story all over the place.

When I tune back into Coach's speech, he's on to the second half now, where we finally got our asses into gear. Unfortunately, it was too late. We got close, within three points, but we just couldn't make it all the way back in time.

"Whatever the hell happened tonight, I expect it to be out of your system. And next week, we come back looking like the team I know you are. Other people may underestimate us, but we never let that be an excuse for doing less than our best. I don't underestimate you. I know just how much effort and sweat and strength and heart you can give me. And I swear to God, the next time we step on this field, I better get it. You understand?"

"Yes, sir," we answer.

"I believe in this team. I believe we can surprise people. That we can be more than the small team in this conference. I believe that each and every one of you is so much more than people ever give you credit for. I've coached a lot of players. I've coached guys who have gone pro and guys who haven't, and I can tell you that the biggest difference between those groups is that those who go on to a future in this game know how to rise to the occasion. They know how to show up. And they do it when they're tired. They do it when they're hurting. They do it when they're distracted. They know how to put all that aside and play. And that's what I need from you all. That's what I expect from you."

Someone to my left, Carson, I think, says, "Yes, sir," and the rest of us follow.

Coach tosses the towel on his shoulder into the laundry cart and tells us, "Clean up. Enjoy the rest of your weekend, and be ready to work on Monday."

We gather closer, not quite in our normal circle because the layout of the locker room won't allow it, but we put our hands out as if we're circled up. Coach counts to three and we break with our usual chant of "No Easy Days."

And goddamn if those words aren't true.

As I hit the showers, I know I'm one of the ones who fell short during the first half. Not because I overindulged last night . . . well, not on alcohol at least. And I sure didn't take things easy last week. The one downside (or maybe upside) of being friends with the quarterback and captain is you don't get to take things easy. Because when the coaches aren't looking, McClain most definitely is. And if not him, Moore or Brookes. And not a single one of those guys would let me get away with dragging my ass if I were ever so inclined. Not that I want to. The goal has always been football. It's not just the end of the road for me; it *is* the road.

No, I was off my game because of Nell. Because I couldn't stop thinking about her. Her skin. Her mouth. Her curves. The barely shielded panic in her eyes when she asked me to stop. The fact that she'd practically run away from me. And that last devastating look she gave me before she left with Dylan and Silas.

All of that would have been enough to do my head in, but it only got worse. I dreamed about Lina. About Nell. About both of them. They kept morphing into each other in my dream, and I couldn't keep up with who was who. I dreamed of that last fight that Lina and I had, when she ended things for good. Only I had the fight with Nell, and then Lina showed up, and everyone was fighting with everyone, and I woke up pissed and confused and hard.

Even in the second half of the game, I played better, but my head still wasn't quite my own. It doesn't help when I exit the locker room with Brookes, just behind McClain and Moore, and we watch them reunite with their waiting girlfriends. They stand there holding each other as we approach, and there's a sting of something that might be envy in my gut.

Lina never much liked football. She came to my games, but she didn't think it was smart of me to pin my entire future on a sport where I could be injured or replaced or just plain not good enough. She was fond of calling it a hobby, not a career. And as much as I loved her, I loved football, too. And in the end, I chose the sport over her one too many times.

Needing a distraction, I look over at Brookes and say, "You need a hug, Isaiah? I could hold you if that would help."

McClain gives me the finger. Moore actually pauses from kissing Dylan long enough to say, "Fuck off, Torres."

I smile, feeling a little more normal, not to mention pleased when the couples end their affectionate hellos.

Dylan says to Silas, "Dallas is going to drop me off at home to get some things and my car, but then I'll head over to your place?"

"I'll be there," he answers.

"Me, too," I say, and Dylan gives me a patient smile.

"I'll see you, too."

Moore lifts his chin to McClain and says, "You and Dallas are welcome to join. It'll just be us. Low-key. Just some TV or something, and Dylan said she'd cook."

Dallas says, "Sure. I think we'd like that."

"Don't expect too much," Dylan says. "I get by, but Antonella's the real cook in our house."

My chest tightens at her name, and the words are out of my mouth before I can help them. "You should bring her with you."

Dylan gives me a searching look, but she doesn't make any more speeches, nor does she tell the group about my little infatuation.

"I'll ask."

Then thoughts of Nell consume me on my drive home, and the whole time Silas, Isaiah, and I spend tidying up the apartment before everyone's arrival. Will she avoid me? Ignore me? What will I have to say to get her to open up to me again? It won't be easy. There will be too many people around, and she's shy, but I've got to figure out some way to talk to her. I'm not okay with leaving things the way they were last night, and if I'm honest, I definitely don't want a few minutes in a pool to be it between us. I need more time. Right now, she hasn't blocked out Lina like I planned. Instead, she's just stirred up even more memories, and I can't live like this. It will keep messing with my head until I crash and burn. Or worse . . . until I call Lina. Something I haven't allowed myself to do in nearly a year now. Because as good as it always felt to hear her voice, the stilted conversation, the space between us, was a knife to the chest. And I spent too damn long being a masochist over her.

Nell is supposed to end that. She has to end it.

Just as we finish cleaning up the living room, Silas gets a call from Dylan, and I listen in to his side of the conversation.

"Hey . . . Oh. Okay . . . Yeah, I'll call McClain and tell him . . . It's fine, Dylan. Really. Is she okay?"

She? Who is she? Nell?

"No," Silas continues. "I'll be fine alone." Even I can hear the disappointment in his voice, which is why I'm guessing there's a longer gap as Silas listens to whatever Dylan is saying. "You're sure? If you need to just be with her—" He gets cut off. "You're sure? We won't just get in the way?" He pauses and then nods. "Okay, I'll be there in ten."

He hangs up and turns to Brookes and me. "Change of plans. Dylan needs to be at her apartment, so she can't come over. But she said you guys are welcome to come over there instead if you want."

He calls Carson, and that's when I get the real explanation.

Nell is drunk, and Dylan doesn't want to leave her home alone. When he hangs up the phone, I can't hide my shock. "Nell is drunk? The Nell that lives with Dylan?"

"Wasted, apparently."

"I'm in," I say, and when we both look at Brookes, he's watching me. And I can tell by the look he's giving me that he knows I've got something going on with Nell and doesn't approve. I lift an eyebrow in the most casual so-what? gesture I can offer.

He nods. "Sure. I'll come." But the words are said to me, not to Silas, and I get the feeling what he actually means is, *Sure. I'll come watch and make sure Torres doesn't do anything stupid.*

We tell Silas to go on ahead, and we'll come along in a few minutes. But as soon as Brookes is in his room, I jog after Silas, and catch him as he's getting into his truck. "You mind if I catch a ride with you?" I lie, "Brookes got a call, and he's gonna be a bit."

While Silas drives, he has me text Brookes and McClain the address. Brookes wants to know why I left with Silas, but I'm not about to tell him that I didn't want to spend the car ride with him harping on me to leave Nell alone.

Because I can't leave her alone. I just can't.

Silas parks the truck, and I follow him up a metal and concrete staircase to a second-floor apartment. He opens the door without knocking, and that's when I see Nell standing on the coffee table with some big red-haired dude, singing Spice Girls at the top of her lungs. We step inside just as she's telling him what to do if he wants to be her *lover.*

I think of her list. She told me getting drunk was on it, and all of a sudden I'm furious that this guy got to help her check that task off instead of me. "Nell," I say, before I think better of it. She twists to see me, and her socked feet slide on the coffee table, and then she's stumbling into the ginger giant, and both of them are going down. I dart forward, but I can't catch up to her. They hit the ground with a thud, a groan, and Nell's too-cute giggles. She's lying right on top of him, and he has his hands on her bare back where her shirt has ridden up from the yoga pants that fit her like a fucking miracle.

She lays her head in the crook of his neck like she's completely forgotten that I'm here. If I stopped to think, I'd have known how crazy it would look to storm over and tear her off the guy. I would realize what my actions would mean to Silas and Dylan. But I don't think. I just know I can't spend one more second watching her snuggled up against this guy without losing my mind. She squeals as I pull her up into my arms, and I don't think her feet are even touching the ground.

"You okay?" I ask, but all she does is laugh again and lay her head on my chest. I catch a whiff of alcohol, a strong one, and I realize she really is completely smashed. She probably doesn't have a clue who she's snuggling up against. Probably can't even tell the difference between me and whoever the fuck is on the floor.

But even if she doesn't realize what she's doing . . . it feels damn good to have her wrapped around me again, and for a few seconds it dazes me. Then I look up to find everyone in the room watching us.

Damn.

I lock eyes with Dylan and say, "How did this happen?"

"I'm still working on that. As far as I can tell, she decided she wanted to invent her own cocktail, and she enlisted our friend Matt's help." Ah. Matt. He's one of Dylan's activist friends. I didn't realize he was close to Nell, too. Nell points to him sprawled out on the floor and adds, "This is what happens when you spend all day trying lots of different mixes of alcohol."

That seems to catch Nell's attention enough to rouse her, because she pulls back and places both her small hands on my face.

"I figured it out. It took me a long time, but I got it. I call it Newton's Third Law."

"Uhh . . ."

"Get it? Yours was Bad Decision. And mine . . . is Newton's Third Law." She descends into giggles again, and I scan my dormant science knowledge to try and remember what she's talking about. I'd taken a physics course last year for my kinesiology major, but I just barely scraped by. Unlike high school, where I was concerned with keeping up to impress Lina, last year I'd been mostly focused on forgetting her.

"Is that the one about actions and reactions?"

"Exactly! Every action has an equal and . . ." She pauses and swallows, and man, she's so far gone. "Reaction. Equal and opposite reaction. So . . . *action*." She gestures to an empty cup on the bar, then to her own drunken state. "*Reaction*."

Then she does this little move that's halfway between a fist pump and a celebratory dance. She's so fucking adorable, it actually hurts. Somewhere between my chest and my stomach there's a knot that twists every time I see her. And I'm starting to enjoy it, the strange pleasure pain of wanting her.

"I don't get it," the dude on the floor says. "She's been going on and on about that law for an hour, but for the life of me I don't get what it has to do with alcohol. And somewhere around the eighth shot, I stopped trying to figure it out."

Christ. Eight shots. I hope to God that Nell hasn't had that much to drink.

She pushes at my arms, wrestling out of my embrace, and says, "Here. Let me make you one."

She wobbles over to the table, where there's half a dozen different kinds of liquor and at least that many mixers. I follow and ask, "Any idea how much she's had to drink?" Dylan shakes her head, and the ginger guy is still lying on the ground, silent. I think he might actually have passed out.

"I'll make sure she doesn't drink any more. Maybe you could get started on the food, Dylan? That will help if we can get her to eat any of it."

"Sure. Of course. You sure you've got her?"

The look in Dylan's eyes as she asks tells me this is anything but a simple question. I don't know what this is with Nell. I don't know how long it will last. But I know I'm not handing her over to anyone else to take care of. No fucking way.

"Yeah. I've got her."

Chapter 13

Nell's To-Do List

- *Normal College Thing #18: Invent an alcoholic beverage.*
- *Remember the alcoholic beverage you invented.*
- *Don't throw up.*

orres is somehow even more handsome than I remember. And at the moment there are three of him, which adds up to a whole lot of handsome. He's talking to Dylan, and I keep getting distracted by his mouth. By the way it so perfectly forms words. It's a really great mouth.

Which is why I just can't help touching it.

I rest my fingers there, wanting to feel it move as he talks, but he's just looking at me, and when I twist my head around, I realize that Dylan and Silas have disappeared into the kitchen.

I turn back and order, "Talk."

"What do you want me to say, sweetheart?"

His breath is hot against my fingertips, and a sudden image of him sucking my fingers into his mouth pops into my head, and holy hell . . . where did that come from? Certainly not from any personal experience I've had.

"I like the way your mouth moves."

He laughs, more warm breath, and pulls my hand away to kiss the center of my palm.

"Like I said before, you are a puzzle."

Then I remember my reason for coming over to the table. My drink! I tear my eyes away from Torres and focus on the bottles in front of me, trying to remember how I made it. I started with something clear. Gin, maybe? Or vodka? I pick the one that's in the prettiest bottle and dump some of it into a plastic cup.

"Whoa there." Torres lifts the bottle from my hands, and I let him have it. I was done with it anyway. "I think you're all good on drinks right now."

"This one is for you," I tell him.

Then I add some orange juice, a shot of the other clear liquor just to be safe, some grapefruit juice, and a squeeze of lemon concentrate. I swish it around with my finger, and then hand the cup to Torres, sucking the liquid off my finger while I watch him. For a moment all he does is stare at my finger in my mouth, and I wonder if he's picturing the same thing I thought of earlier.

I pop my finger out of my mouth and say, "Drink."

He raises the cup to his mouth, taking a gulp, and then pauses for a few moments before swallowing. His eyes narrow, his nose scrunches, and his Adam's apple bobs forcefully.

"Oh God," he says.

"Oh God good?"

"More like oh God please don't let my esophagus melt."

I frown. "It's not that bad." I stand on my tiptoes and dunk my finger in his cup again, pulling it back to my mouth to prove it. But he catches hold of my wrist before I get there.

"Uh-uh. Not that again. I can't take it."

"What?"

"You know," he begins. "Maybe it's not the drink that tastes good, but your skin. I think I need to test that hypothesis."

"I do like hypotheses. Did you know that's the plural of hypothesis? Hypotheses." I hadn't really registered much beyond the last word of his sentence, so he catches me completely off guard when he draws my hand up close to his face and slips my forefinger into his mouth.

"Oh," I breathe, feeling as if the world's previous gentle swaying motion has been pushed into fast-forward, and everything in my peripheral vision is moving fast enough to blur.

Not his mouth, though. That is crystal clear. And lusciously hot around my finger, and when he sucks, it draws my mind back to things he did to my nipples the night before. God, was that only the night before? My breasts feel heavy now, full and hardened at the tip, and there's an ache between my legs. Not a heat or a buzzing or a tingle, an actual hollow ache.

I lean forward, wanting to kiss him, knowing instinctively that he can make the pain go away, but I lose my balance and topple into him, my face smacking into his chest.

"Easy, girl. I've got you."

Heat curls over the back of my neck, but not the pleasant kind. My face feels clammy, and sweat gathers at my brow.

"I need some air," I choke.

"Okay. I've got you," he says again. He tries to draw one of my arms over his shoulder, but he's too tall. Or I'm too short. Or we're both too something. Instead he settles for wrapping his arm around my waist, and I do the same, leaning into his solid side. He's hot, too, and I feel like I'm suffocating in a sauna, but I'm not sure I can walk without leaning on him. Or maybe I just don't want to.

He shouts something in the direction of the kitchen, but my ears have gone a little fuzzy. All I can do is stare at the door, willing it to move closer so that I can feel the cool night air against my damp skin.

I manage a few steps, but when I whimper into Torres's shoulder, he pulls me up and close, so that my feet are just barely skimming the floor. In three long strides, he's opening the door, and I release him to throw myself against the railing of our porch balcony.

It's too high for me to topple over, but even so, I feel Torres's big hands settle on my hips, holding me in place.

"You know, I've never realized how stressful drunk people are," he says. "I suppose that's because I'm never the sober one."

Too many words. I can't process anything beyond the need to gulp down air and the cool touch of wind on my face.

I wish I were naked. Then the brilliant sensation of sweat turning cool against my skin could happen all over. Or I wish I were skinny-dipping again. The thought of that cold water sliding over my bare skin draws a small moan from my mouth. There's a pool in the center of our apartment complex. I wonder if I could convince him to take me there. It's poorly maintained and usually filled with a bunch of drunk college students, but hey . . . that's me right now.

Chalk one up for being normal.

"I wish we were in a pool again," I tell him.

He leans beside me on the railing, pushing some hair off my face and then lifting the thick mass of it off the back of my neck like he knows how hot I am.

"That was a lot of fun," he says. "But I wasn't sure you had fun. After the way you ran off."

I close my eyes, enjoying the lightness of my head and the air flowing over my neck. I hum my approval, and list to one side, leaning my head against Mateo's hand. "I had fun," I tell him. More fun than I've ever had.

"Then why did you leave? I realize things might have been moving fast—"

Because I'm a virgin and you terrify me.

He drops my hair, and I have to jerk myself upright to keep from falling when his hand disappears. "Hey," I whine. "Why did you—"

I look up at him, and I can tell that he's trying to keep a blank expression, but his eyes are wild and dark and just a bit too wide. I frown, trying to puzzle out the change in him. I think back, and when I do, I hear my last thoughts not as if they were in my head, but said in my currently too loud, slightly slurred voice.

Oh God. Oh my God.

And that's right about the time a few more of his friends arrive, calling up at us from the bottom of the stairs. Brookes. Dallas and Carson, too.

It's also right about the time I throw myself against the railing and lose the contents of my stomach over the side.

THE PRIMARY ADJECTIVE people use to describe me has always been "nerdy." Despite this, there's been a surprising lack of mortification in my life so far. I avoid it at all costs because me and embarrassment don't work well together. I blush at the drop of the hat, and it's rarely the pretty kind of blush that makes you look as if you went just a little heavy on your makeup. No, for me, it's the full-bodied, so-red-it's-almost-purple kind of blush. And it always takes forever to fade.

I've always gone out of my way to avoid situations that might stir up that kind of reaction. When I was getting picked on in middle school, I found a teacher willing to let me eat lunch in her classroom during her off period. I didn't really do much dating in high school, because the few times I tried, I couldn't handle the stress of not knowing what would happen next. The mere possibility of embarrassing myself was always enough to make me run in the other direction. I didn't take any chances. Not that kind at least. And now it seems as if my social life is not the only department where I'm playing catch-up.

Welcome to Humiliation. Population: Me.

Thankfully, I'm so miserable that the next few minutes only occur in bursts and patches for me. When I next lift my eyes, Dylan is there, and we're inside the apartment. I blink, and I'm in my room. It's dark, only the lamp by my bed providing light, and she's dabbing at my forehead with a damp cloth that feels like heaven.

"Why did I do this?" I groan. "Why does *anyone* do this?"

She doesn't laugh, though I can tell she wants to.

"Hindsight is twenty-twenty."

"I hate that saying."

"But it's the truth."

"I hate the truth."

She does laugh then.

"Why *did* you do it?" she asks. "I tried to ask Matt, but he sounds like a yeti when he's this drunk. I couldn't make out anything he said."

"I hate yetis," I mumble.

"Yes, well, before you say you hate water, drink this."

She tilts my head up to meet a glass, and half the water ends up running down my neck. And I do, indeed, hate water.

The only thing I don't hate is sleep. Sleep will take away the churning in my stomach, and the awful taste in my mouth, and the flushed heat I know is still marring my skin.

Maybe I'll wake up, and this will all have been a dream. I won't have thrown up in front of the people I'm trying to make my new friends. I wouldn't have told the most attractive guy to ever show any interest in me that I'm a virgin.

Maybe I'll wake up to find that this whole list thing was a long, elaborate dream, and I can go back to being blissfully weird and antisocial and . . .

Alone.

Somewhere between one forced sip of water and the next, I must fall asleep, because I wake up after what feels like hours to the sound of my door closing. Probably just Dylan checking on me, but I'm struggling to find the motivation to move my head the six inches it will take to confirm this suspicion.

Eventually, my bed shifts, slanting to one side, and my head ends up turning of its own volition. I decide I'm dreaming when I see who's seated beside me, because there's no way Torres would be in my room after everything that just happened. I'm sure Dylan wouldn't even let him in. I decide that this must be my subconscious, trying to give me one last good-bye, unreal though it may be.

"I brought you some food," he says.

I groan. My dream can't even do me the courtesy of giving me a pleasant last memory. Or is it normal to be drunk in your dreams when you're drunk in real life?

He breaks the corner off a bread stick and holds it up to my lips. I don't open.

"Trust me," he says. "I know you're tired and probably miserable, but this will help. And the more food and water we get into you now, the less you'll hate yourself in the morning."

"Already hate myself," I say, but I take a bite of the bread stick he's offering. It takes me forever to chew it, and when I'm done, he holds up another. Grudgingly, I eat it.

"That's my girl." And now I know it's a dream.

He offers me water, and I take it, if only to wash down the bread.

"What happened to our deal?" he asks, and he sounds almost angry. "If you'd waited for me, I could've taken care of you. Made sure you didn't drink too much."

Since it's a dream, I don't see the point in being dishonest.

"I don't want you to help me with the list."

"Why not?" Yeah. He's definitely angry.

"Because I don't want you to think I'm a loser."

"Damn it. I think a lot of things about you, Nell. Some of them are certainly not nice, but trust me, they're all complimentary." I shake my head, too tired to pick out the meaning of his words. "You're not a loser, Nell. And I'm going to help you with that list whether you like it or not. I didn't like coming into your apartment and seeing you with that guy. I don't like that he's the one who you shared this first with. *I* want your firsts."

I force my eyes open, and try to look at him with as clear a mind as I can manage. Is this the part where my dream stops being miserable and starts being wish fulfillment? Is that what I wish? That Torres would be my first?

But I can't read anything in his expression, and he doesn't say anything else. No sweet words. No assurances. He doesn't even touch me. He just feeds me a few more bread sticks and some water, and then leaves what's left of the food beside my bed before he turns off my lamp and plunges us both into darkness.

Chapter 14

Mateo

I want your firsts.

Christ.

I'm still thinking about it the next morning. About how she'd looked in bed, her hair spread across her pillow and her expressive mouth drawn down in frown. She'd been so miserable, and I'd *hated* seeing her like that. If I'd been there, if she'd called *me*, I could have taken better care of her. I could have watched her to make sure she drank just enough to get the experience she wanted, but not too much that she'd regret it.

But still . . . what in the world had I been thinking when I said that to her? Regardless of what I want, that V-bomb she dropped is the number one reason I have to stay away from her. It was one thing to use her to forget Lina when I thought it could just be some mutual fun. Hell, even a short-lived relationship. But to be her first? That's some next-level shit, and I'd be a first-rate asshole if I let it happen. I probably should have guessed, but once she'd gotten into our kiss, she'd been anything but shy. Wishful thinking, I guess. I already feel like an asshole for taking things as far as I have. But every time I think back to those moments in the pool, I don't feel guilty. I feel possessive and greedy and territorial, and I can't help but think that I *do* want her firsts. Even if I don't deserve them.

When I shake off those thoughts, I catch Brookes looking at me from his position on the recliner. I'm lying back on our couch, drinking a protein shake after my morning run. I don't like the expression on his face, like he knows exactly what I've been thinking.

As if proving my point, he says, "So . . . Nell."

"Is this a new game where we just say random people's names? I'll bite. So . . . Beyoncé."

"Don't play dumb, Teo. I'm not an idiot. There's something going on there."

"It's called flirting. You should try it sometime. It might turn that frown upside down every once in a while."

He rolls his eyes. "Give me a little credit, bro. I know you well enough by now to tell when you're deflecting. There's something different about this one for you."

Knows me well enough. Bullshit. Brookes has always been like this, even when I'd known him a week. The guy has a gift for reading people. Comes in handy on the field or in the occasional pickup basketball game. In a roommate? It's annoying as hell.

"So I like her. Do I really have to fucking sit here and analyze it with you? We gonna paint each other's nails next? We could both get weaves and then braid each other's hair. Maybe watch some *My Little Pony*. We'd make decent Bronies."

He raises an eyebrow. "You done yet?"

"Not really. We could watch *Titanic*. Lament about how there was totally room for Jack on that door with Rose. He didn't have to die, damn you, James Cameron!"

He sighs and stands. "Okay. I get it. You're not going to talk about it. But do me a favor and think about this one. She's not your usual type. You don't know how to deal with girls like her."

"I know plenty about girls like her, but thanks."

"I'm just saying, she's not the type to be happy with a quick fuck and an even quicker good-bye."

"Jesus. How much of an asshole do you think I am? I like her. I genuinely like being around her. I can get to know a girl without having to sleep with her."

"So . . . you're just friends?"

"We're just none of your business."

Brookes lifts his hands in surrender. "Got it. I wasn't saying anything about you, man. You're a good guy. You two just live at different speeds, and I don't want to see her get hurt trying to keep up with you. And if something like that did happen, I sure don't want to see what this house will be like with Dylan and Silas pissed at you."

"When are you going to start dating someone so I can ask you a bunch of annoying, intrusive questions?"

He only smirks in response.

It drives me fucking nuts that he's always in the middle of everyone else's business, but we know so little about him. But the dude's super private, and I don't have a weird intuitive superpower to just know what people are feeling. That would make my life a hell of a lot easier.

Twenty minutes later, I decide that Brookes is right. I am an asshole.

Because even though I should stay away from Nell . . . I can't.

Which is why I'm standing on her porch now, coffee in hand, knocking on her door at ten thirty on a Sunday morning. Thank God Dylan is an early riser. She swung by the house about an hour ago to pick Silas up for some charity something or other. If I hadn't already heard Silas say he was in love with that girl, I would have known it for sure this morning. Standing in the kitchen, he looked exhausted and ready to murder anything that moved. But when Dylan let herself in, the big guy practically melted at her feet.

I raise my fist to knock on Nell's door again, but hesitate.

I watched Dylan wrap Silas around her finger this morning, and I'm allowing practically the same thing to happen to me, except I'm not in a relationship. I'm not in love. I'm not looking for a future with Nell.

So why can't I just walk away like Brookes wants me to? Why can't I chalk it up to a hot make-out session that's never going to go any further, and cut my losses? Why can't I do that?

The door opens, and my stomach dips at the sight of Nell's bleary eyes and rumpled hair. She squints at me, and then winces at the sunlight, instinctively taking a step back into the house.

I step in after her without waiting for an invitation, and shut the door firmly behind me.

"I brought coffee," I say, lifting the tray up into her line of sight.

"Shhh!" She holds one hand up to me and the other to her forehead.

"I think," she says, her voice raspy, "there's a herd of elephants in my head."

"Welcome to the world of hangovers, sweetheart."

She blinks at me, then says matter-of-factly, "I'm going back to bed."

She shuffles down the hallway, and I follow her, still holding the coffee carrier and resisting the urge to laugh. Then she swings her bedroom door wide, and doesn't bother to close it before tumbling headlong into her bed. Again, I take that as permission, closing the door in case Dylan comes home unexpectedly.

Before Nell can slip back into sleep, I force the coffee into her hand.

"Drink a little of this," I tell her. "It'll help clear up the headache and nausea." She doesn't look like she believes me, but she takes a sip anyway. "Aspirin will help, too, if you have some."

"Bathroom," she says, and I go out to the hallway bathroom. I find a bottle in the second cabinet I open.

When I return to her room, she asks, "You find it?"

"I did. Right next to your box of tampons. The things I endure for you, woman." She rolls her eyes and takes the aspirin, and she drinks about half the coffee before placing the cup on the nightstand and sinking back against her pillows. She must be feeling better because she finally asks the question I'd expected to hear the second she opened the door. "What are you doing here?"

I shrug, toe off my sneakers, and throw myself down on the covers on the other side of her bed. She groans when the mattress bounces, but other than that doesn't complain.

"I knew you'd be miserable this morning . . ."

"And you decided that was something you needed to see?"

"I decided I could be of some help. I've had more than my fair share of hangovers. When that coffee kicks in all the way, we'll get you showered and dressed, and then we'll go out for some greasy breakfast. You'll be good as new in no time."

"You've done this more than once? Are you crazy? I never want to drink again."

"Everybody says that. If you don't, you're not doing it right."

"I don't feel like I did anything right."

"You checked another thing off your list, didn't you?"

She throws an arm over her eyes in lieu of an answer, and after a minute or so of silence, she asks, "Why are you really here?"

"I told you, I—"

"If you feel sorry for me because of what happened last night or what I said, don't. Please. I'd really rather you just leave."

"I can't do that. Sorry."

"Why?"

"Because last time I let you get away from me, you called some giant ginger-bearded monster to get you drunk, and look how well that turned out. Face it. You need me."

She makes a groan that sounds vaguely laughlike. "Matt is not a monster."

"We'll agree to disagree."

She sighs, and rolls on her side to face me. I suck in a breath because even hungover, she's beautiful. And that fiery, challenging look in her eyes always goes straight to my cock.

"And if I had wanted to call you?" she asks. "I don't have your number."

"You could have just thought of me. I would have known and come running. I'm practically a superhero in that regard."

"Riiight."

"Why so disbelieving? Unless you thought of me, and it didn't work? Were you thinking of me last night, girl genius?"

"Not even a little bit."

"I thought about you. Even during the game last night when I should have been concentrating on not getting my ass kicked, you kept popping up. I think I might be addicted to you, Antonella De Luca."

"How do you know my full name?"

"I might have done a little snooping last night while you were out of it. So you were valedictorian in high school, huh?"

"Just how much snooping did you do?"

"Relax. Your list is safe. I promised I wouldn't read it, and I didn't." My eyes drop to her lips, which she keeps pressing together in what I assume is nervousness. "It was tempting, though."

All of her is tempting, and I should probably get out of this bed right now before I drag her beneath me and remind myself just what her skin tastes like.

Regretfully, I pull myself up to a sitting position and say, "All right. Go shower so we can get breakfast. Unless you need assistance, then I'd be happy to—"

She cuts me off. "No. No, I think I can handle that alone."

"Pity," I say. "Well, I'll be here waiting in your bed in case you change your mind."

She stands up and faces me, still all cute and rumpled from sleep. "You are so . . ." She trails off, and shakes her head, turning for the door instead.

As she heads for the bathroom, I call out, "I'm so what? Charming? Devastatingly handsome?"

"You so better be in the living room by the time I'm done with my shower."

Damn. I'd been looking forward to seeing her in a towel.

Next time.

Chapter 1.5

Nell's To-Do List

- ~~Normal College Thing #7: Get Drunk.~~
- Never get drunk again.
- Invent hangover cure. Make millions.

That's it? You don't have anything more exciting on that list of yours?"

Even though Mateo—crap . . . *Torres,* has been quizzing me nonstop over breakfast about my list, I'm having a surprisingly good time. I think I'm gradually becoming acclimated to his outlandishly flirty statements because I'm getting better at letting them roll off my back without blushing . . . or worse, getting turned on.

That doesn't mean I'm about to tell him all the things on my list. I've told him all the safe ones, leaving out all the potentially embarrassing ones and anything of a sexual nature. And I have to admit, most of the new items that have occurred to me in the last few days have been of a sexual nature.

And it's entirely his fault.

"What about coming to a game? Is that on your list?"

For some reason, I don't want to admit that going to a game is already on my list.

"I don't know anything about football."

"I could teach you. I'm sure you'll be a fast learner."

"I suppose I could add that to my list."

In reality, it was one of the first things I added after meeting Torres and the rest of his friends. I want to see them in action. See *him* in action.

"Excellent. What about other campus traditions?"

"Like what?"

"*Like what*, she says." He catches the eye of a stranger passing by our table and gestures to me. "This girl, man. She kills me."

The guy appears to be in his midthirties. He looks at me, and then back at Torres, and says, "I feel you. Stay strong, dude."

I laugh, even though I have no idea what's happening. The guy walks away, and Torres digs back into his food like nothing has happened. He's just so . . . "shameless" perhaps isn't the best fit now that I know him better. He's just confident. Comfortable. He fits everywhere with everyone. What must it be like to live with that kind of ease? To never doubt yourself or your actions? I envy him almost as much as I like him.

"Okay, crazy. Tell me about these campus traditions."

"Well, you've already missed out on all the homecoming ones. You should have met me sooner, girl genius. But there are still a few fun ones. The tunnels, for one."

"Tunnels?"

"Yeah. You've never heard of them? They run underneath the campus. I think they were built in the Cold War era or something, but these days they're just dark and damp with lots of graffiti. And, of course, there are rumors of secret societies and mole people and all that fun stuff. There are two points of entry that are easy to access. One over by the parking garage on the north side of campus. The other comes out just below the bridge on the edge of campus. So what do you say?" He cocks an eyebrow in challenge. "Want to brave the dark, scary tunnels with me?"

"Do we have to do it when it's dark?"

"Absolutely. It's a rule or something. Besides, it's much more fun that way. And you can feel free to hold on to me for protection as much as you want."

I roll my eyes. "Have you gone in them before?"

"Nope." He smirks. "We can have our first time together."

I purse my lips and glare at him. There's no way that phrasing was accidental.

"I guess I could hold on to *you* for protection," he says. "If it bothers you that much. I'm for equality, you know."

I suppose in the grand scheme of things, some light teasing about my virginity is to be expected. And I'd much rather that than . . . well, all of the other reactions I imagined him having. If he's teasing me about it, maybe that means it's not that big of a deal. If he were bothered by it, he would ignore it completely. Or rather, he wouldn't be here at all.

A zing of electricity runs up my spine because . . . he *is* here. And the day after my disastrous slip of the tongue, too. That has to mean something . . . doesn't it?

Dangerous thoughts. I redirect my focus to our conversation and ask, "What else?"

"Big Daddy Rusk, definitely."

I nearly choke on my coffee. "Big Daddy Rusk?"

"That massive statue in the commons."

"Of Thomas Jefferson Rusk?"

"I prefer Big Daddy."

"And what is the tradition where . . . Big Daddy . . . is concerned?"

Torres's grin is infectious, and it pulls a smile to my face.

"Well, you're not supposed to touch him these days. Something about skin oils damaging the bronze or something. That's why they put the little fence up a few years back. But the tradition is to climb up and sit in his hand and take a picture."

"A picture. That seems doable."

"In recent years, it's become more popular to leave a little, uh, token of appreciation behind for Big Daddy."

"Like what?"

"Oh, you know. Coins. Knickknacks. Lacy underwear."

That time I do choke on my coffee, and it burns as it goes down the wrong pipe. I cough and cough, and Torres stands and slides into my side of the booth to rub at my back.

"Jesus, woman. If you try to die on me every time I mention underwear, that's going to make seducing you trickier than I thought."

I gulp in some air and shove him out of the booth.

"People really do that?"

"Oh yeah. They loop all kinds of stuff over the fingers on the statue, especially during homecoming week. The school assigned security guards there this year, but people still found a way."

"That's crazy."

"If you really want crazy, there's always the Sweet Six."

"Do I even want to ask what that is?"

"The six spots on campus where you're supposed to have sex before you graduate."

"Oh, come on. Now you're just making things up to shock me."

"I'm not. Swear to God." He holds one large hand to his chest and lifts the other like he's being sworn to tell the truth. It's not fair that he's this charming. It's not fair that this is all just a normal day for him. He's always this outgoing and fun and spontaneous. I'm just a regular occurrence for him, and God, how I wish I could say it was the same for me.

"I don't believe you," I say.

"One of the Sweet Six spots is the stacks with all the old university records on the third floor of Noble Library."

"What? I study in the lounge on the third floor all the time."

"Well, then. That's a prime opportunity for a study break if I ever heard one. There's also the old stairwells that they have roped off in the chapel."

"The chapel? Seriously?"

"Do you think the Sweet Six should count as six things on your list?"

"No. Absolutely not."

"You're right. They're kind of a package deal. We'll just count them as one."

I drag my hands through my hair and gape at him. "You are . . ."

"You keep doing that. Am I that hard to describe?"

"Yes."

"Is that a yes for the Sweet Six or . . . ?"

I force myself not to react. He likes flustering me, and I won't give him the satisfaction.

"That's a no to the Sweet Six. Final answer."

"What about Big Daddy Rusk?"

I throw up my hands and stand up from the booth. "I think it's time to go. Any longer here and I might murder you. And it wouldn't be smart to murder you with an audience."

I reach for my wallet, but Torres stops me.

"I got this. You shouldn't have to pay on the day of your very first hangover."

I return my purse to my shoulder and smile. "Thanks."

He leaves some money on the table and then loops his arm over my shoulder. "I've got some ideas for how you could thank me. Six of them, in fact."

I laugh, and shove his arm off me, and he calls out after me the entire time I march toward the door, getting louder and more dramatic with every step. He's making a giant scene, and everyone in the diner is watching us. Normally I would be horrified and well on my way to an unattractive magenta blush, but . . . it's different with him.

Everything is different with him.

"I CAN'T BELIEVE I'm about to do this. I've gone crazy. You've made me *crazy*."

Torres's hand lingers at my waist for a long moment before he does what he's supposed to and helps boost me up onto the base of the Rusk statue that we talked about at breakfast a few days ago. The base alone comes about as high as my chest, and I never could have gotten up without him. Or a ladder. The statue's pose is reminiscent of the Lincoln Memorial, with Rusk sitting down, only his hand is open and stretched out, and that's where I'm heading. If I can manage to climb all the way up without falling and breaking my neck. When Texas was an independent republic, Rusk served first as secretary of war and later the Supreme Court chief justice. And when Texas became a state he was elected as one of its first senators.

And now I'm honoring his memory by doing my best to climb up into his lap like he's some giant bronze Santa Claus. I step up on his foot and try to haul myself up onto his knee, but I have a pitiful amount of upper-body strength. As in . . . basically none. I jump, hoping that might help, but I only end up clutching ridiculously at the knee, unable to pull myself up but too afraid to let myself drop for fear that I might twist my ankle landing on the statue's foot.

"I've got you, sweetheart," Torres says, having hopped up behind me with zero assistance. Then his hands are on my ass, and he's pushing me up onto the knee.

"Did you suggest we do this just so you could grope me?" I call down to him.

"Unexpected benefits."

Carefully, I climb to my feet, holding on to Rusk's outstretched arm to keep me steady. Then, after one deep breath, I scramble my way onto his large bronze arm and shimmy my way down into his hand. I sit in his palm, and have to hang one leg over each side. My thighs are a bit too large to fit comfortably, so I feel like I'm wedged into his hand. And one look down at Torres's grinning face tells me what an idiot I am.

I'm straddling the statue's hand.

And while it's holding my weight just fine, there's no way I don't look ludicrous. And probably a little lewd.

"Most people don't actually sit in his hand, do they?"

"It's the knee for most people, true."

"Torres!"

"What? I figured go big or go home. Besides . . . it's pretty fucking hot."

"I'm going to kill you as soon as I get down from here." I start trying to shift myself out of the hand, but my butt really is entirely too large for this thing.

"No! Wait," he says. "Let me jump down and get a picture. You're up there already. Might as well make the most of it."

I try to scowl at him. But it *is* pretty funny when you think of it. And it will make a good picture. When my brother and I were growing up, Leo's room had been covered in stuff like this. Photos with friends. He had a big stop sign on his wall that he and his friends had stolen God only knows how. He had souvenirs from places they'd been and things they'd done. Nothing crazy because we weren't quite well-off enough to travel or anything. But little things that meant something to him even if they didn't matter to anyone else.

Memories.

I had trophies. Medals. Certificates. Those were my memories. But no one takes those kinds of things to college with them. You're supposed to pack them away in boxes because as soon as you graduate, they don't really matter anymore.

But now . . . I have this.

While Torres descends, I look out at campus. It's dark, but there are streetlamps dotting the sidewalk. Noble Library is a few blocks over, and is still open, but otherwise the university seems abandoned. The statue is in the middle of a grassy courtyard, surrounded by old oak trees that have probably been growing since the university was founded back in the late 1800s.

It's peaceful and beautiful, and it occurs to me that I've never just sat somewhere on campus and looked. There's always been somewhere to go or something to do, and I've never taken the time. I lean back on my hands and breathe in the night, and when Torres calls for me to look at him, my smile is wide and genuine.

"Come on! Get crazy," he says.

I throw my hands up and smile even bigger. He laughs and snaps another picture on his phone.

"You're a *real* wild one, Antonella De Luca."

Then something occurs to me, and my stomach tumbles with nerves and a surprising feeling of exhilaration. Can I check two things off my list with this late-night adventure? Can I actually be a little wild for a change? I think about Torres's words. *You're up there already. Might as well make the most of it.* I take a deep breath, shift to sit on my knees, and wait for Torres to slip his phone back in his pocket.

Then I call, "Hey, Mateo!"

When he looks up, his eyes questioning, I gather my courage and the hem of my shirt and lift it up for one, two, three seconds. Then I tug it back down, keeping my eyes squeezed shut because I'm too scared to see his face.

Chapter 16

Mateo

Holy. Fuck.

I blink. And blink again.

And I'm tempted to keep my eyes closed so I can just keep picturing her. Damn. I was already halfway to obsessed with her rack, and now that I've seen it wrapped up in that black, lacy bra, I'm not sure I'll ever be able to look at her without having to fight off a hard-on.

She has her eyes scrunched up tight, and her lips pressed tightly together, and for the life of me, I can't believe she did it. This is the girl that ran away from me at that pool less than a week ago. The girl who won't even tell me half the things on her bucket list.

That girl just flashed me.

While she still has her eyes shut, I jump, and propel myself up onto the statue's base. She opens one eye, and then the other, and her gaze sweeps around the grass, until I climb up onto Rusk's knee. She gives me this shy smile, and I'm undone by how she somehow manages to be adorable and sexy all at the same time.

I wish that damn hand were bigger because I want nothing more than to launch myself up there and kiss her. I wonder if I sat higher up on the arm, if it could hold the weight of both of us. Before I can decide whether or not to chance it, bright lights wash over us, and I turn to see a campus cop car pulling up on the street below. He flashes his lights once and then puts the car into park.

"Shit. Time to go, Nell."

Her eyes meet mine, all that earlier shy sensuality replaced by panic. I reach out and grasp her hand, pulling her out of the statue's hand and onto the knee with me. I jump down to the base below and tell her to throw her legs over the side. I hear a car door open as I wrap my arms around her legs and help lower her to the base. I do the same thing to lower her to the ground, and by then the cop is heading for us.

I grab her hand and pull her into a run.

There's a dirt jogging path cutting through the commons area, and I drag Nell onto it. Dust kicks up around our feet, and she's wearing flip-flops that slow her down, but she doesn't complain.

I can imagine that for a girl like Nell the thought of getting into trouble with a cop (even a campus cop) would feel like the end of the world. Which is why I refuse to let us get caught.

"Come on, babe. Little faster."

She lets me tug her along, but I can tell she's struggling, so when the jogging path curves, instead of following it, I pull her to the right and into a breezeway between two buildings. We move faster on the concrete, and in less than ten seconds we're out the other side.

I lead her across the street, and we run under the lamplit sidewalk up and over a block until we hit the library. I slow us to a walk and guide her through the front door. I'm not sure if the cop is still chasing us, but if he is, I doubt he'd follow us in here. But just in case he does, the best thing for us to do is to blend in with a crowd.

Unfortunately, the library isn't exactly hopping at midnight on a Wednesday. And I can admit, I've never actually set foot in this library myself, so I have no idea where to go. I'm about to pull us over between some bookshelves because I figure that's better than nothing when Nell takes the lead, gesturing for me to follow her over to a bank of elevators.

I keep an eye on the front doors while we wait for the elevator, and just as it dings and we step inside, the campus cop comes through the front door.

Inside the elevator, I jab at the Door Close button.

"The cop just entered the building. I don't think he saw me get in the elevator," I say. "But we should find someplace out of the way or somewhere with people around until he gives up and leaves."

"There's usually a decent number of people in the lounge on the third floor this time of night. That's where the best computers are. We can go there."

She hits the button for three, and I just hope that I was right about the cop not seeing me. If he didn't, he'll likely be gone in a couple minutes. I mean, does he really have nothing better to do than chase us all over campus for climbing on a statue?

Scratch that. He is a campus cop, after all.

When the doors open, I follow Nell along a long hallway lined with offices into the main library area, and then to the right as she heads for a section with computers and comfy-looking furniture. We collapse onto a love seat, and Nell sinks back into the cushions, trying to contain her breathing. There are three people working on the computers, and one more sitting at a table reading a big textbook. Not exactly a crowd, but it should do just fine. And I still doubt that the cop will even search that hard. But I won't take the chance . . . for Nell's sake. I'll never get her to do anything else on the list if I muck things up tonight.

We look at each other, and then we're both laughing. Nell covers her mouth with her hand, trying not to make too much noise as her bright eyes meet mine.

Kiss her. Kiss her now.

She leans her head back on the cushion, sighing as her laughter gives way to a few deep breaths. And the moment has passed. I'm not sure whether I'm proud or pissed at myself for resisting.

"Well . . . that was eventful," I say.

"Seriously, if he'd caught us . . ."

"Oh, I was talking about you flashing me."

She brings her fist down hard on my thigh, and I catch her hand.

"Easy. I'm kidding. Mostly. Okay, not at all. That black lacy thing you're wearing is definitely still winning for most memorable part of the night."

"Do you ever think about anything besides sex?"

She tries to tug her hand away, but I keep it trapped between mine and my thigh.

"Sure. I think about football. And food. But the rest of the time, I'm definitely thinking about your boobs."

"Shhh! Be serious."

"I would never joke about your tits, sweetheart. I take them *very* seriously."

She glances around at the students working. "You're going to get us in trouble. Again."

I hear the elevator ding, signaling a car has just arrived on this floor, and we look at each other. What are the odds that someone other than the cop would be coming up here at this hour? Too slim to chance it.

"Go that way, back into the stacks," I tell Nell, and in seconds we're up off the love seat and making our escape. Her short legs move in a quick exaggerated walk, and her long hair bounces against her back with the movement. I glance behind us, but no one has exited the hallway yet.

We pass row after row, and it's not lost on me where we are. I'd been joking when I teased her about the Sweet Six, but here we are, in the very spot I mentioned. The shelves are lined with old yearbooks, course catalogs, student manuals. There's an entire section of old newspapers and documents, including the university's original charter, displayed under a glass case. In other words, nothing that would interest a college student in the middle of the night unless he was looking for a deserted place to make out.

Nell makes a turn into one of the stacks about three-quarters of the way back, and before I follow her, I take one more glance back. Coming out of the elevator hallway are two Asian girls, whispering quietly, book bags slung over their shoulders. So not the cop, then. I relax, and then follow Nell only to find her leaning against one of the shelves, flipping through some old thick textbook. So I stand corrected. Of course, Nell can find something of interest everywhere.

I take a moment just to gaze at her. She seems absorbed in the book, but I'm not sure whether that's real or just her playing a role in case the cop was to wander by. She's wearing snug black yoga pants again and a baggy T-shirt. I love that she makes absolutely no effort to dress up for me. With Nell, you know exactly what you're getting because she doesn't see any need to mold herself into something she isn't. And it doesn't matter what she's wearing because the image of what she looks like underneath is permanently burned into my mind.

I take the book from her hands and am about to tell her that it was a false alarm when a noise distracts me. A very *distinct* noise.

Breathy and low, it starts out as a little gasping mewl before progressing into a quiet moan. If Nell's suddenly rigid posture is any indication, she hears it, too. I start to return the book to the shelves so we can leave, but Nell's hand on my wrist stops me. Her eyes are focused directly on the opening on the shelf that the book had occupied. It's level with her eyes, but is about midchest for me. I shift behind her, bend a little, and realize that she's got a perfect view of the couple going at it the next row over.

I shove the book on top of another shelf where it doesn't belong because this just got really fucking interesting. Nell's body language is still stiff, but she's holding her breath, her eyes glued to the gap between the books.

A lanky dude has a girl pushed up against the stacks, and they're making out. Like really going to town. I can see the bulge of his hand beneath the girl's shirt, kneading at her breast. I keep waiting for Nell to snap out of it. It's like when you pass a car wreck, and you can't help but look, but then immediately feel guilty for gawking. But the seconds keep passing, and she's not reacting except to keep holding her breath. I lean down, planting my mouth next to her ear, and ask, "So you like to watch?"

She exhales heavily, and I think I've broken the spell, but then she leans back into me and gives this sort of half shrug, half nod. *Fuck.* There's no freaking way I'll be able to keep my hands off her now.

"So what does it for you?" I ask. "Is it just seeing them? Seeing how into it they are? Or is it the fact that they could get caught at any moment? That *we've* caught them, and they don't even know it."

She shrugs.

"Come on, girl genius. Tell me what it is. I need to know."

Before she can answer, the girl on the other side of the stacks turns around, and the guy flips up her skirt, and that finally provokes a reaction in Nell. She spins sharply, pressing her back against the shelves, blocking the opening with her head. Her breaths come fast and frenzied now, and her expression is stuck somewhere between horror and humor.

I step in close to her, and she has to tip her head back to meet my gaze. She has these big honey eyes, and when I'm this close I feel like I can almost see right through them to the thoughts beneath. She's excited. But feels guilty for being excited. It doesn't help that we can both still hear the couple on the other side. They're trying to be quiet, but given how close Nell and I are, the slight squeak of the shelves and their labored breaths are evident. I plant my hands on her hips, holding her in place, and keep eye contact. Whatever just happened . . . I don't want to pretend like it didn't. Again and again tonight, she's been shedding layers of her shyness, and I need it to continue.

I lean in close, and with my cheek against hers and the sound track of horny college kids still going in the background, I whisper, "I'm so fucking hard for you right now."

I can feel her swallow, the way it moves through her whole body.

"Did you do this on purpose? For that stupid Sweet Six thing?"

I grin, and move my hands from her hips to her waist, digging my fingers into her flesh. "You really think I would do something this elaborate to get you here?"

She pulls away slightly so I can see her lift one dark brow in response. "I think that sounds exactly like something you would do."

I lean back to her ear and murmur, "Oh, sweetheart, you've still got a lot to get to know about me. I'm all for fun and games, but when I want something, I don't bother with games. I'm not patient enough for that."

"So this is just a coincidence?"

"There have been a number of unexpected benefits to tonight. And what? Did you think I planned for *them* to be here, too? Like I had any idea that watching other people hook up would get you hot."

"It's not that," she snaps, and at the same time a loud groan comes from the next row over. A series of noises follow that are less sexy and more comical, and I have to bury my face in Nell's hair to keep from laughing. The guy is still groaning, and the girl is whispering for him to wait, to hold on a little longer. He doesn't. The shelves stop squeaking and the girl lets out a distinctly disappointed sigh. We stay silent and listen to the other couple shuffling, whispering, and rearranging their clothes. The thud of footsteps lets us know they're leaving, and as they round the corner and pass by our row, Nell buries her head into my chest, mortified.

When they're out of earshot, we collapse into each other laughing. We're not quiet. Hell, they can probably still hear us, but I don't give a damn. Especially when I pull back to catch sight of Nell's face. Her eyes and nose are scrunched up, and she keeps alternating between pressing her fingers to her cheek and covering her forehead. Her cheeks are flushed with more color than I would have thought possible for someone with her skin tone. Her embarrassment should just be amusing or cute, but somehow even this side of her seems sexy to me.

"So what is it, then?" I ask now that we're alone. "If it's not watching that turns you on, what is it?"

She tries to shy away from me, but I've got her trapped between my body and the books. She chews at her bottom lip, and her chin bobs a few times, like she's trying to pluck up the courage. "I just find it interesting how everything . . . *works.*"

I can't hold in my laugh. "So it's just biology for you? That's what does it? Like watching animal mating habits in a zoo?"

Her eyes narrow, and she shoves me backward. She tries to flee, but I grab hold of her hips and pull her back against my chest. "I'm sorry. I'm not making fun of you. I swear. I just want to know what you like. It's entirely selfish. You've got your list, and I've got mine. And knowing what it takes to get you off is right at the top for me."

Her expression is still wary, but her hands rest against my chest now instead of trying to push me away. "I wasn't talking about how sex works. I've known that since I read a disturbingly informative book in the third grade. It's about how . . . the rest of it works. Attraction. Desire. Pleasure. I'm fascinated not just by the movements and the actions, but what fills in the blanks. What turns something from stimulating to . . ."

I'm not sure how her talking scientifically about sex is turning me on, but it is. Could have something to do with hearing the world "pleasure" come out of those plump lips of hers.

"From stimulating to what?"

"Orgasmic."

Yep. Definitely turned on. That's it for me. I'm fucking done for.

"So you like the idea of watching because it's like an experiment to you? A study?" She nods. "What about doing your own experiment? To see what *fills in the blanks* for you?"

Lifting my hand, I run a finger down the side of her neck, and her hands clench against my chest. I cup her neck in both hands, reaching my thumbs up to glide along the soft skin of her jaw. Her body alternates between surrendering to my touch and tensing up. With each swipe of my thumbs, she wavers. But I can't tell if she's resisting because of nerves or because she doesn't want this for some other reason. One of those, I think I can fix.

"I—" she starts, then cuts herself off with a deep inhale.

Gently, I rub my fingers against the nape of her neck, trying to calm her down, and she sighs. "There are some things I *can* be patient for, you know. On the field, I have to know just the right moment to break away from my defender. Too soon, and he'll catch up to me before I catch the ball. Too late, and I miss my window of opportunity. So, while I do go after what I want full force, I know how to wait until the time is right."

When I'm done talking, my massaging of her neck has her eyes half closed, but she lifts her lids enough to pin me with her gaze.

"Thanks for the football metaphor, now tell me plainly what you're saying."

I swallow a laugh. The way her confidence around me has grown is nothing short of stunning. If I were a more poetic guy, I'd compare it to seeing a flower bloom before my eyes. But that's not me, so all I can say is it's hot. Unbelievably hot. Every time she goes toe-to-toe with me, I just want more.

"I'm saying that I'd love to be the person to help satisfy your curiosity, the one to help you figure out what you like. But I won't ask for more than you're willing to give." I'd like to tell her that she has control in this aspect of things, but I can't promise that. The need to feel her surrender to me is too strong for that. But it requires trust. I need her to be able to turn off the thoughts that are always running through her head, and she won't do that until she believes she can.

I use the hand at her neck to draw her a little closer, dipping my own head down at the same time. "So the question is," I begin, "how much are you willing to give me, Nell?"

Her gaze flicks back and forth between my eyes, as if she might see something different in the left than the right. I draw a thumb over her bottom lip, pulling at it enough that I can feel the warm exhale of her breath on my skin. "This?" I ask her. "Can I have this?"

I lean down to take her mouth. The look in her eyes is response enough for me, but before I get there, she closes her lips over my thumb. The tentative slide of her tongue nearly brings me to my knees. Then she sucks at my finger, and just like that, she's stolen the control right from under me.

I like experimental Nell. I like her so damn much.

Chapter 17

Nell's To-Do List

- *Normal College Thing #4: Do something wild.*
- *Don't get caught.*

It was an impulsive move. I had a hazy memory of him doing this to me when I was drunk the other night, and I remember that it felt like all my bones had gone liquid. My response had surprised me. Never in a million years would I have thought that such a thing could have that strong an effect on me. And I'd just wanted to, I don't know . . . return the favor.

But now my brain isn't blurred by alcohol, and I'm intensely aware that I'm standing in a library where anyone could walk by . . . sucking on his thumb. And I'd just admitted to a hugely embarrassing fascination for watching another couple's intimacy, and *seriously* what is wrong with me? I'm such a freak.

God, I'm doing this all wrong. I don't know how to be sexy, how to be . . . *this*.

Just when I'm about to pull away, Mateo's body collapses against mine, and his teeth nip the lobe of my ear. My mouth falls open on a gasp, and his wet thumb rubs across the circle of my lips before dipping back inside.

Does that mean this is good? That I'm not making a fool of myself?

"You're killing me, Nell." In response, I swirl my tongue around his thumb again, and he groans. His hot breath sends a shiver down my spine. "Do you know how bad I want you? Do you have any idea?"

He drags his thumb from my mouth and moves to press his forehead against mine. Seconds later, the lower half of his body leans into mine, too.

I can feel him, hot and hard against my stomach. He's wearing gym shorts, and I'm shocked by how much I can feel through the layers of our clothes. And while I'm still marveling at the feel of him, he kisses me, his lips demanding my attention.

Our last kiss had been long and exploratory. We'd barely known each other then. And though I still don't know the facts of him—I don't know about his family or his childhood or how he sees his future—I do feel like I know him. And God knows he knows plenty about me. And this kiss? There's nothing slow or introductory about it. His tongue drives into my mouth, punishing and seeking and coaxing all at the same. His hands grip the shelves on either side of me, caging me in so he can press his body flush against mine. I bring my own hands up around his waist to clutch at his back. He changes the angle of our kiss, somehow pushing even harder, and I dig my fingers into his back to hold on.

He makes a noise into the kiss that's almost a growl and trails his mouth down to my neck. He reaches around to take my hands from his back, and then pushes them against the shelves behind me. Pinning my hands out to my sides, he continues his assault up my neck and back to my mouth.

Some part of me had thought that I was exaggerating the rawness of our kisses in the pool. I'd expected that if Mateo ever kissed me again, it would be more like his personality is every day. Teasing and light and just a little overwhelming.

But there's something primal and dominant in him that doesn't come out except in moments like this. I feel like it should make me nervous, especially with my arms trapped against the shelves, but I like that he's in control, that he knows what he's doing whenever I don't.

Against my mouth, he says, "I need to touch you. Let me touch. That's all."

We're in public. We could be caught at any moment. For all I know, someone could be watching us right now. I should say no. *Be smart, Nell. Say no.* "Okay."

Oh, to hell with being smart.

While his mouth conquers mine, building and stoking a fire that feels barely contained inside me, he slides both of my hands above my head so he can hold them there with one hand. I suck in a breath, feeling my spine tense with anticipation. His fingers slide along the waistband of my yoga pants. He strokes gently from one hip, over my slightly rounded belly, to my other hip. Then his hand slips beneath the fabric, beneath my underwear, and his fingers touch me where only I have ever touched. Instinctively, I shy away, trying to pull my hips back, but the shelves behind me stop my retreat.

He breaks the kiss to return to my ear, his hand stilling against me. He kisses the shell and whispers to me, "Just breathe. I only want to make you feel good. Can I do that? I'll be gentle."

I swallow, glad that I don't have to look him in the eye, and nod.

"Not good enough. I need a yes. I need you to say it. Before I make you fall apart, right here, I need to know you want my hand there as much as I do."

I can't bring myself to do more than whisper when I say, "I want it."

Then he's looking me in the eye, and smirking, and his fingers drag over damp flesh. "We'll work on your volume later when we're not in public."

Everything clenches in response to his whispered words. How will I ever be able to enter this library again without blushing?

He circles a finger around my most sensitive spot, immediately homing in on what it took me several fumbling tries to find on my own the first time I touched myself there.

I clench my teeth and force myself to breathe out of my nose to stay silent. His hand above my head shifts, and he turns one of my hands around. "Hold on to this shelf."

He doesn't stop his ministrations down below, so it takes me a few seconds to comply. When I do, he squeezes my hand beneath his, making me grip the shelf harder. "Keep your hands there. Don't let go."

I bite my lip to keep from replying, though at this point I have no idea what I would say. No? Yes, please? Make unintelligible noises?

I hang on tight to the shelf above me and fix my gaze on a point on the ceiling. His fingers circle again, and then slide back to dip inside me for the first time. The muscles in my thighs tense, and I breathe in through my nose.

"Hey," Mateo says at the same time that he slips his other hand beneath my shirt to cup my breast. "Why are you holding back?" He leans in to kiss my clenched jaw. "Relax for me."

He thumbs at my nipple through the material of my bra, and I squeeze my eyes shut. He does it again, pumping his finger inside me at the same time, and instinctively I pull my thighs closer together, whether to trap his hand or resist it, I'm not even sure.

He kisses me hard, but his hands are moving and there's so much going on that I can barely react. I let him kiss me, but I'm too concentrated on the aching pull between my thighs.

Closer. Closer.

After a few moments he pulls back, abandoning my breast to bury a hand in my hair and force my eyes on him. "Relax," he tells me again, his voice so commanding it sends a shiver down my spine.

"I *am* relaxed."

"No, sweetheart. You're not. You're clenching your teeth and your thighs and your hands. You're locked up tight. Is it where we are? Does that bother you?"

I shake my head and answer, "I'm concentrating."

The corner of his mouth twitches.

"On? You know it's guys who try to distract themselves so they won't come, not girls . . . right?"

"That's not what I'm doing." And now I'm blushing. Furiously. Though I'm not sure my last blush ever went away, so more likely I'm just purpling a little more.

"Then what are you concentrating so hard on?"

God, how can I possibly answer that?

"I'm concentrating on . . . on the opposite of what you said."

His brows furrow, and he studies me for several long moments. He sighs and shifts away from me. This time the kiss he places on my lips is short, quick. All that raw, overwhelming feeling? Gone. He pulls his hand out from my clothes, and the loss makes my knees nearly collapse. It's not easy for me to orgasm. I don't even do it to myself that often because it takes too long. It's too difficult. But he had me close in a record amount of time. His voice gruff, he says, "Come on."

Something in my gut unravels.

"But . . . we . . . what?"

He wraps an arm around my waist, tucking me close to his side. "This isn't going to work."

He pulls me out of the stacks, into the aisle. "Where are we going?"

"We're leaving. The cop has to be gone by now."

I frown, but let him pull me along, and the entire time we're in the elevator and during the walk back to his pickup, I can feel something turning and turning in my stomach. Like when you watch people make cotton candy, and the spun sugar just gets bigger and bigger. Each step is another spin, each step builds up the cobwebs of dread inside me.

I knew this was a mistake. I knew it. I just . . . he and I are from different worlds. How could I possibly think that we would be compatible, that me, a naive virgin, would be able to keep up with someone like him?

I should have stuck to my original sense of him. He's dangerous. In ways bigger than I ever realized. I'm smart when it comes to everything else, but not with this, not with him. I feel so incredibly stupid, and it's not something I know how to deal with.

I hate it.

He keeps his arm around me as we walk, but I wish he would just let me go. I'm weird and inexperienced, and I guess we're not as compatible as I thought we were. The only good thing about all of this is that it happened before we actually tried to have sex. I can only imagine how awful that would have been. And now I just want to acknowledge the mistake and move on. I want him to stop touching me because . . .

Because even though I feel humiliated and stupid, I still want him. And with his arm around me, I'm struggling to cut him and all of this off like I should.

We parked in an open lot behind the student union building.

It's as empty now as it was when we arrived. He parked his truck in a corner space, away from the streetlights. It's dark, so I stick close to his side, but he doesn't walk me around to the passenger door. He opens the driver's side, leans over the seat to fold up the middle console, and then helps me climb up and sit in the middle.

Confused, I try to scoot over the rest of the way, but he slides in beside me and stops me with a hand on my thigh. He points to my bag in the floorboard and says, "Get your list."

I hesitate, and the hand on my thigh squeezes. "Get the list, Nell." I reach down for my bag while he turns on the overhead light. I pull out the spiral like he said, but don't open it.

He reaches across me to the glove compartment and pulls out a pen. He hands it to me, and I realize he wants me to mark the tasks off my list. Uneasy, I open the spiral, trying to keep it angled away from him so he can't see, and I search for the items I've completed.

4. Do something Wild.

Yeah. I'd say that one is gone after tonight.

15. Flash someone

Oh God, I'd *flashed* him. Who am I and how do I get normal Nell back?

I skip to the end of the list, to the new items I'd added after talking to Torres.

20. Take a picture with the Thomas Jefferson Rusk "Big Daddy Rusk" statue.

I cross the items one by one, wishing it were that easy to just strike through this night and my mortification. I go to close the spiral, but he stops me, settling his hand over the page. I look up, stiffening automatically, but he's looking at me, not the list.

"I need you to add something else to your list."

I raise my eyebrows and ask, "What?"

What was this about? Surely this isn't about the Sweet Six thing again, not after how poorly things went in the stacks.

"I want you to add 'Have the best orgasm of my life.'"

I drop his pen. I very nearly drop my spiral.

"You want . . . *what?*"

"You heard me, Nell. Now add it."

He's back to the dominant Mateo that comes out when he's kissing me, and the ache he'd started back in the library flares to life between one breath and the next. I reach for the pen, but I'm too distracted by what this could mean.

So we're not over? He still wants me? How could he still want me? My heartbeat speeds up as I mentally dissect our evening up until this point, and when it takes me too long to find the pen, he growls, "Oh, fuck it. Add it to the damn list later."

He grabs the spiral and tosses it into the passenger seat. I sit up, and he pulls at the stretchy fabric on the thigh of my yoga pants, letting it snap back against my skin.

"Take those off."

I blanch. "What?"

"This will be easier without them. You can leave your underwear on if you want. Though I might point out you've already been naked in my arms."

"We were underwater. And it was dark."

He turns off the overhead light, dousing the entire cab in black. "Better?"

I blink a few times, and my eyes slowly adjust. I can see the shape of him in the dark, but no details. I sigh, considering.

He reaches out, finding my shoulder first and sliding his hand up until he can cup my face. "You've got to trust me," he says. "Trust me to take care of you, to make this good for you."

His thumb catches at my bottom lip, and I close my eyes, almost trembling in the dark.

"Okay."

He leans over to kiss me, catching just the corner of my mouth. "That's my girl."

My heart throbs, and I remember my drunken dream. Or what I thought had been a dream. He said the same thing then a few minutes before he said that he wanted my firsts. I'm tempted to ask if him if the memory is real, if he actually said that, but there's a chance he'll say no, and I'm not sure I can take any more self-doubt tonight.

With a steadying breath, I hook my fingers into the waistband of my pants and begin wiggling them off. Beside me, Torres hunches over and adjusts his seat, sliding it back as far as it will go.

When I've deposited my yoga pants on top of my spiral in the passenger seat, I ask, "Now what?"

"Now you straddle me."

I let out a heavy exhale.

"You said you trusted me."

"I do. I just . . ."

Straddle him? That's a lot of trust.

"Think too much. I'm well aware. Now come here."

Tentatively, I rise up on my knees, bending my head to keep from hitting the ceiling. I steady myself with a hand on his shoulder, and impatiently he takes hold of my thigh, tugging until I've got one leg on either side of him.

His shorts are cool and silky against my bare thighs, and goose bumps dance up my spine. His hands start at my knees, gliding up until his long fingers curl around the curve of my ass. This close, I can see the glint of his eyes and the shape of his mouth. Even sober, I still think it's a really good mouth.

"Now listen to me. We're alone. It's dark. No one is going to stumble upon us, so you don't need to think about any of that. No one can hear us, so you don't need to keep your mouth closed or censor your reactions." He tugs me forward until I feel his erection press insistently against my center. "And I want you so bad, it's a miracle I was able to walk all the way here without taking you against the side of some building. Nothing you do or say is going to change *this*." He pushes down on my hips, lifting himself up at the same time, and I catch my breath at the contact. "So you don't have to be nervous about me either. You have absolutely nothing to think about. Nothing to worry over. And you don't need to think about whether or not you're going to come. I'm going to get you there. Trust me. Your job is just to feel. React in whatever way feels right to you. That's it."

I nod, but I'm not sure that's a promise I can keep.

He kisses me, languid and hot, chasing away the gnawing panic that had overtaken me when he stopped in the library. His hands guide my hips, rocking me against his erection in time with our kiss. Under his guidance my hips roll, slow and steady, as if we have all the time in the world, and at the top of each roll, my clit grinds against him, and my limbs practically go numb. It feels like a dance, I realize. This isn't something that follows a set pattern, there's not list of correct things to do. It's more like art, and with his hands teaching me, I realize I have to listen to my body, not my head.

"Put your arms around my neck," he says. "I want to feel like you're all the way around me." I do, and it makes my chest drag over his with every pump of our hips. Even through all the layers, the grazing touch draws the tips of my breasts to a hard point.

He kisses me for a long time, tasting and sucking at my lips and my tongue. And just when I start to wonder when he's going to *really* touch me, just when I start to *long* for it, his hand sneaks under the back of my shirt, and with one quick twist, he unhooks my bra. Then both his hands are gone from my hips, cradling my breasts instead. He kneads and squeezes, pausing every few seconds to roll my nipples between his fingers, and there's a line

of lightning directly between his hands and my sex. He continues kissing me the whole time, and I continue rubbing my center
against his length. Desperation builds high enough that I have
trouble maintaining a rhythm because I want to move faster and
slower both at the same time.

When the buzzing between my legs is so strong that I'm pant-
ing and my hearing sounds like I'm underwater, he says, "Lean
back. Keep holding on to my neck and lean back."

I whimper, unwilling to stop the rhythm of our hips, but he
grips my waist, moving me how he wants me. My bottom slides
closer to him, until I feel the hard ridge of him nestled flat against
me. If my arms weren't around his neck and we weren't in a ve-
hicle, I could probably lie all the way back on his knees. When
my arms are stretched taut, and my body is how he wants it, he
reaches between us and passes two fingers over the damp fabric of
my underwear. He does it again, this time pressing down against
the sensitive nub at the top. I close my eyes and bite my lip, and his
other hand tightens on my waist in response.

"Don't do that," he says. "Don't withdraw. Look at me. Focus
on me."

I try, but looking him in the eyes makes my heart race unbear-
ably fast. So fast it scares me, and I have to close my eyes. Have to.

"If you can't look at me, then listen. Tune out everything else
except for my voice. Concentrate on that."

I close my eyes, deciding this is the much safer route. That
is . . . until he starts talking.

"You're so fucking wet for me, Nell. I wish I could describe what that does to me. It's the best kind of misery, knowing I did that to you." He pushes the fabric aside and eases two fingers inside me. "And God, you're so tight. So unbelievably tight. Someday you're going to take me here." He pushes deeper inside to emphasize his words, and I gasp. "Are you listening to me, Nell? Are you with me?"

"I—I'm listening." And dying because of it. Each time he touches me, each time he says something, it feels like I'm whispering against dynamite, like I'm a hairsbreadth away from utter destruction.

With his fingers still inside me, he circles his thumb against me, and I squeeze my legs against his hips.

"Don't fight it. I know you want to tense, you feel like you have to prepare, but you don't. Let it come to you. Let me bring it."

I try to relax, try to loosen my legs and my arms and everything. I lean my head so far back that it touches the steering wheel. I just breathe. I don't try to describe what I'm feeling, don't try to catalog it. I don't analyze what makes his touch so different from my own. I just let it wash over me.

"That's my girl. Christ, you're beautiful. And you feel so good. Do you know how many times I've thought about you like this the last few weeks? Do you know how often I've stroked myself raw thinking about your mouth, your nipples, this pussy? That's it. You're close, aren't you? You're shaking."

I am, I realize. I'm trembling so hard, I'm afraid I won't be able to hold myself up, that any second my fingers are going to slip from around his neck and I'll fall into the floorboard.

"I'm going to fall," I say. "I can't hold on."

"So don't. Come, sweetheart."

I smile. "No, I'm actually going to fall. My hands are slipping."

He tugs me up and against him, and I bury my face in his neck. The movement changes the angle of his fingers inside me, and all it takes is one more stroke, and I'm gasping out his name, squeezing him with my hands and my arms and my legs and all of me. And the explosion I've been flirting with goes off in my brain, somehow silent and loud all at once, and the aftermath tears through my limbs.

My body jerks and arches, and I have absolutely no control over it. I'm all reflexes, all reactions, and through it all Mateo is whispering in my ear, calling me *beautiful, perfect, hot*. And somehow just the sound of him prolongs it. The knowledge that it's his lips against my ear, his fingers inside me . . . it keeps my body clenching and clenching until it hurts so beautifully.

Then slowly, the maelstrom recedes like the tide, drawing me with it until I collapse exhausted and unable to move against Mateo's chest. His mouth stays pressed to my temple as I try to catch my breath, but I'm not sure I'll ever breathe the same way again.

He was right. Undeniably the best orgasm of my life.

Chapter 18

Mateo

Damn, Speedy." Ryan claps me on the back as I wipe at my face and neck with a towel. I'm in such a good mood that I don't even mind the nickname that he's been calling me since last year. It hasn't caught on, but that hasn't stopped him from using it day in and day out. Persistent, that one. Not that it's a bad nickname, per se, certainly better than "Blocks," which is what he calls Brookes. But between "Torres" and "Teo," I've got enough different names. Anything else would have to be really good to be worth the hassle. "Hell of a game," Ryan says. "Keep playing like that, and we'll be in for a bowl game for sure."

I grin as I pull off my pads. It *was* a pretty awesome game. My best since starting at Rusk. Everything had just clicked. Mc-Clain and I were practically of one mind, we were so on fire. And no matter who the defense put on me, I kept managing to break away. Everything that *could* go our way *did*, and we won by forty, and on the other team's turf, too. And considering this game put us at seven wins for the season, officially past last year's record, our locker room is louder than I've ever heard it.

Coach keeps his speech short and sweet, as he tends to do when we win. After a quick round of showers, we load up on the bus to head back to the hotel. It was an evening game, and too long of a flight for us to head back tonight, and I can tell by the knowing glances the coaches keep giving one another that they know it will be hard to keep a handle on us tonight. I should be as eager to party as everyone else, but at the moment I just wish we were taking a red-eye flight home. I can think of much better ways to celebrate this win.

The Rusk crowd at the game was small, but a ton of them stuck around, and they're chanting "Bleed Rusk Red!" as the bus pulls away. We yell with them for a while, banging on the ceiling and the seats. We even keep it up when we're long out of the parking lot and on the highway heading for the airport hotel where we're spending the night.

The overhead lights come on, and Coach stands next to his seat at the front of the bus. We yell for him, too, and he laughs, raising his hands to try to get us to quiet down.

"All right. All right. Settle down. A few housekeeping things. We've got a late-night supper already set up for you guys in Ballroom A in the hotel. If you want to run to your room before you eat, it's at the back of the hotel, past the workout area. Our flight home leaves at seven thirty in the morning, which means we leave this hotel at five thirty. I won't tell you how late you can stay up, because you guys deserve to do a little celebrating. But I sure as hell better not have to come find any of you guys in the morning. If your ass isn't on a seat in this bus at five twenty-nine A.M., you better believe you'll regret it. And your teammates will, too. So roommates, take care of your own. Is that clear?"

"Yes, sir."

"The usual rules apply. No leaving this hotel. No drugs. No alcohol. No girls in your room. You can make use of the pool and other hotel facilities until they close for the night, but I better not get any calls from the hotel about any of you causing problems. Is that also clear?"

"Yes, sir."

He smiles, and we pull up in front of the lobby of our hotel. "Well, then gentleman, enjoy your food and enjoy your win."

If anybody in the hotel was already asleep, they most likely aren't now. The noise we make as we leave the bus is enough to wake the dead. As soon as I climb off, Coach Cole falls into step beside me.

"Oz gave me your final stats. Eight catches for two hundred and eight yards in total. An excellent game, son."

"Thanks, Coach." I like Coach Cole. I know I can be a pain in the ass, and I rarely know when to shut my mouth, and he's been cool about it. But we've not really had that much one-on-one inter-action. It's mostly just been him telling me to be quiet or calm down or quit dancing. He gives me a serious look now, and I don't know how Carson doesn't piss his pants every time he's near Coach. I find him intimidating, and I'm not dating his daughter.

"You keep matching that level of play, stay consistent, and you'll be in good shape for the draft when you graduate in two years."

My heartbeat thunders in my ears, loud enough to drown out even the overwhelming noise of my teammates. *Draft?*

"That something you're interested in?"

I stumble over the words because I try to get them out so fast. "I—I am. Yes, sir. I am."

"Good. Right now, concentrate on the next game, on this season. The best way to get you noticed is to get this team noticed as much as possible. But keep up the good work, stay serious, and we'll talk in the off-season about what else we can do to get you ready."

I'm still saying my thank-yous when Coach nods and turns back toward the bus.

It's the kind of thing you dream about hearing. I can still remember being in high school and thinking that it was only a matter of time. I was going to get recruited, play some college ball, and then go pro. I was so certain that all I needed was a shot, and it would happen. Certain enough that I made it my everything. Then there were scouts and recruiters, but they weren't the big schools I always expected them to be. The powerhouses. Instead, it was a mix of Division II schools, and a handful of Division I schools with less than stellar programs, like Rusk. Then suddenly things didn't seem so certain anymore.

Lina had pushed hard then, tried to get me to admit that maybe deciding my life based on football didn't make that much sense anymore. I didn't listen. I buckled down and shut her out, shut everything out. But that didn't stop her words from ringing in my head day after day. So that when I started freshman year here at Rusk, I was dragging the weight not only of a broken heart with me, but of Lina's doubts heaped atop my own. And the only way to deal with it, the only way not to drown under it had been to pretend like it didn't matter. I had to pretend that nothing mattered. That everything was a joke because if you can laugh about something, it can't hurt you.

But now everything could be about to change. And I'm scared to think about it because . . . getting my hopes up over something like this? Over something that *matters*? That's a hell of a lot of hurt I'm risking.

AFTER DINNER, a group of about ten of us end up in McClain and Moore's room. We're crammed onto the beds, the chairs, and anywhere else we can fit. I settle myself against an open spot on the wall. Last year, we would have been down at the pool or with the girls that somehow always know where the team is staying. But now half my friends are among the girlfriend-ed, and well . . . I don't have much of an interest in flirting with groupies tonight. Before I can join the conversation, my phone buzzes with a text. I smile when I see it's from Nell.

> I heard someone had a good game.

> It has been a pretty great week for me.

> How so?

Been hanging with this hot girl. Escaped the cops. Scored some touchdowns. You know, the usual.

That does sound eventful.

I can think of a pretty good way to cap off the night.

Do I even want to ask?

You wouldn't happen to have sexting on your list, would you?

Ha ha . . . ńo. Try again.

Oh, come on, girl genius. Give a guy a break.

Never going to happen.

I'm going to text you dirty things all the time. Eventually you'll have to reply.

Eventually I might just block you.

> You like me too much to do that.

> We'll see.

A pillow hits me in the face, drawing my attention back to the room.

"Dude," Keyon says. "I called your name like five times. Don't tell me you searched your name on Twitter again."

I flip him off. "Yeah, that's what I'm doing. So, leave me alone with my adoring public."

> So what are we checking off your list tomorrow?

> I have to study.

> Don't tell me you're already getting tired of me.

> Some of us actually mean it when we say study.

> I could help. I could quiz you. Reward you when you get it right.

> I really do need to study. If you come, you can't distract me.

> Who? Me?

I get nailed with another pillow. "Seriously, guys? What are we, children?"

"Wait. Hold up. Did Torres just accuse someone else of immaturity? Is the world ending?" Silas asks, and everyone bursts into laughter. I throw the two pillows back at them.

"Who are you texting?" Brookes asks.

"How do you know I'm not on Twitter like Keyon said?"

He just raises an eyebrow, and damn his creepy perception.

I sigh. "You guys are the worst, you know that?"

"Wait," McClain says. "Are you implying what I think you're implying, Brookes? Does Teo have a girlfriend? An actual, real-life girl? Not just a booty call?"

I glare at Brookes, and he shrugs.

My phone buzzes, and I stand up. Stretching, I say, "It's late. I'm gonna crash."

As I head for the door, I hear groans and prods behind me to stay, to spill about the girl. With my back turned, I wave and leave for my room. When I'm settled onto my own bed, I look at the text from Nell.

> I suppose I can at least take a break.
> Dylan does dinner with her parents on Sunday night, so if you'll come over then, I'll cook.

> It's a date.

Chapter 19

Nell's To-Do List

- *Normal College Thing #11: Go on a date.*
- *Figure out how to reply to Torres's text about whether or not I'm wearing panties without sounding like a complete idiot.*
- *Make sure to actually wear cute panties just in case he checks.*
- *Oh God. Stop freaking out. Stop it.*

I should be studying. Mateo or Torres or whoever he is won't be here for another hour, and I should be studying because even though he's promised not to distract me, he's just naturally distracting, and I'm not sure how much work I'll get done tonight.

That's what I should be doing. Instead, I'm putting on makeup. Real, actual makeup. On my face. Like a normal person. Or trying to anyway. I haven't used my mascara in a couple months, and it's gone all clumpy inside. I make a few passes over my lashes, but no matter how much gunk I wiped off the brush, it still comes out all clumpy and awful on my eyes.

When I find myself actually considering running to the pharmacy down the street to buy a new tube, I press my hands to my face in frustration.

I look at myself in the mirror and say, "Stop this. I don't need this to impress him. I don't need to impress him, period."

Clearly he hadn't needed me to wear makeup the other night. Granted, it was dark, and he could probably only see the outline of my face, but still. Besides . . . it's not as if I'm trying to . . . I don't know, *keep* him. This isn't about that. It's about experience and discovery. And yes, maybe I'm no longer envisioning a future spent alone, married to my job; maybe that's not what I want anymore, but I'd be crazy to start picturing a future with this particular guy.

What if he goes on to play football professionally? I might not watch football on TV, but it doesn't take a genius to know that all of those guys date supermodels and actresses and people much prettier and more interesting than me.

I don't expect to have a piece of his future. I'm just going to enjoy the piece of him I have now.

After a quick trip to the bathroom to wash off the mascara monstrosity on my eyes, I decide to go ahead and start cooking. If I can't be productive and study, I can at least do something useful. Originally I'd planned to wait to start dinner until Torres got here. I relished the idea of putting him to work. But it's probably a good thing I'm starting now. Somehow I can't imagine Torres doing anything in my kitchen except making a mess. An image pops into my head of my counter covered in ingredients, and the food burning, while he kisses me into oblivion.

I shake away that thought and begin prepping ingredients. One of the things I did love about growing up in and around a restaurant was learning how to cook. It's not as big a part of my life as it is for my parents and the rest of my family, but it's something that puts me at ease. There's a science to it that has always appealed to me. Measurements and mixes and observation. It engages my hands and my mind, and at the moment I could use that kind of distraction.

I'm making tortellini Bolognese because I figure since he's an athlete, his diet is probably pretty carb heavy. And Bolognese is a sauce I used to help my mom make all the time. She used to spend hours on that sauce, letting it simmer and steep in flavor. She'd be horrified to know that when I make it these days, I'm usually done in a little under an hour.

I focus on the vegetables first. Chopping and dicing my way through onions, carrots, celery, and garlic. It takes a little while, but eventually the motions of my hands and the concentration finally push the thought of Mateo (and his mouth and his hands) out of my head for the first time in days. By the time I toss the vegetables in the pan with olive oil and a little butter, I've lost myself in the task. I've made this dish often enough that I don't even have to look at the recipe. I move on from the vegetables to the meat.

Mom makes hers with ground beef, pork, and veal, but on my college-student budget, I've settled just for ground beef.

I think of Mateo again, but this time I'm calm enough to do it objectively, to wonder what's made me so nervous in the first place. It's not that he's coming over or that I'm cooking for him. It's more about what happens afterward.

Dylan texted just before the makeup debacle to say she was staying the night at Silas's again. The words caused a stab of regret . . . until I realized what they meant. An apartment all to myself with Mateo. No one would be coming home to interrupt us. And after what happened in his truck earlier in the week, I was practically suffering withdrawals from his hands and his mouth and all of him.

How is it that I could be addicted to him already? That I could crave him this much? I don't know, but I do know I've never had this kind of physical connection with anyone. And maybe he is dangerous. Maybe he's a much bigger catalyst than I bargained for, but I'm willing to risk it. For the orgasms. And okay, the laughs and the companionship and the adventure, too. And for him. That indefinable, overwhelming, annoying, and endearing thing that is just Torres.

I'm ready to sleep with him.

The thought hits me out of nowhere and has my heart behaving erratically again, so I force my attention back to my sauce.

I've finished adding the milk and tomatoes and spices and have left the sauce to simmer while I clean up when the knock comes at the door. My hands are covered in the remnants of my ingredients, and my stomach swoops so low I could swear it settles somewhere around my knees. I nudge the sink faucet with my forearm and start washing my hands as I call out, "Come in."

I hear the door open, and I close my eyes and take a few quick, steadying breaths as I soap up my hands. I tell myself to open my eyes. That he's going to come around the corner any second, and I'm going to look ridiculous washing my hands with my eyes closed, but everything inside of me is in a frenzy. And I know . . . *know* that "butterflies in your stomach" is just an expression, just something parents say to their kids, but all the same, I could swear that I feel every flap of their wings.

My eyes are still closed when I feel the buzz of his presence at my back, then his large hands settle onto my hips, curling around to stretch across my lower belly. I feel something ghost over the skin at my neck. His lips? His nose? And then he murmurs against my ear, "Something smells delicious."

I swallow, fighting off a shiver. This is . . . it's . . . so strange. And yet, somehow not. It shouldn't feel natural to have him in my house with me while I do everyday things like cook. He's from this other world, and in my head he's so intertwined with the list that is so *not me*. He shouldn't fit here.

But I'm learning that the difference between what should be and what *is* matters very little where he is concerned.

"I'm making tortellini," I tell him, belatedly realizing I should have asked him if he had any allergies or dislikes or—

"Sounds great."

I finally open my eyes as he wraps his arms fully around my middle and noses some of my hair to the side to kiss the corner of my jaw.

"Do you need me to do anything?" he asks.

Make me feel like you did the other night. Put me out of the misery I've been in the last several days without you.

"No, the sauce is pretty much done. I'm about to put the pasta on to boil. When that's done we'll be good to go. I might throw together a salad."

He turns me around and presses me back against the sink. "So what you're telling me is that we'll have a little time to kill while the pasta is cooking?"

He leans down to kiss me, but I put my hand up to block him. "I haven't put the pasta on *yet*."

"Well, do that so we can get to killing time." He punctuates the command with a swat to my bum, and I gape at him.

"You did *not* just do that."

"I did. And I liked it." He rubs his hands together like some cheesy movie villain and says, "In fact, I think I might want to do it again."

I dart away from him, spinning so that he's nowhere near my ass.

"You stay there," I order, opening the fridge to get the tortellini. Even though inside I'm thinking, Screw the pasta. Screw everything. Clearly I'm not the only one craving the next course after the other night, and I'm so very tempted just to abandon dinner to drag him back to my bedroom.

"You've got one minute, woman. And then pasta or no, I'm coming for you."

My heart thumps with nerves or anticipation or something else I can't identify. Something that has only ever happened with him, so I don't know what to call it.

I start opening the package of tortellini and say, "I can't put it in until the water is boiling. And even then, I'll still have to stir it occasionally."

"Fifty seconds."

"If I don't watch the pot, they could stick to the bottom or stick together."

"Forty-five seconds."

"Torres!"

"Five-second penalty. It's Mateo to you."

I glare at him, and rush to fill a pot with water. By the time I put it on the stove, I only have a few seconds left. I get the burner turned on, and then I'm practically tackled by a six-foot-two (maybe six-foot-three) overgrown child. He crowds me against one side of the archway that separates the kitchen from the little dining nook, and his hands slide unabashedly down to cup my ass. He kisses me, but I break away, turning my face to the side so I can laugh.

"You are ridiculous. And you can't blame me if the food ends up being horrible."

"I won't blame you for that. I'll just blame you for torture."

"Torture, is it? Really?"

He catches my bottom lip between his thumb and forefinger, tugging lightly. "Keeping me away from this," he says. "Definitely qualifies as cruel and unusual."

I close my eyes. How am I supposed to remain cool around him when he says things like that? *How?*

"One minute," I tell him. "You've got one minute. Then I need to check on the sauce and start on a salad."

Cockily, he lifts one dark brow and says, "Guess I better make that minute count."

His hands slide from my ass down to the tops of my thighs, and he heaves me up so that I'm forced to wrap my legs around his waist. I throw my arms over his shoulders to hold on, but he keeps me up with just his hands and the crush of his body against mine as if I weigh nothing at all.

"Fifty seconds," I tell him. I mean for it to sound sarcastic, but instead it comes out breathy and soft, and he groans in response.

"Cruel and unusual," he says again before slanting his mouth over mine.

I expect the kiss to be fiery and hot and fast, but instead it's teasing and sensual. He seduces me one stroke of his tongue at a time. Quick. Slow. Quick. Quick. Slow. And every time he withdraws, I arch up into him, trying to keep him with me. In seconds, the kitchen disappears, and it's only me and him and all the places our bodies are touching and all the places they aren't. His fingers dig into my thighs, and the small bite of pain somehow heightens everything else. I drag my hands over the slopes of his shoulders, down to his muscled biceps and back up again, and when he slows the kiss, it's my turn to dig my fingernails into his skin. Because I don't want slow. I want everything.

He pulls back, grazing his lips over mine again and again without actually kissing me. I groan in frustration, and he says, "Minute's up."

I tighten my legs around him and breathe, "Have another minute."

When we finally come up for air, I've boiled half my water away and have to refill the pot. This time I manage to resist him long enough to make a salad, get the water back to boiling, and toss in the tortellini. Fifteen minutes later, we fill our plates and head for the table. Once we're sitting, I realize that I'd been so ridiculously worried about what I was going to say when I saw him or how I was going to look and how the night would end that I didn't even think to be nervous about the other scary part of the evening.

Dinner. Like an actual dinner date. With conversation. And awkward silences. And *more* awkward silences. I pick up a fork and push at my food, trying to think of what we could possibly talk about. Then he groans.

"Good?" I ask hopefully.

He gestures with his fork while making another series of appreciative noises that despite not being words somehow read as *Oh my God, yes.*

"It's my mother's recipe."

"It's amazing. *You're* amazing."

I look down at my plate, hiding a small, satisfied smile. "Thank you. But it's just pasta. It's not as if I made the tortellini from scratch."

"None of that," he says, pointing his fork at me. "This is excellent. The end. Full stop."

"Okay. Thank you," I say again.

"One thing, though. You have to promise me never to cook for any of our friends."

My stomach clenches at the word "our." I still haven't checked off that particular item—"Make new friends"—despite the Frisbee game and the party. I'm waiting for it to feel right. For it to feel like I belong to them and they belong to me. But I realize then that Torres counts. Whatever else he might be . . . we're friends.

"Why can't I cook for them?"

"Because then they'll always want you to cook. And *this* . . ." He circles his fork over his plate. "This is *mine*."

I smile and shake my head. "So selfish."

"With you? Hell yes."

"With my food, you mean."

He suddenly looks serious. "With *you*. No more calling that ginger dude to help you with your list. I don't like him."

"You don't *know* him."

"Sure, I do. Matty something or other. He came to a few parties earlier this year with Dylan. And what kind of name is Matty anyway?"

"Selfish *and* jealous. You're not doing so hot tonight." I lift my eyebrows in mock disapproval. "Anyway, Matty is just a friend. And it's not like you have to do *everything* on the list with me."

"It *is* like that."

"No, Mateo. It isn't. Besides, you're busy. You have practice and games and classes. You might not always be around. School is out in about a month, and then . . ."

" And then what?"

"And then I graduate."

When a stunned silence follows, I realize I maybe should have broached that particular topic with a bit more finesse. Until now, he'd been continually shoving pasta into his mouth and still managing to hold up his end of the conversation. Now he does neither.

"You're twenty," he says finally. "You can't be graduating."

"I am. I came in with all my requirements pretty much out of the way. And since I don't have a job, I petitioned to take more than eighteen hours each semester."

"So that's what the list is. One last hurrah. And then what?" He fiddles with the napkin beside his plate for a second, and then continues: "You leave?"

Am I imagining the tension around his mouth and his shoulders?

"Not immediately. None of the graduate programs I'm applying to allow me to start in the spring semester, so I got a job as a research assistant for one of my professors. That will last me through the end of the school year. I've applied for a few summer internships, and hopefully one of them will work out, and then after that, theoretically, graduate school."

"Damn. You never stop, do you? It's one thing after another. Now I get why . . ."

He trails off, and all my worst fears are coming true. We've barely been at the table for ten minutes and the differences between us are already abundantly clear. We do fine when we're just joking or flirting or kissing, but beyond that? What do we have?

"Now you get why I need a list just to have a life?" I finish for him. "I did warn you that I'm usually pretty boring."

"No, that's not it at all. And you're *not* boring. Stop saying that." He places his fork down on the table forcefully enough to make a thud. After a pause, he continues, "I was going to say that now I get why you're . . . starving."

I squint at him and shake my head in confusion. "I'm starving?"

"Yeah. For adventure. For connection. I saw your face when you were sitting up on the Rusk statue. It was such a little thing, but your expression was like you were on top of a mountain, like you were taking a break and opening your eyes for the very first time in your life. I get it now. I understand. That list? I don't think you're doing it to have a life. I think you're doing it as a last resort, like those shock paddles they use at hospitals. I think you're trying to wake yourself up. Before it's too late."

It's as if he's just reached into my chest and handed my heart to me, and all I can think is . . . touché. I tore him down when we first met, pinpointed his flaws, so I suppose turnabout is fair play.

"You're giving me too much credit. You're right . . . I have missed out on a lot, and it has made me *eager* to make up for what I've lost. But that list is just a list. It's a challenge to myself to explore a different side of life. Not a cry for help."

"You're a smart girl, Nell. You don't think it's possible that you latched on to that list as a lifeline because a part of you needed it? Otherwise, if it was just about having a little fun before you graduated, why step so far outside of your comfort zone? You could have just made more of an effort to hang out with Dylan and stupid-name Matty. You could have done things you already know you enjoy. There's a middle ground here, and you jumped right over it into the deep end. No one does that unless they're already drowning in some other way."

I think a tiny piece of me falls in love with him then. Because despite how different we are, despite the fact that he's known me just two weeks (two crazy and overwhelming weeks), he's managed to put words to the choking feeling that had me crying to my mother not long ago. My life has always been about forward motion. From the first time I walked into a cafeteria alone and realized I didn't have anywhere to sit. In elementary school, we were seated in alphabetical order, according to our last names. It didn't even occur to me that middle school would be different until I stood there, tray in hand, and realized that there was no one I wanted to sit with, and no one who wanted to sit with me. So lunch became a time to focus. To study. Then it was that way after school, too, while I waited for the bus. Then it was Saturday nights. As long as I stayed busy, I didn't have to acknowledge that I had no other options. It was work and study or . . . nothing. That was all I had.

I only function when my mind is focused on a goal, and I'm driving toward it. And yet, for the past few weeks, I keep getting sidetracked. And maybe he's right. Maybe that list is my way of putting on the brakes. I'd thought as long as my schedule was overflowing with assignments and commitments and projects, it meant that I was full. That there were no holes in me. But all those goals are just temporary distractions. Sand through a sieve. The minute the sand has passed, the holes are visible again.

"I like my major," I tell him, my tone defensive not because of anything he's said, but because of the way I can feel my thoughts pulling back to that place I try to avoid. "I like the idea of being on the edge of the future. There are so many possibilities in biomech. One of the summer internships I applied for involves biomedical research with NASA that could completely revolutionize space travel. *NASA*. I think that's so cool, and it sounds right up my alley. Most of the time, I'm eager to get started."

"And the rest of the time?"

I take a deep breath, brace myself, and say, "The rest of the time I doubt everything."

He pushes his plate aside and scoots his chair a little closer to mine. His hands slide halfway across the table toward mine before stopping.

"You know, yesterday my coach said he thinks I stand a chance at going pro. I can't tell you how long I've been waiting to hear someone besides me say that. It's all I've ever wanted. When I figured out I was good at football . . . it gave me an identity. It gave me definition. I have sisters, have I mentioned that? Six of them actually. I was the only guy in this huge family of women."

"That explains why you're so comfortable around them."

He reaches one hand out then and snags mine, pressing my knuckles on the table and drawing his fingers over my palm.

"It's hard to live in a house with that many people. I was smack-dab in the middle. Not the oldest. Not the youngest. And for a long time, I felt like just one in a crowd. I had my sister Victoria's eyes, and Sofia's nose, and my personality was mixed and matched and patched together from other people in my family. And I just kind of . . . *was*. Until I found football. It was something that was mine. I didn't have to share it with any of my siblings. And Fridays were the one night a week when my big family got to revolve around me. It gave me confidence. Pride. Purpose. Football gave me everything."

He hesitates, drawing his fingers from my palm, closing them over my own, and then folding my hand into a fist. "But that was then. I was just a kid, and now I'm not. And over the years, I've given up so much for football. Things that I can never get back, things that have changed me as a person. And I can't help but wonder what else I'll have to give up before all is said and done. And as amazing as it was to hear someone else bring up going pro, a part of me wishes Coach hadn't said anything. Because it's a lot easier to be certain from afar, but when things get real, when they're within your grasp . . . it's a totally different story."

"That's it exactly. I've always been so sure. I've never wavered. I decided what I wanted to do, and I put my head down, and I got to work. But now . . ."

"It's real."

I nod. "It's real."

And so I went searching for something that wasn't. Something that was so completely different from my life that it might balance the scales and stave off reality.

I look at Mateo then, his big body folded onto our measly kitchen chairs. His eyes are so warm and open and understanding. And it occurs to me that I went searching for something artificial with my list and found far more truth than I know what to do with.

I don't know what I'm doing when I stand up from the table and hold out my hand to him. Our plates are still sitting there, and normally I would go straight to washing them and cleaning up after dinner, but I've already waited days for him.

And I'm tired of waiting. Time to really jump in the deep end.

Chapter 20

Mateo

I can't read Nell's expression when she stands up next to me. It's
not a look she's ever given me, but just like everything else where
she's concerned, it makes me want her. I take the hand she offers
and am shocked when she begins pulling me down the hallway in
the direction of her bedroom.

I try to control my reaction, to stop all my blood from rushing
south. She could just want to show me something. She could . . .
fuck. I'm sure there are any number of reasons she could be taking
me back to her room, but I can only think of one. And her bed,
and her skin, and her taste on my tongue, and the cries I'm determined to wring out of her.

She nudges the door open, but instead of turning on the overhead light, she moves toward the bedside lamp. She flicks it on,
and the amber glow shines up on her, bathing half her face in
light. I stay by the door. One last-ditch effort to control myself in
case this isn't what I think it is.

She doesn't say anything. And the seconds of waiting, the anticipation, only make me harder. I watch her struggle to decide on what to say, and when she sighs, I think maybe she's changed her mind. That she can't bring herself to ask for what I think we both want.

But I should know by now that Nell will always find a way to shock me. She reaches for the bottom of her sweater, and in one quick move pulls it up and over her head. My gorgeous shy girl has done more than bloom. She's fucking brilliant. Brighter than the sun, strong enough to pull me right out of orbit. She's wearing the same black lacy bra that she'd flashed me the last time I saw her. But this time I get more than a glimpse—oh no, I look my fill. Her long neck gives way to dainty shoulders. The bra has her tits pushed up and together, and praise Jesus for Victoria and her secrets. My eyes drop to the narrowing of her torso, the flare of her hips, the soft indentation of her belly button. Her skin looks smooth there and paler than her arms and her face, and I have the strongest urge to leave my mark there, to tease that uncharted skin with my tongue and teeth. Her jeans rest at her hips, stopping my further exploration, but I can remember the vague outline of her legs in the dark of my truck. I certainly remember the feel of them, squeezing at my hips as she came.

That memory snaps me back into action, and I step fully inside the room and close the door. I hear her exhale, and look back to her gaze.

"I thought maybe you . . ." She trails off.

"Would say no?"

She nods. I cross to her and use one finger to tip her chin up so that she faces me. "I told you before . . . nothing you could do can make me not want you." I take her hand and draw it to my cock, straining at the confines of my jeans. She smoothes her hand over it once, and then again, no hesitation.

"You're already . . ."

"Hard? Yeah, sweetheart. I pretty much always am with you."

"But we haven't even kissed."

"I've been thinking about kissing you again since the moment our last kiss stopped."

I'm trying to think of a less crude way to tell her that her tits always do the trick, too, when she unfastens the button at the top of my jeans. I suck in a breath at the slight ease in pressure and hold it as she slides my zipper down. Her knuckles accidentally bump against my erection, and I groan. She pauses and looks up at me, and her eyes are calculating. This time her touch is not accidental. She drags a finger over the bulge in my boxer briefs, and the jolt of need I feel is so similar to hunger that I barely resist the urge to pin her to the bed and taste her.

She moves her fingers to the waistband of my jeans and pushes them down. While she does that, I reach back to grab my shirt and pull it over my head. I kick off my shoes and step out my jeans, and it's my turn to stand still while her eyes study me. Slowly, as her gaze moves over my chest, she lets her fingers trail in its wake. Tentatively, she circles her finger over my nipple in the way that I've done to her, and I fight a groan.

She smiles. "None of that, now. If I'm not allowed to hold back, you aren't either."

I can't wait another second to kiss that smart mouth. I wrap my hand around her neck and drag her closer. Her lips instinctively part under mine, her tongue eager and seeking, and there's such a fucking change in her from the other night. She throws everything into the kiss, running her hands up my abdomen and over my chest and down my arms. I have no doubt that she's absolutely in this moment. She's not thinking about anything else, and my cock pulses in response. She breaks away with a gasp, and looks down between us.

There's such wonder in her voice when she says, "It moved," that I can't stop my laugh.

"It does that."

She reaches out to touch me again, but it's not enough to feel her fingers over the fabric. I want her warm skin, those small fingers. But first, I want us on an even playing field.

"Take off your jeans," I tell her.

While she's shimmying them off her hips, I lose my underwear, gripping the base of my dick tight when her legs come into view. She bends to push her jeans off the rest of the way, and her chest nearly spills out of her bra.

I shift my eyes toward the ceiling because now I'm picturing her on all fours, the way her breasts would fall, waiting for my hands to cup them as I slide into her from behind. *Damn.*

I have to fight not to let my thoughts run ahead of my actions.

But it's hard. There are too many things I want to do to her, too many ways I want to have her.

But she's a virgin. And I've never been someone's first before. Not even with Lina. And the thought of it now feels too big to comprehend.

While I'm still looking up, her hand wraps around my cock, pulling me back to the present, and I shudder out a breath. Her eyes are trained on her hand where it touches just above mine, and I release my hold to give her control. I flex, and I move in her hand this time, and she makes this small noise of satisfaction.

"If I wanted to use my mouth on you," she says, "would you teach me?"

Holy fuck, I'll never get tired of how direct and honest she is.

"I will teach you absolutely anything you want to know." She starts to drop to her knees, but I catch her around the waist, pulling her in tight against me. "But not right now. Tonight is about you. I'm the one who gets to learn now."

She looks disappointed at first, but when I caress her thigh, sliding up the curve of her ass, she doesn't complain. I shift her backward until her knees hit the bed, and then I guide her to sit. Her bed is low enough that she's in the perfect position to take me into her mouth, and even though I want it—*God*, I want it so bad—I force myself to step back.

I kneel in front of her and pull her in for a kiss. Some of my need bleeds through, and our movements are fast and hard instead of the slow seduction I'd been aiming for. But as much as

I long for control, it's not something I know how to keep around her. I want her too badly.

When we both need air, I break away from the kiss and push her backward until she lies flat on the bed. Her arms fly out to her sides, and the rise and fall of her chest makes my mouth water, and as much as I love her in that bra, I want her out of it. Leaning over her, I slide my hands beneath her back to the clasp. She parts her legs around me, hooking her ankles behind my back.

The hooks of her bra come undone at the same time that she lifts her hips, arching her body up so that her center rubs against the muscles of my abdomen. She wants the friction she found that night in my truck, and it would be so easy to shift a little higher, lay myself on top of her, and align our hips. But there's something beyond sexy about the needy way she writhes against me. I can feel her damp underwear against my skin, and I want to just stay where I am and glory in her uncontrolled actions. Before, I had to work to get her loosened up, to get her to give herself over to the pleasure, but not anymore.

I had intended to taste her, to bring her to the edge that way so that the rest might be easier for her, but now I have a different idea. If I can survive it.

I tell her to move back on the bed, up toward the pillows, and then I crawl onto the mattress beside her. I pull her onto her side to kiss her, and I feel her naked chest crushed against mine for the first time since our night in the pool. It had been good then. Incredible really, but it's nothing compared to this. Reaching down,

I trail my fingers down her thigh until I get to her knee, then with one swift pull, I drag her leg up and over my hip. She gasps and digs her fingernails into my bicep, but I'm not done. Not by a long shot. Slowly, I roll to my back, gripping her hips to bring her with me until she's astride my hips.

"Sit up," I say.

She looks nervous, but she complies. And *fuck*, she looks good on top of me. Her hair is wild, and her tits are flushed a pretty pink.

"Put your hands on my chest."

She does, laying her palms flat against my pecs. Holding her hips, I shift her until my cock is trapped between her and my stomach, the length pressed against her pussy. The only thing between us is a pair of black silky underwear, slick with her arousal.

Guiding her hips like I did in the truck, I whisper, "Move."

Tentative at first, she flexes forward, sliding along my length.

"I want to watch you," I tell her. "I want to see you take what you want. Don't think. Just react. Listen to what your body tells you. Move any way that feels good."

This time she's bolder, leaning her weight into her hands so that she can grind her hips down into mine. The pressure on my cock hurts so fucking good, and I have to struggle to keep my breaths steady. She arches her back, pushing herself down the length of me before rocking back up. Faster, she does it again. And again.

Her breasts swing with her movements, and I reach up to cup

them in my hands. She cries out, increasing her pace, until the friction of her dragging against me is almost more than I can bear.

But she's too gorgeous like this. I can't stop her. I won't. Not when she's so completely lost to her desires. I roll her nipples between my fingers, and her movements become erratic, her thighs flexing on both sides of me, and she whimpers something too low for me to hear.

"What, beautiful? What is it?"

"Please," she whines, her dilated eyes meeting mine. "It's not enough. *Please*."

I drag her down for a kiss, and she clings to me, her hands wrapping around my shoulders and squeezing tight. Then, while her mouth is against mine, I reach down and rip the seam on the hip of her underwear. I throw it away, and then the head of my cock brushes against her slick center.

She breaks away from the kiss with a gasp, resting her forehead against mine as she pants against my mouth.

"It's going to hurt," I tell her. "But you're in control. You want to stop. You stop. You want to move. You move."

She nods, and I guide myself to her opening.

"Wait!" she cries. "Condom."

Fuck. *Fuck.* I have never in my entire life forgotten a condom. It's always at the forefront of my mind. Something about her throws me completely off my game.

"Sorry," I say, at a loss. "I didn't mean to . . . I just . . . Jesus, Nell, you're so fucking glorious to watch, I lost my head."

I start to shift her off to the side, but she stops me. "There's some in the drawer of my nightstand."

I lift an eyebrow, and she shrugs. "I like being prepared."

And it's a good thing she is. Because the last thing I want to do is climb off this bed to rummage through my jeans. She leans over to open the drawer, and then pulls out an entire box.

"I wasn't sure what kind to get, so I did some research on the Internet."

I groan. I can only imagine the kind of research she's done, knowing how thorough she likes to be.

"They're perfect," I say, impatiently tearing open the box and removing a packet. She shifts back onto my thighs, and her eyes watch, fascinated, as I roll the rubber down my length.

I never could have predicted how good this would feel with her. I knew I liked her, I knew my attraction to her was off the charts. But it's the little things, the way each moment holds inter-est for her. Each new touch, each new experience . . . she soaks it all up, and it turns my head around. I can't help but feel like I need to imprint every moment of this evening on my memory, too, to make sure I remember how perfect she was, how much joy there is in her. I don't want to forget one second of what it's like to be her first.

I drag her back into place and up to my mouth and whisper against those plump lips, "You're beautiful, Nell. Thank you. Thank you for this."

And then for the second time, I guide myself to her wet heat and begin the slow, torturous slide inside her.

She's tighter than I could have imagined, and even though she's practically melting around me, it's not easy to push forward. I dip my head to pull her nipple into my mouth, and she rocks back a little, drawing me a little farther inside.

"That's it. Push back while I push forward."

I suck at her breast again, before trapping it between my teeth. Her hips bear down against mine, and she cries out. I push my hips up, driving forward a little harder, and our combined movements push me almost all the way inside.

I collapse back on the bed, stunned into stillness for a moment at the mind-numbing pleasure of being clasped inside her. She sits back, and the last inch of me slides inside, until I can feel our bodies press together.

I force myself to look for her reaction, even though my instinct is to thrust, to pull her down against me and drag myself back through that exquisite tightness.

Her eyes are closed, and her hands are back to resting on my chest. Her expression is pulled tight, and I know she's in pain.

"Talk to me," I tell her. "Tell me what to do."

She shakes her head, her expression tensing even more, and I can feel my stomach drop right through the mattress. She's shutting me out again. I should have known the pain would be enough to undo all the easiness in her. It's hard enough for her to let go when all she's feeling is pleasure.

I sit up, intending to hold her and talk her through it, but she gasps at the movement.

"That felt good." She sounds surprised.

I wrap my arms around her middle and kiss the corner of her mouth. "It will all feel good. Just give yourself some time to adjust."

But as usual, Nell doesn't know how to take things slow. She only knows how to move forward, and I'm grateful for that particular attribute when she rises up on her knees a few inches before sinking back down against me.

Somehow, in the time between that first thrust and now, my memory of how tight she was dimmed, but now it's back in full force as her body squeezes around me.

"Fuck. You feel so good."

"I do?"

"Yeah, girl genius. Better than anything I've ever felt in my life."

And it's true, not just an in-the-moment utterance. This . . . *this right here* . . . is the best I've ever felt in my life.

She does it again, lifting a little higher this time, dropping a little faster, and I groan. "How do you feel?" I ask.

"Strange."

"Good strange?"

"I think so."

I run my hand up her spine to thread my fingers through her hair. I tilt her face down to mine so I can see her expression. Our gazes meet, and she swirls her hips experimentally, and *fuck*, I lied.

This is the best I've felt in my entire life.

Looking into her eyes, seeing the way they glaze over as she rubs her clit against me, feeling her chest brush against mine, all while being held so perfectly inside her.

I must think that phrase a dozen times, two dozen, as she loosens up, and we begin a slow and steady rhythm. Each moment sends pleasure tearing through my limbs, eclipsing the moment that came before.

Eventually, the position is too restricting for our mutual need to go faster, harder, so I roll, pressing her back against her pillows, and brace my arms on either side of her body. Then I'm slamming into her while her nails score my back and she throws her head back in pleasure. I can feel her getting tighter around me, and I speed up my movement, watching the way her body absorbs my hard thrusts.

She says my name, and that alone nearly drags me over the edge, but I manage to hold on, pausing while I'm buried deep inside her.

I reach between us, rubbing at the sensitive spot between her legs, and am rewarded with the bucking of her hips. I drag myself out, slow and steady, rubbing harder against her. I know she's close when her legs start to move at my sides. Her hips twist and lift, like she's reaching for something.

"Mateo," she says again, and I press my thumb down hard as I slam back into her.

Then her body clutches impossibly tight around me, pulsing and rippling, and I'm gone with her. The pleasure jerks at the base of my spine, and then roars through the rest of me. It burns through my blood, swallowing me up whole, and my last thought as I collapse against Nell's soft form and take her mouth in a kiss is that I've told my final lie.

This.

This is the moment.

Chapter 21

Nell's To-Do List

- ~~Normal College Thing #5. Lose my virginity.~~

wake up hot. And sweaty. And sticky. Exhausted, I start kicking at my covers, but the muscles in my legs are sore and heavy.

Hold on.

Hot, sweaty, sticky, and sore are *definitely* not part of my normal morning routine. I don't do anything that can make me sore on a normal basis. (Work out? *Please.*) And I sleep with the air-conditioning set low because I *hate* waking up hot and sweaty. I continue trying to wiggle out from under the covers, pondering these four oddities, and I become aware of a fifth.

I can't kick the covers off properly because there's a heavy weight over my legs—and over my waist, too, now that I think about it. I try to lean up onto my elbow, but when I move, the weight around my waist squeezes so tight that I'm abruptly awake. *Very* awake. And there's a bare chest inches away from my nose.

"Stop moving," a deep voice growls above my head.

I do stop. I stop so fast that my sore muscles spasm momentarily when I freeze up.

Torres. In my bed.

"And she freaks out in three . . . two . . ."

I push the arm off my waist and sit up straight. That's about the time I process my nakedness, when I feel the cool air of the bedroom fan over my sweaty skin. It feels good, but I'm more concerned with just how very bright the morning light has made my room. Scrambling, I pluck at the sheet and pull it up to cover my breasts.

Torres groans behind me. (Torres? Mateo? God, why are names so stupid?)

I feel the barest touch low on my spine, just above the curve of my bottom that I know is entirely visible to him. He begins dragging his fingernail up the length of my spine, and I straighten, resisting the urge to squirm under that small exploration. But I can't control the goose bumps that pebble over my skin or the breath that catches in my throat when the bed shifts and I feel his mouth begin the same trek up my back.

I clutch at the covers, needing something to ground me, and instead I end up gripping his calf. He chuckles, and the puff of his breath in the middle of my back tickles, and I break my resolve to stay still.

"Did you know you squirm when you're about to come?"

I don't know how to answer that. My brain is still too foggy from sleep. Do I stay silent? Tell him that yes, I noticed it last night, or no, I've never done "that" before him, so I don't know if it counts? Or do I just tell him to shut up because he's embarrassing me?

I *don't* like being embarrassed.

I tell myself I shouldn't be. What we did last night, it was . . . brilliant. Better than I ever could have imagined. And he's made no move to rush out of my bed, so that has to be a good sign. But I can't get over the fact that I'm sticky in places I shouldn't be sticky, and the sheets against my skin are damp with sweat, and *dear God*, was that his tongue on my back? Doesn't he know I'm sweaty and gross?

Just when I'm about to bolt for the bathroom, his mouth reaches the nape of my neck, and I feel his tongue and then teeth graze the side of my neck.

"Should I assume your silence is a yes? That you know your arms and legs flail when you're right on the edge, as if you're about to fall over an actual cliff?"

I shrug. That's what I'm reduced to. Master of intellect right here.

His mouth trails along my shoulder, and then I feel the graze of his stubble as he lays his cheek against my back.

"Come on, girl genius. Answer me. It's important."

Then, finally, I find my voice. Scoffing, I say, "How could that *possibly* be important?"

"Because I want to fuck you in the shower, but I'm worried you won't be able to stay standing when you come."

I make a noise that not even I can identify, and drop my head into my hands. I hear him chuckle behind me as he flops back on the bed.

"You are such an ass," I say into my hands.

Then, before I know what's happening, I'm being slid and tugged and rolled, and my naked body is draped on top of his. My legs fall to each side of his hips, and large hands squeeze my backside. "What did you say about your ass?"

Annoyance is finally beginning to dilute my embarrassment, and I try to push up from him. His arms won't budge. Instead I end up with my forearms pressed against his pectoral muscles, and his face just below mine. "I said *you're* an ass."

"Hmm . . . no. I like the way I heard it better."

I squirm, trying to slide off him, and instead he rolls, trapping me beneath him, and insinuating his hips more firmly between my thighs.

"This is . . . a lot for me," I say. "I would appreciate it if you could put the joking on pause for a little bit."

His eyes are dark as his gaze glides over my face. There's the barest shadow of stubble along his jaw and neck that I'm not used to seeing, and just the sight of it makes something flutter in my belly. One corner of his mouth tips up, and I know he felt the subtle shift in my hips as I reacted to the sight of him hovering over me. He leans in close, brushing his lips back and forth over mine in a not quite kiss.

"I don't know why you think I'm joking, sweetheart. I love your ass. Have ever since you wore that short little schoolgirl skirt and nearly gave me a heart attack when you walked away from me. And as for fucking you in the shower . . . I was *definitely* not joking about that."

A blush blazes over my cheeks, and he smiles. "I get that this is new for you, Nell. I do. But I'm not going to lie or hold back telling you how much I want you. I can't."

I swallow. "I'm just not used to talking about this kind of thing."

"I believe you scientific types would say the only way to really get comfortable with something is through exposure. *Practice*." He lowers his body against mine, props himself up on his elbows, and cups my cheeks. "And for the good of mankind and these gorgeous red cheeks, I'm willing to do whatever it takes to make you comfortable."

His gaze is so piercing, so serious. I am constantly amazed and undone by the different facets of his personality. He can flip-flop between joker and romantic so easily. He's so comfortable as both. Then, as if proving my thoughts, he adds, "And I'm willing to have shower sex as many times as it takes until you learn to stay standing."

I shove playfully at his shoulder, and as he tips over, he once again brings me with him. We roll so that I'm on top, and I can feel the hard length of his erection nestled in the heat between my legs. We're inches away from tumbling off the bed, and one of my legs hangs over the side, my toes brushing the carpet.

He's still got one hand on my cheek, and he uses it to start drawing me down toward his mouth, and I can't explain why it makes me panic. It just does. Last night was good. Great. And it was exactly what I wanted. But I haven't had time to think about what's next. I *have* to think about what's next . . . don't I?

"I need to shower and get ready for class. If I don't hurry, I'm going to be late."

He keeps pulling me closer, until my mouth is just over his, not quite touching, but so close I can feel his every breath against my kiss-chapped lips. The promise of that nearness distracts me, and I feel my body melt into his, my soft stomach pressing against his harder one.

"Skip it," he breathes.

"I—I can't. I've never skipped a class. Not ever." But it's tempting. So very tempting.

"Is there a test today?" His lips swerve left, touching my cheek.

"No."

"Do you have to turn in an assignment?" His tongue traces the sensitive spot at the corner of my jaw.

"No, but—"

"Skip it," he murmurs against my ear. The heat of his breath makes me shiver and press closer. "Skip it and stay here with me."

"Mateo—"

He hums. "I like my name in your mouth. Come on, girl genius. Think of your list. You've been doing a lot of things you've never done before. Give me one more. Let me thank you for last night."

His other hand has found its way to my hip, and he uses it to rock me against him. And just like that . . . I find myself giving in. No, not just giving in. Throwing myself at him. Because even though I'm tender, it feels unbelievably good as he glides through the wetness between my legs. And he's in my bed. And the morning light is playing over his bronze skin, and his eyes are dark and sleepy. And that's another piece of Mateo Torres I want to lay claim to. I want to own this memory of him playful and pleading in my bed.

"Please," he breathes, his voice strained and gravelly. "You want to make me beg, is that it? Is that on your list? Because I just might do it. For you."

"No more after this."

His grip on my hip tightens, and the hand on my cheek slides into my hair. "What do you mean?"

"I can't skip any more classes after this. I won't."

He exhales, and the tight hold he has on me loosens. He thought I meant sex, that I meant no more of *that*. And his reaction, the way his whole body stiffened, takes away the last of my unease. I'm not the only one on edge here. I'd thought after the way I pulled him in here last night, the way I initiated things, that he had all the power. But I've got some, too.

"Shower?" I ask, and I can't help but think of the night that I'd turned on all the lights in the house. His smile sweeps away the loneliness in a way that never could.

I CHECK OFF another first in the shower when Mateo kneels in front of me and teases me with his mouth and his fingers. I'm sore, and when I wince he places an apologetic kiss just below my belly button. He only uses his mouth from then on, and it takes me a long time to come, long enough that I try to stop him on more than one occasion because I feel bad for his knees, but he only laces his fingers through mine and pushes my hand back against the tile wall. When my orgasm does come, it's slower than last night's. Less detonation and more crashing wave. It starts at his mouth, and crests in my belly before, flowing out through all the rest of me. My legs don't flail this time, but they do go numb, and if my back weren't against the tile, I'm certain I wouldn't have been able to keep my balance.

I want to return the favor, but I'm so deliciously exhausted from his long exploration of me with his mouth that my hands are shaky.

"I'm sorry," I say. "I don't know what I'm doing."

He takes my hand and wraps it around his erection. He has me squeeze harder than I expected, but under the fall of the shower, he slips through my fist easily. I try to kneel, but Mateo grabs my hips and keeps me upright.

"I'm already close," he says. "A few times I thought I might come just with my mouth on you."

He gets harder in my hand; bigger, too. And I'm embarrassed that for all I know about biology, I'm still surprised by his body, by how it works. Then he stiffens. He presses a hand into the wall by my head and leans his face into the crook of my neck as he groans. He jerks and pulses, and comes against my stomach.

And even though I'd been exhausted moments before, now I'm alert . . . and curious.

This is what I wanted to know. When I'd added losing my

virginity to my bucket list, it had been no more than a mechanical act. It had been about the body, and that side of things is interesting enough. I do want to touch and explore and discover more, but it's everything else I'd been naive about. Sex is about more than bodies.

And I don't mean love, though I'm sure that does change the equation, too. I mean . . . he was on the edge just from giving me pleasure. He hadn't even touched himself. I know because I remember vividly having his hands on my hips and our fingers tangled together and his grip on my thighs.

That's the side of sex that fascinates me, what made me curious enough to watch that couple in the library. Pleasure isn't just about touching the right places or making the right movements. There's another element to it. And I don't know what it's called or how it works, but I want to.

I want to know everything.

Chapter 22

Mateo

I t's amazing how one night can change everything. Not just the sex, but everything, from the moment I first entered her apartment.

Talking to Nell about her doubts somehow inadvertently lessened mine. Neither of us found any solutions at dinner that Sunday, but talking about it, commiserating with someone else who's facing a similar situation, makes it easier to bear.

And of course, the mind-blowing sex didn't hurt either.

I find myself using Nell as my mental shield. As the next game approaches and the pressure mounts to perform as well as I did last week, I use her face to push away the thoughts of failure. When I start to stress about living up to the expectations of my coach and my team and myself, I think about her in her kitchen or her spread over my lap in my truck or her taking her own pleasure against me in her bed.

When I think about her, nothing can fucking touch me.

Then I have to think about something else entirely for a while because thinking of Nell like that while I'm in public always presents a problem.

I live for the moment when I can see her again, when I can park my fears and stresses at the door and lose myself in her arms. Somewhere in the back of my mind, I know I should be thinking about what this means. She's graduating next month, and even though she's not leaving immediately, she will leave eventually.

But I tell myself I've got time. I'll figure out exactly what it all means later.

Whatever she's doing to me, it consumes me enough to overcome my insecurities and fears. She pushes everything else out, delays the doubts, and I ride that solution all the way to another win on Saturday. I end up with a few less catches, but two of them were huge plays with major yardage. And at the end of the game, Coach claps a hand on top of my shoulder pad, and the look in his eyes says it all.

It's happening.

We're now 8–2, and one of those losses wasn't even conference play. With two games left, we're finally starting to make some waves. They're calling us the "big surprise" of the season and the "little team with big heart." And it feels like we're on the verge of something huge.

Something *real*.

Which is a little how I'm feeling in all aspects of my life lately.

The Monday after the game, I'm feeling high on life and on Nell. As I promised her when we'd been texting after our last away game, I spent the week texting her dirty things. She hadn't quite texted me anything dirty back yet, but she'd asked a few questions. Why I said certain things, what I liked. I figured I was close to getting her to text me back.

I send her one quick text before I lock up my phone for practice.

> Still want me to teach you how to use that pretty mouth?

I'm about to put the phone away when I'm surprised by her immediate reply.

> Yes.

Fuck. How the hell am I going to be able to concentrate on practice now? I'm an idiot.

I toss my phone in my cubby as Brookes comes to stand next to me.

He says, "So, I guess this means I was wrong."

"About?"

"Nell. That's who you were texting, right?"

I shrug. Because Nell and I haven't really talked about how we're going to play this with everyone else. She'd had a big project due today that she spent last week working on, and I'd been gearing up for the game, so we'd only seen each other a couple times.

"That's a yes," he says.

"Tell me something, how do you know this shit? It's fucking creepy, man."

He smiles. "I pay attention."

"To what? My Internet history? Do you have my phone tapped? Did you bug my room?"

"To your face, bro. It's all there. When I mentioned her name, you reacted for a split second, and then immediately covered it up. That told me I was right."

"Why are you here playing football instead of working in the CIA or something?"

He smiles. "Football is more of a challenge."

I laugh. And make a mental note to Google him and make sure he didn't just randomly spring into existence a few years ago.

"Seriously, though," he says. "I'm sorry I gave you shit about Nell. I read that wrong."

"Me or her?"

"The two of you together. You didn't make sense when I considered you separately. But whatever is going on with you two . . . it's good. I can tell."

"You're like some weird version of *The Wizard of Oz*, aren't you? There's some old dude somewhere spying on us all with video cameras and telling you what to say. Or you're secretly a robot or an alien or something."

He raises an eyebrow. "What kind of messed-up *Wizard of Oz* did you watch as a kid?"

"You two," Coach Oz barks as passes by us. "Quit gabbing like a bunch of little girls, and get on the field."

We finish changing clothes quickly as Oz leaves, and when the door slams behind him, I whistle. "Man, Oz needs to get laid. Dude scares me when he gets like that." Brookes makes a non-committal noise. "I'm serious. Look at Coach Cole. Guy is still scary as fuck, but since he's been dating that dance professor chick? *Way* cooler."

The silence after my statement is a bit too *silent*.

"Coach Cole, are you right behind me?"

"Yes, I am, Torres."

I shoot Brookes a glare, and the prick doesn't even bother hiding his grin. I spin. There aren't many people in the world who can make me feel small, but Coach Cole is one of them. We're roughly the same height, but the dude has Hulk shoulders and a beard that just screams, "I could kick your ass."

"Sir, I don't know if you're aware of this. But 'scary as fuck' is a slang term that means incredibly well respected."

His expression doesn't change. Not at all. Freaking stone.

"And 'dating that dance professor chick' is slang for—"

"Just shut up and get your ass on the field, Torres."

"Yes, sir. Of course, sir. Because I find you *scary as fuck*, sir."

He takes a step forward, and I bolt as calmly as I can for the door. I call back, "I was using that as a slang term, remember?"

For a moment I think I see the twitch of a smile beneath his mustache, but it's gone a second later, and I decide I'm better off hightailing it out onto the field.

"You never know when to stop, do you?" Brookes asks, jogging up beside me.

"I prefer to view that particular gift of mine in a positive light. More like . . . I cross lines no one else is willing to cross. I go where no man has gone before. All boldly and shit."

"I literally have *no clue* how you and Nell work. None."

He's joking, I know. But that particular jab slips past my defenses, and bangs around in my chest for a while as we walk out onto the field. I'm not looking for anything long term from Nell, but if events up to this point are any clue, she'll probably be done with me before I'm done with her. And even though I'm not trying to get serious, I can't say I'm looking forward to that. It's gonna fuck me up to see a girl like her walk away, serious or not. And I can't afford that. Not right now. Not when I'm on the verge of finally proving myself.

If I were smart, I'd take that thought and end things now. But I do enjoy flirting with that dangerous line.

Maybe that's what makes me reckless. I don't know. Maybe it's Nell, and how freaking powerful she makes me feel. Maybe I'm so eager to prove Coach right, prove Lina and everyone else wrong. Maybe Nell's assessment of me that first day was right, and I enjoy showing off too damn much.

Whatever the reason, I play hard during practice. As hard as I would play during a game. I take risks, go for catches that I would normally let slide during practice.

After one particularly spectacular catch, my helmet cracks hard against the cornerback tackling me, and my head jerks inside my helmet before my whole body slams hard into the turf.

For a second my ears ring and my vision crosses and crosses even though I'm staring straight ahead. I blink, but it doesn't stop, and there's a pressure in my head that feels like I'm a hundred feet underwater.

I climb to my feet carefully, and the grass moves like waves in front of my eyes. I let myself shake my head once to try and clear the fog, but when that only amplifies the pressure, I know that wasn't just any hit. I struggle to appear normal, to not let on that my head is swimming, and that the weak light from the November sun suddenly feels piercing to my eyes.

This can't be happening. Not when everything was going so good.

Not now.

Coach blows the whistle, and it cleaves my head open.

I get lucky, and Coach moves on to working on a new play where the first look is to Moore, and the second option is to Brookes. So as they work out the kinks, I'm really only running my route. No one mentions or seems to notice that I'm running a little slower, that my route isn't quite as straight as it should be. Their eyes are elsewhere, and it helps me hide what experience already tells me.

I have a concussion.

I've had two before, and the second, which occurred late in the season last year, was bad enough to leave me vomiting, and the nausea lasted for days. It also had me out for a game, which we ended up losing while I stood on the sidelines. If we hadn't had an open week the next week, Coach might have even benched me for two games.

This one is mild by comparison. No nausea, just that fuzzy, dazed feeling, sensitivity to light and sound, and the familiar pressure in my head. But the coaches and the trainers are serious about concussions. With my history, they might hold me back from playing this week, mild or no, just to be safe.

And we're so damn close. We've got two games left in the regular season, and we've got a damn good chance at getting a bowl game this year. If we win both games, we'd end the season at 10–2, a record that might be good enough to get us into one of the major bowls, a first for Rusk, whose program had always been lackluster prior to Coach Cole's arrival. That kind of bowl appearance could change the conversation completely.

About the team. About me.

We'd get a lot more attention coming into next season, and the bulk of our team's strongest contenders will still be here next year. Our most prominent senior this year was Jake Carter, and he's already been suspended, and we're doing just fine without him. We could potentially make a go for the title next year. It would be crazy. A long shot. But not impossible, and I can see it all shaping up in my head. I could go into my senior year in a program that gets just as much attention as those powerhouses I'd always dreamed of playing for. The ones that didn't want me in the end. And all the years of doubt would be worth it.

I'm still thinking of those possibilities when Coach calls practice to a close. I keep my head down in the huddle so no one sees my unfocused eyes. The fatigue is starting to set in, and I have to dig down deep to stand from my kneeling position when Coach dismisses us.

Now is when I'm supposed to tell someone. Even if I'm familiar enough with the symptoms to know what's happening, I'm supposed to get checked out by the trainer. They won't send me to the hospital. They would just send me home to rest, probably assign Brookes or Moore to check on me every couple of hours through the night to make sure my symptoms don't get worse. And then they'd limit my practice time this week to make sure I don't exacerbate things, and if they're worried enough . . . bench me.

But it's Monday. I've got plenty of time to recover before Saturday. So instead of going to Coach, I keep my helmet on until I'm off the field and into the dim hallway that leads to our locker room. The darkness is a relief, and only then do I gently pull off my helmet. My head throbs for a few moments, and I slow my steps, but the pain is manageable by the time I step into the locker room.

The trick is not to let anyone look me in the eye. Luckily, the guys have been razzing me about my more low-key behavior ever since that night in the hotel room when I was texting Nell. They're finally starting to lose interest, and no one comments on how quiet I am as we shower and clean up. As quick as I'm able, I gather my things and head out to my truck, where I'll at least have a little privacy. I pull myself behind the wheel and immediately reach for the sunglasses I keep in the center console.

Now I have to figure out how to hide it at home. I could go straight to my room, but that would be suspicious. Unless I just don't go home. I could go to Nell's instead. Or take her home with me. Then they wouldn't question me going straight to my room. But then again, bringing Nell home is likely to inspire questions, and if Brookes got a look at me, there's no way he wouldn't know something is up.

No, the best thing would be to go to Nell's place and hope she doesn't mind me crashing there. It takes me a while to find our text conversation on my phone. The screen is too small, and my slight double vision makes it hard to read the words. Once I find it, I type my message from muscle memory and hope that for once autocorrect does its job and fixes any mistakes.

> I need your help. Can I come over?

I drum my fingers on the steering wheel while I wait, but even that small noise in the closed cab is grating. She answers. And I can tell by the length of the blurred text that it's just one word. After some squinting and moving the phone around, I finally make out the word.

> Sure.

With a relieved sigh, I start up my truck. Luckily, I don't have to get on the highway to get to Nell's place, and I'm familiar enough with the roads to know from memory where all the stop signs are. The double vision isn't as bad when I'm not looking at things up close, so while the cars around me are slightly fuzzy, I can see them just fine. Even so, I drive at half my normal speed.

I can already imagine that Nell won't be happy that I've driven at all. But I couldn't risk leaving my truck at the athletic complex. That definitely would have been noticed. It takes me about ten minutes to get to her apartment, and I pull into an open parking spot with no cars nearby.

For a few seconds I just sit there, zoned out, forgetting why I came here in the first place. Then my phone buzzes, and I snap out of it. I don't bother trying to read the text. Instead I climb out of my pickup, keeping my sunglasses on, and head for Nell's apartment. I hold tight to the railing on the stairs and make myself focus on the steps. At the top, I brace myself before I knock, knowing the sound will hurt.

Nell answers wearing jeans, and a snug long-sleeved shirt, both of which hug her curves perfectly. All I want to do is sink into her, see if she can chase away this, too.

"Hey," she says, her voice bright and cheerful and too loud. "What's up?"

I step past her, removing my sunglasses, but before I can say anything, another voice cuts in. "Hey, Torres."

My eyes find Dylan on the couch, and *damn it*, I didn't even think about her being here. I should find something clever to say, something normal, but my mind is too sluggish, and I'm too tired to mine for the words, so I settle for returning, "Hey."

I turn back to Nell and gesture toward the hallway that leads back to her bedroom. "Can we?"

She frowns, but nods. "Sure."

I don't look back at Dylan as I follow Nell out of the living room. I drag a hand along the wall of the hall to help steady and straighten out my steps. Inside her room, I collapse onto her bed and drop my head into my hands. I hear the door click closed, but Nell doesn't move after that. She stays at the other side of the room, and when I look up her arms are crossed over her chest and her expression is decidedly wary.

"I'm scaring you," I say. "Sorry."

She cuts straight to the point. "What's going on? Are you . . . Are we . . ."

Aw, shit. She thinks this about her.

I follow her lead and cut straight to the point. "No. God, no. We're good. Great . . . I have a concussion."

Her arms drop, and her entire posture changes. "*What?*"

I wince at the sharp word, and her voice is lower when she asks, "What happened?"

I shift and lean back to lie on her bed. "Practice," I mumble. "Rough tackle."

I hear her feet shuffle toward me as my eyes drift close. "Why are you here? Shouldn't you be at a hospital getting checked out?"

"It's mild. I've had these before. I know how it goes."

And I know that I want to sleep, and now that my head is cushioned on her pillow and I'm lying flat on my back, I'm seconds away from doing just that. The bed dips slightly at my feet, and it jostles as she crawls up to kneel beside me.

I remember Dylan sitting out in the living room and add, "Don't tell Dylan."

"Why? Hey, look at me." She nudges my shoulder, and I pry open my eyes.

She places both hands on my cheeks, tilting my head toward her and looking into my eyes. "I haven't told Coach. Or the guys."

I'm thankful when she doesn't ask me why. Instead she moves straight into medical mode. "Your pupils appear to be the same size. So, that's good. Any nausea? Vomiting?"

"No. I told you. It's mild."

She leans over me, tilting my head so that the ceiling light shines more on my eyes. "Humor me. What are your symptoms? Blurred vision?"

"Yes."

"Sensitive to light or sound?"

"Both."

"Headache?"

I hesitate.

"Mateo? Do you have a headache?"

"Yes, but it's manageable. I'll take some aspirin and be fine."

"Has it gotten worse since you were first hit?"

"No. I swear I'm okay."

She pulls her bottom lip into her mouth, and it's amazing how even with my head as foggy as it is, I can zone in precisely on that movement.

"You'll need someone to keep an eye on you. Monitor your symptoms to make sure they don't get any worse."

And here comes the hard part. "I was hoping that might be you. What do you say, sweetheart? Can you play nurse for me?"

Chapter 23

Nell's To-Do List

- *Throttle Mateo. Hug him. Do something to him. I don't know. Crap . . . I'm in deep.*

It's remarkable how even at times like this he can make a joke. I want to ask him *why*. Why he came here. Why he doesn't want to tell anyone about his concussion.

Why me?

Okay, so maybe that last question is less about his concussion and more about . . . everything. We haven't slept together since last Sunday (well, Monday morning, I guess), though the few times we've seen each other, he was certainly very *hands-on*. But I can't help but find myself wondering why he would choose me. This, taking care of him, feels distinctly in girlfriend territory. Or am I overreacting? Didn't I just admit the other day that we were friends above all else? Maybe this is just what friendship with him is like. Sure, he's taught me more about my body in a few encounters than I ever could have imagined, but I can put that aside for a friendly gesture.

Oh God, who am I kidding? If this were Matty in my bed, my heart wouldn't be trying to rearrange my rib cage.

I don't know how to deal with these insecurities because they're different from the fears I feel about my future or everyday worries about tests and homework and other trivial stuff. These fears are different because . . .

Because there is no correct answer. I like solving problems. I *love* solving problems. But not like this . . . not when there's no guarantee I can be right.

Because Mateo Torres is loud, and I'm quiet. Because he's reckless, and I'm cautious. Because he belongs everywhere, and I don't.

Because I think I'm in danger of falling in love with him.

So, no . . . this is much worse than fears about classes or jobs or the future. Those things might stress me out on occasion, but when push comes to shove, I'm confident enough in myself to believe that it will all work out, that *I* will figure it out.

But I don't think I'm the kind of person who can fall in love. Or at least I didn't think I was. And even if I'm wrong about that, and I *can* fall in love, I feel fairly certain that I'm going to be really bad at it.

Falling in love.

I'll be too clingy or not clingy enough. I'll have trust issues (trusting him and being trusted *by* him . . . both are likely to be disastrous). I'll say stupid things. Or I'll say smart things that make him feel stupid. I'll ignore him in favor of doing my work. Or I'll ignore work for him.

So I can't fall for Mateo Torres. There are limits to this little experiment, and that has to be one of them.

I won't be cliché enough to fall for a guy just because he took my virginity. I am ruled by my head above all else.

As I ignore my own issues and focus on him, the pinch of pain at the back of my throat that comes from seeing him like this tells me that the danger is very real. I have to fight a tide of rising panic even though I know he's right. His symptoms are mild, and with bed rest, he should recover just fine. But it's just . . . I've never seen him this vulnerable. And I want . . .

I am ruled by my head. Nothing else.

He has this glazed look in his eyes, and even though he seems coherent enough and is making an effort to appear as normal as possible, I can tell how tired he is. My freak-out will have to wait until tomorrow. For now, I need to be practical. For his health's sake. My brain quickly cycles through the necessary information. He needs to rest, but I'll also need to wake him up periodically to make sure he's still coherent, still able to be woken up. Which means he'll be spending the night here. In room. *In my bed.*

Only this time, Dylan's here. And I'll have to tell her something.

"Okay," I say. "Let me get you that aspirin."

As I make my way to the door, he says, "Thank you. You're amazing."

"Don't thank me yet. If I think you're getting worse, I'm taking you to the hospital. I don't care how 'fine' you are."

His mouth twitches, an almost smile. "You think I'm fine?"

I roll my eyes, even though a part of me finds it adorable that he's still flirting with me even after we've already slept together.

Ruled by your mind, Nell. Focus.

I leave to retrieve the medicine and some water. On my way to the kitchen, Dylan catches me, "Is he okay?"

"Hmm?" Crap. What do I tell her? "Oh yeah. He's just tired from practice, I think. And . . ." Here goes nothing. "Well, I know you told me to stay away from him, but I like him. We're . . . *seeing* each other."

There. Neither of us has really talked yet about telling other people that we're sleeping together. We're both so busy with my classes and his football stuff that we didn't want to have to split our limited free time by answering questions about ourselves. But this is the only explanation, besides the truth, that I have for why he'd show up here and want to go straight to my room. It will justify why we're spending hours cooped up in my room, and keep people from disturbing us.

"That little bugger, he pulled it off."

"What?"

"He asked me about you. Wanted to know how to talk to you. I honestly didn't think he had a chance, or that he was serious enough to wear you down, but he did it."

Oh, he was *plenty* good at wearing me down.

She asks, "And you like him? For *real* like him?"

I have to fight the urge to drag her onto the couch and spill everything I'm feeling, to ask her what love feels like, just so I'll know that what I'm feeling isn't it. And if it is . . . damn it, now is not the time.

"Yeah. I like him. Listen, he needs my help with something, can we talk about this later?"

She gives me a smirk, and I'm sure she's thinking of a very different something that I might help him with, but she says, "Sure. I think I'll go over to Silas's. Spend the night there."

I'm stunned for a moment at how supportive she is of all this. From the way she'd first talked about Mateo, I figured she would think I was crazy. That was a big part of why I hadn't told her before even though I was dying to talk to someone. But now she's practically throwing me into his arms, leaving us the apartment all to ourselves.

With a glass of water in hand, I make my way back to my room to find him struggling to stay awake. I close the door behind me and move to his side.

"Hey." His smile is sleepy and soft, and it makes him look sweeter. Less intimidating. I might want to be ruled by my mind, but there's a fist around my heart, and the poor little organ seems to struggle to beat against it, to beat against how terrifying it is to want a person this much. I shake out a few pills and hand them to him along with the water. He pops the aspirin into his mouth and then leans his head up far enough to swallow a mouthful of water.

Then I reach down to pull off his sneakers. They're longer

than the length of my forearm, and they look even bigger when I place them on the floor beside my bed.

"Nurse Nell," he murmurs in his deep, gravelly voice.

"Do you want to be under the covers?" I ask.

"Depends. Will you be under there, too?"

I roll my eyes. "You need to rest."

"I can multitask."

And *oh*, I want him to. But we can't. He's ill, and I'm . . . me.

He shifts up to a sitting position, and though he could probably do it by himself, I pull back the covers when he stands. I wait for him to climb back into the bed, but instead he steps closer to me and lifts a hand to my cheek. He leans down at the same time I tip my head up, and he rests his forehead against mine. His eyes are closed, and mine are open. And this close I can see his dark long lashes, and I can see the slightest hint of stubble on his cheeks and jaw. He doesn't say anything. Nor does he move to do anything more than touch me. He takes a deep breath, and I place a hand on his chest to feel the way it expands and then falls. He breathes again, and it feels like he's taking a piece of me into his lungs with him, and just when I'm about to close my eyes, he pulls away and crawls into my bed.

That fist squeezes. As if it's trying to get me to admit it. To think the words that scare me far too much to say.

Something tugs low in my belly at the sight of him there, and somehow those few seconds of being close to him, of breathing with him, feel just as intimate and huge as it felt to have him inside me for the first time.

How is that? In what universe does that make *any* sense?

In this one, my mind says as I watch his eyes fall closed.

And even though I should let him rest, even though I should use this time to study or read or make one epic pros and cons list, I set an alarm on my phone for two hours from now, and I round the bed to crawl in beside him.

He takes up over half of my full-size bed, so that even if I didn't want to be touching him, it would be hard to avoid. Not that I try.

He lifts his arm, and I immediately crawl under it, to lean against him. I lay my head on his chest and press my body close to his side. His arm settles down around me, his fingertips brushing along my spine.

We've lain like this once before, that first night after we had sex. That was the only time he stayed the night, and it feels different now, to have him hold me like this when it's still light outside and when we're both fully clothed, and my mind isn't numb from pleasure. I'd been so exhausted that night that I fell asleep almost immediately, no time to think or analyze.

"Now, *this* is what I call full-service medicine."

"This is the part where I would hit you. If you weren't already hurt."

"Go ahead. I can take it. I like a little pain with my pleasure."

I don't even think before I ask, "Do you really?"

He sucks in a breath, and his chest lifts beneath my cheek.

"We can talk about what turns me on another time. When I can do something about it."

"You could make me a list."

He groans, and pulls me tighter against him, and my heartbeat kicks into high gear. I know nothing is going to happen. Nothing *can* happen. But my body recognizes his, remembers how good we were together.

"Damn, woman. You're going to be the death of me."

"Sorry," I answer sheepishly. "Go to sleep. I'll shut up."

Please, dear Lord, let me shut up.

"We're having this conversation again later. I like this list idea a lot. But only if we make one for you, too."

"You already know the things that turn me on. Better than I do probably."

"No, I don't. Not yet. But I will. We both will. You can count on that."

Another squeeze from that fist.

I nod against his chest, embarrassed and pleased and eager all at once.

And as he falls asleep beneath me, I get to know him in a way that friendship and flirting and sex haven't allowed, completely undone and made honest by sleep. I learn the rhythm of his breaths, the unhurried beat of his heart when he's completely at rest. I discover what his face looks like when it's free of his usual charm and bravado. I study how he looks when he is entirely his own, not the entertainer, not the athlete, not the flirt. And like music stripped of its enhancements and frills, he's somehow better in this simple form.

I'm still awake when my alarm goes off for the first time. I prop myself up on my elbow and gently but firmly shake his shoulder.

"Mateo."

He groans and mumbles something, and I shake him a little harder. His eyelids lift, and he regards me a moment, before smiling in this brilliantly sexy, sleepy way. I lean across him to flip on the bedside lamp. He winces at the light and clamps an arm around my waist, trapping me in my prone position. With his eyes squeezed shut he says, "Turn it off."

"Let me see your eyes first."

He complies, but doesn't release his grip on my waist, so I'm practically on top of him as I study his pupils. They're still not reacting to light as much as they should, but they're the same size, which is good.

"How old are you?" I ask.

"Nineteen."

I blink. I hadn't known that he was younger than me. He's so much more experienced and confident that I assumed he was older.

"I see that look," he says. "I'll be twenty in January, so don't go thinking I'm too young for you."

"I'm not. I just didn't know. That's all. I assumed you were older."

It also occurs to me that my whole point in asking was to see if he could think clearly, but since I don't *know* how old he is, I have no way of knowing if he's lucid.

"Do you know what day it is?"

"Monday."

"And do you know where you are?"

He smirks. "Your bed." He tugs one of my legs over him until I'm straddling him. "Between your thighs."

Well, he certainly *seems* coherent. But just for my own curiosity, I ask, "How tall are you?"

"Six two."

Ha! I was right.

I smile and he asks, "Do I pass inspection, Nurse Nell?"

"You'll do, I suppose."

He smiles, and lets his eyes fall shut. I set my alarm again for two hours later and reach out to turn off the light. It's dark in my room except for the low glow of a streetlamp outside filtering through a crack in my curtains. I try to slide off him, but his arms are still tight around me. When I start to pry his arm away, he rolls onto his side, taking me with him. One of his arms ends up under my head, and the other goes around my waist and burrows up the back of my shirt to touch my bare skin.

"Better?" he asks, his words a mumble against my forehead.

Both of my arms are curled awkwardly between us, and there's definitely no way I can sleep like this. Even if I could find something to do with my arms, I feel like I can't breathe this close to him. The air between us is too warm and thick, and I'll never be able to stop thinking.

When I've gone several long seconds without answering, he pulls his hand away from my back and leans away a little. "Sorry."

"No. It's just . . . I don't know what to do with my arms. I've never slept in a bed with another person. Well, except for the other night with you, but I was, um, so tired I didn't really think about it."

"Another first. Roll over. I'll give you a lesson in spooning."

I flip to my other side, and this time when he slips his arm around me, there are no awkward limbs. There's no space between us either. His chest is pressed flat against my back and his legs curled around mine, and I can still feel him breathe like this. And not just his chest either . . . like this I can feel all of him, touching from top to toes. I can feel him half hard against my bottom, too.

"This okay?" he asks.

"Yeah. It's okay."

Better than okay. And with his arms around me, the fist finally eases enough that I slip into sleep.

Chapter 24

Mateo

A miracle happens.

Nell skips all her classes the next day to sleep late with me. Even though she'd sworn last time that it would never happen again. I didn't even have to ask. When the alarm went off, she reached over and turned it off like she'd been doing all through the night, but instead of getting up and getting ready for school, she crawled back into my arms.

She didn't say anything. Didn't announce what she was doing. She just turned the thing off for good and settled back in with me.

Sleeping was not how I wanted to celebrate her loosening the reins a bit, but it was my only option. And something about just lying together like this felt better anyway.

By the time we're awake for good, my symptoms have eased to nuisance level. The sensitivity to light and sound is the worst, but still bearable. My thoughts still occasionally wander off, but it's rare enough that most people will just think I'm distracted. I've skipped all my classes, though that has less to do with the concussion and more to do with Nell, but there's no skipping my daily workout and practice.

But I'm having trouble leaving Nell's room.

There's no need for her to monitor me for another night, but twice now I've slept with her beside me. I know what it's like to wake to her soft thighs pressed against mine, to be surrounded by the smell of her hair and skin—I can't *un*-know something like that. And I want it again. Even though, as a general rule, I don't spend the night with girls. I made an exception that first night because it was her first time, and I didn't want her to feel like I was running out on her. But that was supposed to be it. *Supposed to be.*

But Nell is never easy to put into a box. Just when I think I know where she fits in my life, she rearranges things. And really, what would it hurt to break this one rule? Just every once in a while. Not all the time. I want to enjoy the feel of waking up to her again when my mind isn't battered and foggy.

She's sitting cross-legged on her bed with her laptop, e-mailing excuses to her professors. Her long, dark hair is twisted into this thick knot on top of her head. There's one lock that didn't make it in, and it falls loose and curly against her long neck. Before I really know what I'm doing, I'm climbing onto the bed behind her and reaching for those rogue strands. I settle in behind her, one of my legs on each side of hers.

"Tunnels tonight?"

She frowns, tilting her head slightly back toward me. "We can wait for all that stuff until you're fully recovered."

I lift my hands to her shoulders, kneading gently. "Hell no. You're on a deadline, after all. Gotta get all your wild and crazy out before you graduate." She opens her mouth to respond, but then closes it. And I wonder if she can hear the slight edge to my voice when I talk about her graduating. Not that I have a right to be pissed about it, but I can't help it. I don't like having a deadline. I don't like not having a choice about how much time I get with her. I decide to keep talking so she doesn't have time to dwell on it. "Besides, it's not like the tunnels are going to be physically demanding. If I can make it through practice, I can definitely walk down some concrete tunnels. And then who knows, maybe I'll even feel up to some more *physical exertion* afterward."

I lean down to kiss her shoulder, but her back straightens, and she shifts to look back at me. Ignoring that last statement, she says, "You're going to practice?"

"First I've gotta go lift." And I am so not looking forward to the sound of the weight room—all clangs and thuds and scrapes. It's going to be a nightmare. But a necessary one. "Then practice, yeah."

Her eyebrows furrow, and I can see her debating about saying something before she finally spits it out. "So, you're not telling your coach at all? Do you think that's smart?"

It would be cute that she's worried, if she weren't voicing the thoughts I've done a lot of work to keep myself from thinking.

"I told you. I've had concussions before. This one is so mild I'll probably feel good as new within the next few hours."

"Yeah, but if you were to hit your head again shortly after your initial injury, it could cause serious damage. You could die. It could—"

I lower my mouth to hers, cutting her off. For a moment she resists, not quite kissing me back, but not completely immune either. After a few seconds she relaxes and one of her hands travels up to my neck. I get a little lost in her mouth. In the softness of her lips. The taste of her tongue. The quickening of her breath.

I pull back before I get carried away and give in to the urge to toss her computer to the ground and strip her naked.

"I'll be fine, Nell. I know my limits. I promise I'll be careful. You'll see. You're worrying about nothing. You and me. The tunnels. Tonight."

Her eyes flick over mine, narrow, but then finally she nods.

DESPITE WHAT I told Nell, I don't feel good as new in a few hours. I take it easy during my workout. They're unsupervised—at least technically—so no one will call me out for going at half strength. But even taking it easy, I'm exhausted before I get halfway through my hour. I'm worn out by trying to appear normal while my nerves feel more and more raw by the second.

When practice starts, I very nearly spill to Coach. But then I tell myself that it's laziness talking. I'm strong enough to power through this. My reasons for staying silent are the same today as they were yesterday. So I stick to my guns and suffer through practice. I think it's obvious to everyone that I'm not up to par, but I hope they chalk it up to a bad day rather than to the fact that I'm avoiding getting tackled as much as possible.

If you don't catch the ball, not much point in someone taking you to the grass.

I even take a nap after practice, but it barely takes the edge off, which is why I'm exhausted when I get to Nell's later.

I can tell by her worried look when she sees me on her porch that this isn't going to be good.

"You ready?" I ask.

She fixes me with a silent, assessing gaze.

Maybe I should have canceled. I knew she would give me grief over "knowing my limits," but I wanted to see her. So I figure I can take a little grief.

"Come on." I hold out a hand to her. "I'm excited about this. Both of our first times, remember?"

"Mateo . . ."

"We're just walking. It's nothing strenuous. We'll walk a ways in, explore a bit, and then we'll leave."

"And you'll sleep?"

I jump at the chance to spend another night with her.

"If you'll be my nurse again."

Her eyes lift in a smile even though her mouth doesn't, and I know I've won. In my truck, I flip my heater on to full blast. Some hint of winter is beginning to creep in, and the night air is crisp and there's a cold breeze. She's wearing a light jacket, but I can tell as I drive that she's cold. So I flip the middle console up, and tell her to scoot over, and I drive onto campus with her huddled close to me. We park near the tunnel entrance by the north parking garage, and I find a Rusk sweatshirt in the backseat to pull over her head for extra warmth. It swallows her, falling all the way to her knees, but the dark red looks good against her skin, and I like seeing her in it.

Even with her jacket and my sweatshirt, she loops her arm around mine and snuggles closer. I lead her down to the mouth of the tunnel, which at first glance looks like an oversize drainage pipe. A concrete-covered ditch runs for about fifty yards before the entrance to the tunnels, and a thin line of water runs down the middle. As we stand at the entrance, the tunnel looks dark and dank. Hardly the most romantic place, but it pricks my sense of adventure, and some of my fatigue gives way to anticipation.

"You're sure this is safe?"

"Now that you mention it, I keep thinking of that disaster movie where one of those underwater tunnels in New York collapses and there's a huge wave of water coming down the tunnel."

"Fantastic. Exactly what I wanted to think about."

I laugh and pull out the flashlight I brought with me. I direct the beam down the tunnel, and it shines far enough to show that it splits into three tunnels a little ways in. As far as I can tell from here, they're parallel, but that doesn't mean they don't branch off somewhere farther down.

"Let's go, sweetheart."

Fifty feet in, we find our first piece of graffiti on the concrete wall. In faded black spray paint, it reads "College Is Okay If You," then the writing gets too faded to read, leaving the secret to making college "okay" forever mysterious.

When we get to the split, I have Nell choose, and she picks the middle.

We stumble upon a zombie horde painted on the wall, and I squeeze her arm. "Good choice."

She wrinkles her nose, and I laugh. The sound echoes eerily off the walls around us and causes a twinge of pain in my head.

Nell sees it.

"We shouldn't have done this."

"I'm fine," I assure her. "Let's keep going. Maybe the Batcave is somewhere down here. Or the Chamber of Secrets."

She doesn't react to my Harry Potter reference even though I know she's read the series because I saw them on a shelf in her room. Stubbornly, she says, "You're not fine. I did some research after you left this morning. You said you've had concussions before. And with each one, no matter how mild, your risk for brain trauma increases. The next time you hit your head a little too hard, the symptoms might not go away for months or at all. They could be permanent. I read an article about one football player who not only can't play anymore, but he has to have a tutor in all of his classes even though he used to be a straight-A student. He can't concentrate. Can't retain facts. And it's been three years since his last concussion. He can't play football, and football has made it so that he'll have a hard time doing anything else."

"I know, Nell."

She stops abruptly, pulling her arm away from mine. "You . . . *know?*" She sounds like my knowing this is some kind of betrayal.

"Yeah, I know it's risky. But I'm a wide receiver. Not a rough-and-tumble tackler. I don't take frequent hits to the head."

"Frequent enough," she says.

"In a good game, I make maybe six catches. A great game could be eight to ten. Some of those don't even end in a tackle. And yes, I'm tired now. And I'm still showing symptoms, but I've got several days before the next game."

"And what about practice?"

"I'm taking care of that." Though I'm not sure how long I can get away with underperforming like I did today. One bad practice is fine, but any more and I might jeopardize my chance to play this weekend even if I don't mention the concussion.

"It only takes one hit, Mateo. Just one. I get that you're this big, strong athlete and you think you should just tough it out, but you're wrong. This game can't possibly be that important."

"It is." We've both stopped walking and she's dropped my arm to square off with me in this dark and dreary corridor.

"Football's your dream, and I get that. And I know your coach mentioning going pro the other week has you excited, but you also have to be realistic. It's just not smart."

Her words stir up long-buried memories, and in an instant all the things in her that remind me of Lina come to the surface, similarities that I haven't thought about in a long time. But I've had this fight before. Maybe not about a concussion, but that dig about being realistic is always the same. People think it's the nice way to help you manage your hopes . . . that they're doing you a favor by being honest. But that's fucking ridiculous. It assumes that you're stupid or naive, that you don't have reality beating down the door to your thoughts day in and day out. It takes fucking work to dream, and I don't need anyone else shoving the unlikelihood of success in my face, because I do that to myself enough already.

I need someone to believe with me. To believe *for* me when I can't believe myself.

"You have to take care of yourself, Mateo, if you want to—"

"You know what?" I say. "Turns out that I *am* pretty fucking tired." I gesture to the tunnel walls. "I don't know why I gave a shit about this anyway."

I turn back toward the entrance, and I don't pause to take hold of her hand or let her grab my arm. I need the space.

"Mateo. You can't just keep deflecting like this. It's not enough just to rest. You need to tell someone. You need to take precautions against—"

And then I just snap. I whirl around and pin her with the beam of the flashlight. "You know fuck all about what I need, Nell. Jesus, you've never even been to a game. You don't know anything about football, and you don't know anything about me."

For a moment she looks small. Too damn small. The black of the tunnel looms around her, threatening to swallow her despite my measly light. Her arms are wrapped around her middle, and in that big sweatshirt she looks like she needs protecting.

From me.

And just when I'm about to go to her, to say something, to take back my harsh words . . . anything . . . she lifts her chin in that familiar proud way of hers.

"I've known you from the moment we met, Mateo Torres."

How could I have forgotten? "A puppet? That's what you called me, right? Letting other people pull my strings. Sorry, sweetheart, but I pull my own strings."

"Maybe you do. But you're still performing for other people. You play class clown for others, thinking it makes them like you or makes you fun. But history has a word for that . . . you're playing the fool."

That hits me harder than any tackle, and for all her words about it just taking one hit to knock me out, it's ironic that she would be the one to deliver the worst blow.

"Fuck this. I don't need any of this."

I take off down the tunnel, heading back for the small hole of light I can see in the distance. My feet splash through puddles, and the noise from my movements amplifies in the small space, becomes harsher and distorted as it echoes. Then I hear Nell hurrying along behind me. She calls out, "I'm not saying you *are* a fool. Mateo, would you stop? Listen to me for a second. You're smart and kind and wonderful, and I—I . . ." She sucks in a breath, probably from trying to keep pace with me, but I don't stop. "I'm just saying you don't need to play that part for other people. Your friends care about you. *I care about you.* You don't need to pretend for us."

I jerk around, and she barely skids to a stop before slamming into me. And my voice is too loud, and she's too close, everything is too close as I yell, "*It's for me*, damn it. It's not for you. It's not for my friends. Did you ever think of that while you were dissecting me? My life? The way I am . . . I do that *for me*."

My heart thuds in my ears so loud I'm surprised it doesn't echo in the tunnel, too. Nell swallows, and I can see those big eyes working, studying me, moving around the pieces of me in her head to fit this new development.

"Why?"

One damn word. Just one damn word, and it's the absolute last thing I want her to say because I know how my answer will sound. Pathetic boy with a broken heart pretending so it doesn't hurt. It's so goddamn ridiculous.

"Because it helps. Helped."

She lifts a hand like she wants to touch me, but then seems to second-guess herself, and it stays hanging in the air between us as she asks, "With what?"

Then I tell her everything about Lina. With my eyes on the ceiling and the walls so that I don't have to look at her, I tell her how in love I was.

"She was this brilliant, confident girl. The kind of girl that when you look at her, you know she can do anything, *be* anything. She had the whole fucking world in the palm of her hand, and she had me there, too. From the moment I met her. But you can't . . . you can't love someone like that without feeling like you have something to prove. To her. To the world. I needed everyone to know that we belonged together. That even if I wasn't some genius, even if I had zero hope of going to the Ivy League schools that were practically begging for her attention, I was important. I was going places. So when it looked like football could do that for me, I threw everything into it. I had to play college ball. I had to go pro. There was no other option. She and football were linked in my head, the two great loves of my life, and I would have done anything, given whatever it took, to keep them both."

I break off, and I realize that my breathing is ragged, that my heart is pounding hard enough to put a dent in my ribs.

"What happened?" she asks.

And finally, I look at her. Only she's not looking at me; she has her arms wrapped around herself and her gaze on the circle of light my flashlight makes on the ground.

"I got too caught up in it all. I was so focused on proving myself that I didn't realize I was losing everything in my attempt to gain it. Lina and I started fighting. Every time I brought up football, she would tell me to be realistic, that I needed to have a backup plan in case it didn't work out. But all I could hear was that she didn't trust me to be good enough."

"For football? Or her?" Nell's voice is small as she asks.

I sigh and drag my hand over my face. "Both. It was always both."

"Senior year, I narrowed it down to two schools. Rusk, which had the bigger program and was closer to home, and a smaller Division Two school that was not too far from the university that Lina had chosen. I was torn. Rusk was the better place to prove myself, but it was too far away from her. The Division Two school had a good football program, but the chance of getting noticed in Division Two was a lot smaller. I could have possibly swung a transfer to a bigger university eventually, but it was a risk. In the end, though, it didn't matter. She broke up with me the night before I was going to commit to the Division Two school. She said that we wanted different things out of life. Her exact words were something about her moving on from high school to bigger things. But I was so stuck on football that I didn't know when it was time to let go. She didn't want to hang around while I relived my glory days for as long as I could."

"That's awful."

It *was* awful. Most of the time our fears come from within us, but she planted the seed that day. And every time I'm feeling low, I water it with thoughts about whether or not the best parts of my life are behind me.

"To be fair," I say, "I wasn't exactly the best boyfriend there at the end. I let the recruiting game go to my head. I was so wrapped up in being the best athlete that I could be for her that I didn't realize I was ignoring her in the process. I tried to fix it. God knows, I tried. I would have done anything, maybe even given up football, if she had shown even the slightest interest in giving me a second chance. But she didn't. So I committed to Rusk, and tried to put it all behind me. And when I got here, I thought I was starting over. I hid my broken heart behind parties and jokes in the beginning because I wanted to make a good impression. No one likes that mopey guy who misses high school during freshman orientation. After a while it became second nature. And some days, it was almost like I'd never known Lina at all. In fact, I'd almost forgotten her completely."

"Until you met me."

"I—"

I don't know what to say. Is it better to be honest? To lie? Either way makes me an asshole.

"The day we met, after I got hit with the Frisbee . . . you said I reminded you of someone. It was her? Wasn't it?"

I don't answer because words will only make this worse. And I wish my earlier joke about that disaster movie would come true, that some pipe would burst or there would be some freak flood, and a wall of water would come and just drown this all out.

"I think I'd like to leave now."

She takes the flashlight out of my hand and walks past me, and for a few long moments I stay where I am. I let the light fade away. Her footsteps, too. And as silence moves in around me, I realize that what just happened was nothing like the fights I had with Lina. Our fights had been loud and aggressive, and they'd left me burning up. And when things with Lina had ended, I felt like I'd been at the center of some explosion, and all the pieces of me were scattered everywhere, and that everyone had to see it, see how broken I was. I was alive, but in pieces.

Fighting with Nell is like . . . it's like drowning. And each word that pushed us further apart, each step she took, was another gulp of water into my lungs. And just like someone stuck underwater . . . I knew I should stop. I knew that each gulp was killing me, but I just couldn't.

And now that she's gone, I'm not in pieces. There was no explosion. No battered and bleeding pieces of me to hold together. No, I would almost prefer that there were.

Because she's taken the last of the air with her, and inside now I'm as still as the dark tunnel around me, and just as lifeless and empty.

Chapter 25

Nell's To-Do List

- *Stop making to-do lists. They suck. A lot.*

Between the time that Torres left my bed the morning after his concussion and his return later that evening . . . before everything fell apart, I'd added something to my list.

And I know I can cross it off because even though I hate him, even though the thought of him brings every doubt and insecurity roaring to life in my head . . . that damn fist around my heart still squeezes.

So I guess I can finally admit it. Late, though it is.

23. Fall in love.

Been there, done that, wish I had never written a single word of this stupid list. But I'm committed to it now, so I add yet another item.

24. *Get my heart broken.*

Then I cross them both off at the same time. Whoo-hoo life experience. Sure glad I have that now.

I knew this whole experiment would all go bad. There's no way it couldn't, not with me at the helm. God, I should have realized this sooner. I should have known that he and I wouldn't fit together under normal circumstances. The only reason he ever looked twice at me was because of *her*.

There are still items on my list that I haven't completed, but I feel like I've done my part. I've stepped outside of my comfort zone. I've taken risks. And I've paid for it.

And I was right all along.

I'm better off committed to my work. And now I'm going to graduate early. I've narrowed down my grad school choices to two programs, and I'll be filling out those applications . . . soon. Anytime now. I'm going to do the things I always planned to do, and I'm never going to look back.

That's the first lie I tell myself.

I'm no longer worried about my future. I know everything is going to work out.

That's the second.

The next day, I lie when I tell Dylan (and myself) that I changed my mind. That Torres and I, while attracted to each other, just aren't compatible.

I lie when she asks if I want to eat ice cream and watch chick flicks, and say instead that I need to work on grad school applications. Then, when she's gone, I break out my sweatpants and the ice cream and settle down on the couch to watch a special on the Discovery Channel about lions hunting their prey. (Okay . . . so I wasn't lying about the chick flicks, but all the rest of it . . .)

It's a lie each time I go to bed and promise I won't think of him.

It's a lie each time I wake up and convince myself that he was *absolutely* not the first thing on my mind.

It's a lie that I'm not disintegrating with worry the night before the football game thinking about all the things that could go wrong, the ways he could be hit, how it could affect him.

I don't care.

I don't care. I don't care. *I don't care.*

(More lies.)

So, even though I hate my list . . . even though I said I was through . . . when Saturday comes, I make plans to check another item off my list.

10. Go to a football game.

After this . . . I'll be done.

TAILGATING.

Dallas tells me that it gets its name from everyone camping out at their trucks, setting up food and drinks on their tailgates to party before a football game. Personally, I think it's absurd to make the name of an inanimate object into a verb, but no one asked me. I also think it's absurd that in a sport called football, the majority of the game has very little interaction between balls and feet. But again . . . not my choice.

Dylan, Matt, Dallas, Stella, and I carpooled together, and I follow them to a section of the parking lot where the student union is throwing a huge tailgate party. From the few things I've picked up over the years, I had expected the game not to be very female-friendly. I mean, it's sports, for one thing. But so many commercials and photos I'd seen played up the cheerleaders in skimpy clothing, and I figured that kind of stuff would run rampant. Ironically, there are a lot more half-naked guys than there are girls.

There's one large group of shirtless guys whose chests are painted a dark red to match the school's colors. Each guy has a single letter on his chest in white, and while I'm sure this was not their intention, the four closest to me spell out the word "suck."

I get a hot dog, but decline alcohol, and the five of us sit down on those concrete slabs that are placed in front of parking spots. As I eat, I survey the group of shirtless guys again, taking in all the letters, and working anagrams in my head trying to figure out what they might say. They've shifted again and instead of "suck," there's now a group sporting the word "scat." Again, I'm doubting (and also weirdly hoping) this was their intention. There are somewhere between fifteen and twenty guys, and they keep moving around, which is putting a serious damper on my anagramming.

"What are you staring so hard at?" Stella asks beside me.

Everyone else has kept up a steady stream of chatter, but the two of us have been quiet. I heard Dallas mention something about this being the first game Stella has attended in a while. According to Stella, it's only been like a month and a half, which doesn't sound like that big of a deal to me, but everyone else seems to think it's significant.

"I'm brainstorming possible combinations of the letters on those shirtless guys that are really extraordinarily drunk considering how early in the day it is."

She smiles. "What do you have so far?"

"Well, this group here and that one over there could combine to spell 'scrotum.' But I feel confident that's not their intended message."

Stella chokes on her soda. "Oh God, I hope it is."

I think about how much of a kick Torres would get out of this, and my heart rattles.

"More realistically, though, they're spelling something to do with the school. Rusk. Those letters match up. There's not a Y that I can see, so I don't think it says 'university.' There's an F and two Os, so I'm betting 'football' is part of it. But that still leaves some letters unaccounted for."

"Wildcat," Stella provides. "The team mascot, I think the rest spells 'wildcat.'"

I scan the letters again, and she's right. I nod. "Mystery solved."

Then I go back to chewing my hot dog. And chewing and chewing because I don't know what to say. I should be working on that whole friendship thing. That's the one thing that might be salvageable from this whole list disaster. Everything else might have backfired, but I know now that I can't let myself go back to being lonely. I can't work that way, and it was foolish to think that I could.

"I'm nervous," I tell Stella. "About seeing this game."

"Don't be. Football isn't as complicated as it seems. You'll get it in no time."

I shake my head. "It's not that. I was sort of, briefly, dating Torres."

She coughs and thumps her hand against her chest a few times as if she's choking. "You were? Seriously? How did I miss that?"

I shrug.

"Damn," she continues. "I'm off my game. Usually, I'm the first person to know that kind of stuff."

"Well, there's not much to know anymore. We got in a big fight, and it's over. Really, it was doomed before it ever started because . . . well, it just was."

Because me and emotions don't mix.

Because I was just a stand-in.

Because we're too different. Way, *way*, too different.

She says, "I know a thing or two about being doomed before it starts."

"It's awful, isn't it?"

She glances over her shoulder, almost like she's checking to make sure her friends are still busy in conversation. Satisfied, she turns back to me and says, "It's like . . . you have plans, ideas for how something is going to unfold. And you're patient, you don't try to rush things because you know they'll happen when they're supposed to happen. But then what happens is something altogether different. And it doesn't just affect your old plans, it obliterates them. *It* makes the choice for you. And you're left feeling stupid that you ever even considered those old options, that you ever got your hopes up."

Stella and I are both short, roughly the same height, actually, but she seems so small next to me. My first instinct is to attribute that sense to her emotions . . . except she's not really showing any. Her hands don't shake as she continues eating. Her expression is neither wrought with feeling nor purposely blank. Her eyelashes are long, but she's not blinking like she's fighting off tears. She seems normal. *Fine.*

But she got her hopes up for something.

And I know how that feels. I spent all that time wondering whether *I* was capable of a relationship. Whether *I* had it in me. I was stupid to not be prepared for it to be him that got in the way.

I never would have done that in an experiment, let a factor like that go unconsidered.

"I don't think you were stupid," I tell Stella. She stiffens beside me, and I keep going. "I don't really buy into that word. There are only wrong answers and right ones. Stupidity and intelligence, those are attributes we add to make ourselves feel better. Making a stupid decision doesn't make you stupid. Just as making a smart decision doesn't necessarily make someone smart. Our bad choices don't make us stupid, they just make us wrong. About that one thing. Not about everything."

"I want to believe that. That one choice, one *thing*, doesn't define you. But everything is just like fucking dominoes, and they keep falling, one after the other, and I can never get ahead of it. So as much as I want to believe what you say, *I can't*."

The two of us sit in silence as we finish our food.

And maybe Stella is right. There's a reason the social sciences exist, because people are unpredictable. They're not like math and physics and biology. They're different, separate. You can't depend on people to be consistent or rational. So much of what I'm learning in school deals with medicine's attempt to remove humans from the equation as much as possible to prevent human error.

Maybe that's where I went wrong, trying to approach life the way I approach science.

In science, every action might have an equal and opposite reaction, but not in life. Life is unbalanced. Life is complicated. A little lie can cause a lot of pain. A big event like an important game or losing your virginity can have an enormous impact or it can turn out to not mean that much in the end.

"There's no predicting it," I say aloud. "How one thing can affect your life. There's no way to know until it's too late."

"Life's a bitch like that."

I tap my water bottle against her Dr Pepper can, and for the rest of the tailgate party, Stella becomes my partner in silence. She doesn't push me to talk, and I don't push her, and when we head for the stands, I'm relieved to be seated by her.

And when the players exit from the locker room, and my eyes pinpoint Torres in his uniform, she bumps her shoulder into mine. "You okay?"

I shake my head, then nod, then shake my head again. "I don't know." I'd thought coming to a football game would give me some kind of closure. I'd get to see him again to ease the ache in my chest, but I'd also see how different our worlds are. That realization was supposed to help me let him go.

Instead, I watch him stretching and my own heartbeat sounds suspiciously like *Love him, love him, love him*, in my ears. This isn't going to give me closure. It's just going to give him more power over me.

Torres is my catalyst. He set my life spinning, and there's only one way to counteract that kind of momentum.

Friction.

I've got to fight back. Resist the urge to miss him, to seek him out. I've got to resist. I stand up as the band starts playing next to the student section, and at first no one hears me over the music, so I have to say it again, louder. "I can't be here!"

I can't sit up in these stands, watching him risk his own health for a game that could never be more important than his future. There are two things I know for certain about Mateo Torres:

1. He has a type (my type, apparently).

2. He will always put football first. He did it with his ex, and now he's doing it again with his health.

And there's one thing I know about me:

1. I don't dwell on setbacks. I move forward. Always, always forward.

Stella stands, and hooks her fingers around my elbow. "Come on. I'll go with you."

"Wait. You're leaving?" Dylan asks. "But you're the one who wanted to come."

I shrug. "Sometimes you make the wrong decision. And that's okay, as long as you don't keep making them."

"Stella?" Dallas asks. There's a bigger question in those two syllables, but whatever it is, it passes just between the two friends. Then Dallas nods even though Stella hasn't said a word, and the two of us begin inching past all the people in our row.

"Let's get out of here," I say.

Chapter 26

Mateo

My mind tries to wander to the empty bed I woke up in this morning, but I don't let it. There's nothing good down that path. Standing in the locker room, I focus instead on the fact that today is my third day without symptoms.

I did the right thing. There's no reason I should miss this game. I'm fine.

Physically, at least.

My head is a little blank. A little numb. But that's not the concussion. That's Nell.

I keep waiting for it to feel like Lina, like my life has just detonated. But no, Nell isn't the type to leave shrapnel, well, not unless you count the final words she said to me Tuesday night when I dropped her off at home.

I get that you loved her. But any kind of love where you have to prove yourself to be worthy is the wrong kind. And you're better off without her.

No, Nell didn't leave me with any wounds. Instead, she healed them. Losing her was the final thing I needed to heal all the damage Lina did to me. Nell fixed me, which is kind of what I'd been hoping she'd do all along. Only this was better. This wasn't just blotting out memories, it was putting them into context. It was taking away their power.

Because what I had with Lina? That wasn't love. It was infatuation.

And I hate that it took losing Nell to see just how different things are with her. I know I still need to talk to her. It isn't fair the way I left things. I don't want her to think that Lina was the only reason I was with her, that she was only a replacement. Because she fucking wasn't. She was something new. Something better. I'd known that from the night she'd given me her virginity. I spent years trying to forget what it was like to be with Lina, and no other girl had ever been able to do anything but blur the memories.

Nell obliterated them.

But not because of any similarity to my ex, just because there isn't room enough in my head and my heart for old hurts and new hopes, and I'm so fucking gone for Nell that she takes up every damn inch.

She's on constant repeat in my head, cycling through every single second of our time together. I can close my eyes and recall just how fast my heart was beating the first time we kissed, the sounds she made that night in my truck, the way her sheets smelled waking up the morning after she gave herself to me.

No, Nell didn't leave me with scars.

She left me *empty*.

She took with her my ability to laugh, the ease with which I can make a joke, the joy that comes from making that perfect catch. She took my ability to pretend that I'm okay, that I've got it all together. She took it all.

And there's no fixing that kind of thing. I can't blot over it with distractions or remake it with someone else. I've got to get it back. Pure and simple.

I've got to get *her* back.

As soon as the game is over tonight, I'll find her. I don't know yet what I'll say. We both said things in that fight that we probably shouldn't have. But I know that what we have is worth salvaging. I don't know how I'll get her to give me a second chance, because God knows, she's smart enough to say no.

But I'll do it. I have to.

THE NORMAL RUSH of adrenaline and anxiety I feel before a game is gone. I reach for it, but I can't get it back. Not even when the team starts yelling and psyching one another up in the locker room. Not even when I don my pads and uniform. Not even when Coach gives a particularly good speech about rising above our underdog status. Win this game and we're 9–2. We'd almost be guaranteed a bowl game. Win another, and we could even get picked for one of the big ones.

But I can't quite see the future stretching out in front of me like I could a few weeks ago. There's a wall, and I know I won't get past it until things are right with Nell.

She's part of my future.

That's why I can't picture it.

Coach Cole stops me before I head out onto the field and asks, "You ready?"

I nod as much as my helmet and pads will let me. "Yes, sir."

"Listen, if we get the coin flip and receive first, I'm putting you out to receive."

"Sir?" I ask, confused.

"Gregory has some kind of stomach bug. He's out. So I need someone fast who can replace him on the kickoff. I need a playmaker. Think you can handle that?"

"Yes, sir," I answer immediately, but inside I'm saying no.

Well, not me precisely, but it's Nell's voice in my head.

Coach heads for the tunnel that leads out onto the field, and I follow him, but the dark corridor is too much like the one where I'd lost everything earlier this week, and I find myself gasping for breath.

Returning a kickoff is one of the most dangerous plays in football, so much so that there's been talk of removing it from the game altogether. When the kick returner catches the ball, they're usually in the end zone. The defense is coming full speed from the other side of the field. The returner can take a knee, and his team will automatically start at the twenty-five-yard line. But the good returners can gain more than twenty-five if they're quick, can find the holes, and break through tackles. But with players coming at full speed, and all that extra field to gather momentum, kick returners take some of the hardest hits in football.

I tell myself that maybe we won't win the coin flip, maybe I won't have to worry about it. *Yet.*

But we do. The setting sun glints off the flipping coin, and Mc-Clain says, "We'll receive."

Then I tell myself maybe it won't come to my side of the field. Maybe the kick will end up outside my territory, and someone else will return the ball.

And then I'm taking the field. My cleats sink into the grass, and the thud of my heart echoes all the way up into my head and fills my helmet until I can't hear the crowd, can't hear anything.

I see the opposing team begin to move, watch the kick of the ball, track the high arc of it with my eyes. It's coming right for me. And I watch the ball spin end over end, and as it begins its descent toward me, I hear my fight with Nell on fast-forward.

And somehow it's there on the field with that ball speeding toward me and all the fears crammed into my skull that I realize . . . Nell wanted me to be realistic about the concussion. I'm such an idiot. I wasn't fighting with Lina; this wasn't about me giving up football completely for something she deemed smarter or more worthy. Nell's last words before I cut her off and started to yell were "You have to take care of yourself, if you want to—"

What would she have said if I hadn't cut her off? *If you want to keep playing? If you want to stay healthy?*

The whole fight had started because she thought *this game* wasn't worth the risk, not because me and my dreams weren't worth the risk to her.

For too long I connected her with Lina, but by that night, I knew just how different they were. How much more caring and kind and joyful Nell is. And yet when push came to shove, I lumped her right in with my ex, and I assumed that they were the same. That they felt the same way about me.

God, I couldn't have been more stupid.

But I'm done with that. No more stupid mistakes. Not even for football.

As soon as the football falls into my hands, I grip it tight, and instead of chancing the run, instead of worrying about what it will mean for my spot on the team or my future in the game, I worry about how I'll ever be able to convince Nell that I love her if I don't even listen to her.

Then I take a knee instead of running it.

I toss the ball to the ref and sprint to Coach Cole on the sideline. I pull off my helmet and say, "I have a concussion."

"What?"

"I got a concussion in practice Monday, but I didn't tell you because I didn't want to chance not playing, but that was stupid. I'm sorry."

His brow furrows and his mouth pulls into a straight line, but he doesn't answer me right away. Instead, he pulls up one of the backup wide receivers to take my place on the field, and grabs McClain to fill him in. Then he starts barking orders to the other coaches and players, and I know he's pissed.

He yells for the trainer and gestures me toward him, and I turn to go, swallowing down my unease, but he stops me with a hand on my shoulder pad.

"I'm mad as hell right now, Torres. You should have told me as soon as it happened. You never should have been practicing. You sure as hell shouldn't have been on my field. But I'm glad you came to your senses. You did the right thing. I want you on this team, but I want you healthy. You come first. Always. Do you understand?"

"Yes, sir."

"And if you ever lie to me again, you'll learn just how scary I can be, got it?"

Oh, I got it.

Chapter 27

Nell's To-Do List

- *Forget about Mateo. Or Torres. Or whatever the hell his name is.*
- *Maybe I should try getting drunk (even though I promised to never drink again).*

T ell me honestly . . . was it seriously the best orgasm of your life? I need to know because . . . some reasons."

Stella becomes the first person besides me to see the list in its entirety.

"It really was," I say with a sigh as Stella and I walk aimlessly through section after section of the stadium parking lot. "Well, at that point anyway. The ones that came later were pretty fantastic too."

NORMAL COLLEGE THINGS

1. ~~Hook up with a jock.~~
2. *Make New friends.*

3. ~~Go to a party (and actually stay more than half an hour).~~
4. ~~Do something Wild.~~
5. ~~Lose my virginity.~~
6. ~~Drink alcohol (And not at church).~~
7. ~~Get Drunk.~~
8. Do a Keg stand.
9. Play Beer Pong.
10. Go to a football game.
11. ~~Go on a date.~~
12. ~~Go skinny-dipping.~~
13. Pull an all-nighter.
14. Sing Karaoke.
15. ~~Flash someone.~~
16. ~~Cuss someone out (and mean it).~~
17. ~~Kiss a stranger.~~
18. ~~Invent an alcoholic beverage.~~
19. ~~Explore the underground tunnels.~~
20. ~~Take a picture with the Thomas Jefferson Rusk "Big Daddy Rusk" statue.~~
21. ~~Have the best orgasm of my life.~~
22. ~~Skip a class.~~
23. ~~Fall in love.~~
24. ~~Get my heart broken.~~

"Okay," Stella says. "Well, first things first. We're marking out this whole 'Make New Friends' thing. You've *made* them. Past tense. I officially declare us all friends." I hand her a pen, and she draws a line through the words. "And I vote that tonight counts as going to a football game. You tailgated. You had tickets. You went inside. The game is currently happening, and we are close-ish to the action. That one gets marked off, too."

She scans the list from beginning to end again and says, "Okay. It looks like all you have left is keg stand, beer pong, all-nighter, and karaoke. That's pretty awesome, Nell. Look at this list. Look at all the stuff you've done. I guess I can't claim to know you super well, but I still feel qualified enough to say, 'Damn, you go, girl.'"

I laugh. "Thanks. It is kind of crazy. To be honest, I don't think I ever really expected to finish it."

"Oh, you're gonna finish it, honey. In fact, you're gonna finish it tonight. You and me. Karoake first. Then we'll hit up a party and get your keg stand and beer pong out of the way. Then we'll come up with a few more crazy things to do since we're not going to bed until the sun is up."

I laugh, but she's serious. "I don't know."

I'm proud of the list. Silly and vapid though most of it is, it's a testament to my determination. Proof that I am more than just my ability to study. More than just the things I've memorized and learned. I'm a person capable of fun and adventure and risk and . . . mistakes.

I can make mistakes, and they won't break me. Not completely anyway.

"Okay," I concede. "I'm in. Let's do it."

*   *   *

THE KARAOKE BAR Stella takes me to is largely empty. I don't know whether that's because most people don't care to go to a bar that's all karaoke all the time, or if it's just because it's still early. Either way, I'm glad for the relative emptiness of the bar when she drags me up to sing.

I'm not a singer.

Not at all.

I sound like I swallowed a frog and it had babies in my throat. (Honestly . . . that frog might even sound better than I do.) But karaoke is on my list, and I'm *going* to do it.

We start with a breakup song that I'm only vaguely familiar with. But it repeats the words "forget you," oh, about a thousand times. So I let Stella handle the verses, and I chime in on the chorus.

After that we start singing older stuff. Spice Girls. TLC. Boy bands galore. We sing so long, so loud, and so badly that I'm surprised no one kicks us out. But the longer we sing, the less I care about how I sound. I'm having fun.

I'm having fun doing something I'm not good at. And I *never* thought I'd say that.

Eventually, my throat starts to hurt, and the frog with babies lodged somewhere near my vocal cords starts to sound like it's been joined by a plague of locusts, so Stella and I vacate the stage in favor of greasy bar food and a corner booth where we can stretch out our legs.

"So wait . . . the cop followed you guys all the way into the library?"

"Yes! I thought for sure we were going to get caught. And then we ended up hiding back in the stacks and—"

"And let me guess . . . *bow chicka wow wow.*"

I blush, and lean my elbows onto the table to get closer to her. "I have a question. And it's embarrassing, but honestly, I think I'm past embarrassment with you. Have you heard of a thing called the Sweet Six?"

"OH MY GOD, YOU DID THE SWEET SIX WITH TORRES?!"

I slap my hand over her mouth as her words echo around the deserted bar. "Shhh! Keep your voice down, would you?"

When she nods frantically, I remove my hand. Then in a whisper, she says again, *"Oh my God, you did the Sweet Six with Torres?"*

"No, I didn't. But he mentioned it. And we might have messed around a *little* back in the library, but that was it. I honestly wasn't even sure if it was a real thing. I thought he might be teasing me."

"Oh no. It's a real thing. Trust me. I've still only knocked off one myself, but I always planned . . ." She trails off. "Never mind. It's—that was something—not really in the game plan anymore."

I have a feeling her sudden silence connects with all that stupid talk from back at the game. I shouldn't push. I pride myself on not being a pushy person, actually. But I can't help asking, "Why?"

She shrugs. "It's complicated. Everything is so fucking complicated."

I nod, and eat another mozzarella stick while she fiddles with her silverware.

"I wish I could make a list," she says. "I wish my brain worked that way, and I could just decide what I needed and wanted, and I could write it all up in one place. But I don't work that way. Because for everything I want, there's part of me that doesn't want it. For everything I think, something in me disagrees. I'm like a pair of magnets in one body, and . . . I'm a mess, Nell. A god-awful mess."

"To messes," I say, holding up the vodka cranberry Stella ordered me. "May they always get cleaned up."

"To messes," she agrees. "And karaoke and keg stands and beer pong and all-nighters."

I DON'T LIKE it, but under Stella's direction we end up at Torres's house. I guess technically, it's not only his house, but that's the only way I can think of it.

"It's going to be fine," she tells me. "I'd take you to a different party, but the only ones I know of are frat things, and Dallas and I have a deal that we don't go to that kind of thing alone. This is the only place I knew of to get you your keg stand and beer pong. And trust me, the guys will be so busy celebrating their win that we won't have any trouble dodging Teo. I got your back. I promise."

"Okay, but we do the beer pong and the keg stand, and then we go do something else. I don't want to hang out any longer than necessary."

"Deal."

The party is about the same size as the one on Halloween, but it doesn't feel quite as intimidating. On Halloween, I'd only stayed in the kitchen for a little while before retreating outside, and I spent the rest of the time . . . well.

Anyway, it's crowded as we move through the living room, and I don't see Torres anywhere. It's dim and loud, and he might not even notice me if he walked right past me. Slowly, I begin to relax.

"I think we should do the beer pong first," I say. "Unlike the keg stand, it requires a certain degree of skill. I'd rather be fresh for it."

Stella laughs. "You're competitive, aren't you?"

"Incredibly."

"I guess it's good for you then that I am a master at beer pong." She mimics throwing a Ping-Pong ball and says, "I've got a light touch."

We find the beer-pong setup in a room toward the back of the house just off the living room. Stella hesitates at the door, shooting me a look. "Oh, come on," I say. "Let's get this over with."

"Okay. If you're fine with it, I got you."

I don't know why she's so tentative all of a sudden, but I'm just eager to play the game, finish my list, and get out of here. The two of us call dibs on the next game and wait our turn. I survey the room while the current game wraps up. There's a bed pushed into a far corner, and a few girls are piled on top of it talking.

The Ping-Pong table is situated in middle of the room, and there's a group of about seven people hanging around it. A small enough group to manage most of the nervousness I'm feeling about playing. I already knew all the rules (thank you, Internet research). Logically, it seemed like a piece of cake. But since I've never played, it was impossible to know the weight of the ball and how much force I'd have to put behind it.

When it's Stella's and my turn, we're up against two guys. Stella knows one of them. He's tall and lanky with a beanie pulled over a mop of longish hair. He smiles at Stella and lifts his chin in a hello to me.

"Ladies first," Beanie Boy says.

Stella looks at me and holds out a white Ping-Pong ball. I take it, weighing the thing in my hand. It's light. So light the air circulating from the ceiling fan overhead would be enough to blow it off course. I miss the first time out, but luckily the other team misses, too, so we're safe from having to drink anything yet.

Stella sinks her first shot on the next round and winks at me. "Told you. I'm a pro."

When the guys again fail to sink the ball in one of our cups, the one in the beanie picks up the cup Stella's ball had landed in, and he downs it in a few long swallows.

On my next turn, I take a breath, analyzing my last throw and adjusting my technique in my head. It's all physics really. Force. Gravity. Arc. I shake out my shoulders, let out that breath, and send the ball flying. It plops into the cup right at the top of the other team's pyramid.

Stella cheers, and we high-five, and even though the guys sink their shot, too, so neither of us has to drink, I still feel good.

We don't miss a single shot for the rest of the game, and by the time I sink the ball into the other team's last cup, the small group in the room has grown to a crowd, and the cheer they let out makes me jump in surprise.

Stella squeezes me into a hug and cries, "Oh my God. You have to be my beer-pong partner forever. No one will ever beat us." She pulls away.

The guys we beat have come around the table, and they congratulate us. The one in the beanie gives me a hug. "Impressive game," he says.

Stella claps and yells, "Who's next? We'll take on anybody!"

"I'll take that challenge!"

My back locks up one vertebra at a time. I can't see him. But I know that voice. I can't forget it.

"Nell, do you wanna?" Stella gestures toward the bedroom door at the same time that Torres steps into view.

"No," I say, placing a hand on her arm. "It's okay."

Torres leans on the other side of the table, and he's so big, his arms so long, that he grips both sides of the table easily. His gaze meets mine, and he raises an eyebrow. "So that was your *first* time playing beer pong?"

There's an edge to his voice that I don't like. It makes it hard for me to swallow, and I've got goose bumps even though it's warm in the crowded room. "It was."

"Beginner's luck, I say."

Stella scoffs. "You wish, Teo. She's a natural."

He smiles, and holy crap, it hurts. It hurts that he can stand there like nothing's changed, like I'm just another girl for him to tease. And the fact that it hurts makes me *furious*.

"Are we going to play or what?" I ask.

"Who's on your team?" Stella asks Torres.

"Oh, I think Ryan is around here somewhere. He'll do."

It's Stella who stiffens this time. The blond guy with curly hair that I always see around her steps up beside Torres. His lips are pressed together as he looks across the table at Stella, and I can't read his expression at all.

A few beats of tense silence pass before Stella claps her hands. "Let's get to it, then."

I add, "You guys can go first."

Torres shakes his head. "Oh no, we'll decide this the official way. With the eyes."

My brows furrow. I don't remember seeing this in the set of rules that I read online.

"What's that?" I ask.

He picks up a ball and gestures for me to do the same. "First throw is decided by eyes. One person from each team gets a ball, and you have to stare into your opponent's eyes and toss the ball without watching where you aim. First one to make a cup goes first."

"You've got to be kidding me. If you think I'm going to believe—"

Stella cuts me off. "It's true." I shut up fast. "I'll do it. Give me the ball."

"No." Torres plants a firm hand on the table, and the whole thing sways slightly under the pressure. "Nell and I are doing this."

I don't get why he's being this way, why he's so tense and

pushy. I mean . . . I get that I probably shouldn't have come to his party. This is his territory, and I'm trespassing. But he could have just asked me to leave. He could have avoided me. Anything but this.

"Fine," I say, and I hate that my voice is quiet. I roll the ball between my fingers and step to the center of the table. I take a deep breath and face him. His eyes are dark, but more than that, the look he wears is dark.

Shit. He's mad. Really mad. I should just leave. Screw beer pong and keg stands and my list. This is a bad idea.

But I don't look away. My gaze stays locked on his.

Ryan puts a hand on his shoulder and says, "Sure you're up for this, man? You should probably—"

"Oh, I'm up for it."

He shoots me a cocky grin, and I nearly bolt. Nearly.

I'm not scared of him. I'm not scared of this party or fitting in or being different. I'm not even scared of being scared. I've got this.

"You ready?" I ask.

"On the count of three," he says.

Then he proceeds to give the slowest count in the history of the universe. I swallow because his eyes are piercing. There's no other word for it. And I've never been good at looking him in the eye. I remember that night in the pickup truck when he let me close my eyes so I didn't have to, and I very nearly give in to the impulse to close them now. But I stay steady, and when he says three, I toss the ball, doing my best to find the rhythm that I'd felt in the last game.

Both our throws end up in cups, so now it's up to Stella and Ryan to decide.

We end up forfeiting first toss when Stella breaks eye contact with Ryan as she throws. It's a closer game than our last one. Torres and Ryan are stronger opponents, and their presence seems to have put both me and Stella off our games.

When Torres sinks a shot and mine bounces off the rim of a cup and misses, I have to drink my first beer of the night. It tastes just as bad as I remember, and I have to close my eyes and force myself to chug it quickly. When I set the empty cup on the table, Torres's expression is drawn in dark edges, and I think he's somehow even angrier at me than he was before. Which makes no sense because it's *his* fault that I had to drink.

Gah. Men.

The game stretches on longer and longer, and the room is now packed full of people. Tension that's about more than just competition spreads taut between us, and by the time we get it down to one cup on each side, my nerves are frayed. It's just a game, but it feels bigger than that. As if we've all got something on the line. Pride, I guess. Our remaining cup is directly in front of me, and theirs is in front of Ryan.

Torres steps up to take his shot, but his eyes find me instead of the cup. I wait for him to look away, but he doesn't. He keeps his eyes on me as he tosses the ball, and it hits the rim of the cup and bounces off.

This is my chance. With his miss, I could end the game if I throw the ball into their last cup.

I close my eyes. I've had to down three cups of beer in all. They weren't very full, so I think I'm still fine, but I also don't want to be overconfident. I blow out a breath and focus in on that cup. I think about the trajectory I want, how soft I want my throw so it's more likely to bounce into, rather than away from, the cup if it hits the rim, then I let go.

It falls perfectly into the cup, and Stella throws her arms around my neck at the same time as our audience goes crazy.

My eyes pass briefly over Torres, and I could swear he's smiling, but I don't let myself look back to check.

"Keg stand, and then leave," I tell Stella.

She nods, and while she tells the crowd that we're done for the night, I start making my way to the door. Stella's small hand grips my elbow a moment later. "You okay?"

I nod. "Yep. I just want to do this and get out of here."

"The keg's usually in the backyard. Come on."

I resist the urge to look back over my shoulder. I'm hoping Torres won't follow. Stella told everyone we were done for the night, so maybe he'll leave me alone if he thinks I'm leaving. Even so, I walk a little faster. There were a lot of people in that room, and even if he does follow me, I have every intention of being outside and out of sight before he can catch up to me.

Chapter 28

Mateo

F uck . . ." She's long gone when I finally push my way out of my room. I spin, scanning the party for her dark hair, her curvy form. "*Fuck.*"

It had been such a shock to walk into my room and see her there. She'd looked vibrant and confident and unbelievably sexy. And everybody was watching her, and that asshole friend of Ryan's with the beanie hugged her, and it took all my self-control not to suffocate him with that beanie.

I hadn't had any intention of partying tonight. I was coming into my room to drop off my bag, and then I was going to go to Nell's apartment. And by some miracle that I still didn't understand, she was already here.

What did that mean?

She certainly wasn't here at the house to see me. The way she'd tensed up when I volunteered to play told me that. But why would she come here if she didn't want to see me? Was it to rub my face in the fact that she's just fine, and I can't walk or talk or do fucking anything without thinking of her? Because she sure as hell looked like she was doing just fine without me.

I knew she'd gained a lot of confidence and was more comfortable in her skin than when we first met, but I still never would have expected to find her completely at ease playing beer pong at a party like this.

God, I'd spent the whole damn football game thinking about her, aching to go after her. I thought about her as the team's trainer examined me on the sidelines and went through all our concussion protocols. I'd thought of her when Coach said he'd rather not chance sending me back into the game. She'd been the only thing that kept me sane on the sidelines as we traded points with the opposing team. Our defense had an off game, and our opponent's wasn't particularly strong to begin with, so it ended up becoming about who could score the most points.

And in a game like that, you're never safe. Even when you're ahead, things can turn around so fast. I paced and paced and paced, and I thought of her. I planned out what I was going to say to her. During halftime, I grabbed a spiral from my bag and wrote it down. Then time ran out, and we won, and all I could think about was talking to her. But Coach wanted to talk after the game, check in on how I was doing, and give me the nonabbreviated version of the lecture he gave me on the field. And all that fucking time that I'd been sitting in his office, she was here in my house. She's still here somewhere . . . unless she's already left.

I hear cheering and clapping in the backyard, and follow the pull in my gut to the door. When I walk out onto the back porch, I catch sight of her immediately, hands balanced on top of the keg, and her perfect fucking legs straight up in the air. Stella stands beside her, but she isn't tall enough to keep a hold on her, so some other dude I don't recognize has his hands around her ankles, holding her up.

I see red.

It's bad enough that she's in my house, and all these other people are here, so I can't just grab her and devour that damn pouty mouth of hers. But no one else touches her. No one. Jesus, I'd take a concussion over this any day.

I fly down the stairs at the same time as she stops drinking and the guy starts lowering her feet toward the ground. She's laughing, and her long hair is wild and twisted over her face. She pulls it away so she can see, and while she does it, Keg-Stand Guy keeps a hand on her lower back like he needs to steady her.

I march over to them and grip both her shoulders to spin her away from him.

"What the fuck, man?" he calls at my back.

But now I've got my hands on her. A few locks of hair are caught between my fingers and her shoulders, and I just want to bury my fingers in those thick tresses.

"What are you doing?" Nell asks.

She's breathing heavy, probably from being upside down and chugging beer, which she doesn't even like. *Damn it,* everything about this night is pissing me off.

"That's two more firsts tonight," I growl.

She tries to pull away, but I tighten my grip.

"Stella and I were just about to leave. We are leaving. Now."

"Oh no. Not yet, girl genius. You and I need to talk."

Maybe she's all good. Maybe I'll be making a complete fool of myself in a matter of moments, but I've got to do it. I force myself to let go of her shoulders and reach down to take her hand.

"Come with me."

"But—I—"

"Nell? You okay?" Stella asks from nearby.

"I just want to talk. Then you can come back out here to Stella. You can do whatever you want."

She worries her bottom lip between her teeth, and I fight off a groan. "It's okay, Stella."

Everyone outside is watching us. I can't just take Nell over to a quiet spot in the yard, not like this. So I squeeze her hand and lead her up the stairs and back inside. We pass through the living room, where the music is thumping to a fast beat, and I lead her back toward my room. There's not as many people inside as there were when we were playing beer pong, but it's not empty, which is what I want.

"Everybody out! I need the room."

"Come on, man." It's Keyon, a true freshman running back, and he's holding a Ping-Pong ball, ready to throw. "You said we could play."

"I know. I'm sorry. But now you can't, so get out."

I know my voice is stern, and I probably seem like the biggest asshole around, but I don't care. The people grumble as they leave, and Nell pulls her hand out of mine to retreat to the far side of the room. The longer it takes for people to leave, the more pressure builds in my head that has nothing to do with my recent injury. Two girls on my bed are the last to leave, and they linger at the door, looking at me.

One look at my hard face, though, and they disappear. I shut the door, and with my back still to Nell, I take a deep, fortifying breath.

I turn, and take in the red plastic cups scattered around the room, which looks like a damn tornado has moved through it.

"Sorry about that. The Ping-Pong table is mine, so whenever we have parties, I let people use my room to play."

"You didn't have to kick them out for me," she says

"If I hadn't, you would have disappeared without saying another word to me, right?"

She shrugs in answer.

I cross to the table and start stacking empty cups just so I'll have something to do with my hands. I've been thinking about talking to Nell all day, but now that she's here, I don't know how to start.

I can't screw this up.

When I go too long without talking, she says, "Listen, I'm sorry about showing up like this. Stella and I were just planning to get in, check a couple things off my list, and be on our way."

That snaps me out of it. "She knows about your list?"

She's leaning against my far wall, a few feet to the left of my bed, and the sight is messing with my head. Especially because her hands are pressed up against the wall behind her like she needs it to keep her from falling.

"I told her today. We're going to finish tonight. In fact, I've just got one item left."

"What is it?" I ask, and she hesitates. "Come on, you already cheated me out of two firsts today, at least tell me this."

If it's something sexual . . . if she's planning on checking it off without me . . . *Fuck.*

"I didn't cheat you out of anything. They're *my* firsts."

Before I know what I'm doing, I'm crossing the room and planting my hands on the wall right beside her head, caging her in. She sucks in a breath, like she's trying to take up less space so we won't touch.

"We've covered this before. I called those firsts. You were supposed to do them with me."

"Oh my God, do you hear yourself?" She tries to shove me away, but I don't budge. "The world does not revolve around you, Mateo Torres."

"Oh, so first I was a puppet, now I think the world revolves around me."

"You don't get to *call* my firsts. They're mine. And why should I let you be first in anything when I'm just a second for you? It's not fun being second choice, is it?"

She pushes on me again, but I reach up and grab her wrists, holding her hands on my chest. "You're not my second choice, Nell."

"My bad. I forgot about football. I guess that really does make me third, doesn't it? Excuse the mistake in my math."

"Nell," I growl.

"I'm glad to see you're doing okay, though. You know, silly girl that I am, I actually came to your football game today."

That rattles me. "You were there?"

"I was. But I left before the game started. I just didn't feel like having to endure hours of watching you endanger yourself, to watch you put a sport above me, above yourself, above everything."

"I didn't."

"You can justify it however you want, but I don't want to listen to it."

"Nell." I drop her wrists to clasp her cheeks and force her eyes up to mine. "I didn't play."

She frowns, and that indentation between her brows pops up, and she lifts her chin stubbornly. "I saw you. You were in your uniform. Warming up. You were going to play."

"I was going to, yeah. I had planned to play, and then as soon as the game was over, I was going to come find you. But then I realized that I couldn't expect you to listen to what I had to say if I wasn't willing to listen to what you said. That fight . . ." I shake my head and drop my hands from her face. Taking a step back, I say, "It was my fault. I wasn't really listening to you. I was hearing what I wanted to hear. Things between us were getting real, fast. And it scared me. And then you were trying to tell me to be realistic about playing with a concussion, but I just heard Lina telling me to be realistic about football. About my dreams."

Nell crosses her hands over her chest, and with her chin tilted up, she looks strangely vulnerable despite the fire in her eyes.

"So I have her to thank for why we got together, and why we broke up."

"No." I shake my head, fighting the urge to press her against the wall again. This would be so much easier if I could just kiss her, and that kiss could tell her all the things I'm doing such a shitty job of getting out of my mouth. "It's not like that. You might have reminded me of Lina in the beginning, but not anymore. And what we have, what I feel, it's not because you're like her. It's because you're *not*. I should have known that you would never say that kind of thing, but that word . . . *'realistic'* . . . it's some kind of trigger for me. And all I could think was that you were going to end it, just like she did, because you're so much better than me, Nell. And I don't fucking deserve you. But that doesn't mean I'll ever stop wanting you." I do cross to her then because I need to touch her, have to. I run my knuckles over her cheek, and her eyes flick down to the floor. "I didn't play today. I was on the field for a handful of seconds before I walked off and told Coach Cole everything. I didn't play, and I should have listened to you, and I'm sorry. I'm so fucking sorry, Nell."

My voice is raspy by the time I finish, and I'm barely fighting off all the emotions clamoring for control.

When her eyes don't lift to mine, I start to panic. I back away and pace along the length of the Ping-Pong table for a few moments, dragging my nails over my shorn head. I cross to the closet where I'd deposited my bag as soon as I came into my room and saw Nell. I unzip my duffel, and the spiral is lying there on top of my clothes and shoes and other junk. I pick it up and turn back to her.

"Ah, hell. I'm not good at this kind of thing, Nell. I know how to joke and flirt and screw around, but I haven't had much practice being serious in a while. I don't know how to get the words out, how to find the right ones. Not when there's so much I want to say, and so many ways I could screw it up. I'm sorry that I yelled at you and started that stupid fight. I'm sorry that I didn't listen about the concussion. And I'm sorry I didn't tell you about Lina. But mostly, I'm sorry that I let you go at all. I should have stopped you when you walked away or pulled you into my lap again in my truck or followed you back into your apartment. Anything but what I did."

She lifts her chin, not quite to its normal haughty heights, but enough that I can tell she's still holding back.

"Okay," she answers.

"Okay?"

"Yes, okay. I accept your apology."

But she doesn't look like it. I'd thought if she accepted my apology, we'd be kissing by now. Why aren't we kissing now?

"Damn it. I'm fucking this up, aren't I? Just . . . read this, okay? I wrote it during the game, and it says it better than I can."

I shove the spiral at her, no finesse, no charm, just fear and panic and desperation. She opens it to the first page, and her eyebrows furrow.

"Oh, not that one. That's the only notes I ever took in my Spanish class. It starts on the next page. Sorry."

She flips the page, and I can't help but feel like she's holding my heart in her hands, and it's just as fragile as the paper between her fingers, just as easy to tear in two.

Chapter 29

Nell's To-Do List

- *Yeah . . . I've got nothing.*

His handwriting is messy. Slanted and hurried, and it's nearly as hard to decipher as he is. My hands are shaky, and my heart won't work properly no matter how many calming breaths I take.

Ways to Prove that you love Nell De Luca

1. *Tell her. Every day. Three times a day. As many times as it takes.*
2. *Never choose anything else over her. Not football. Not your own stubbornness. Nothing.*
3. *Be there whether she wants to go skinny-dipping or wants to study. Make sure she knows that she's the adventure, not anything else.*
4. *Always tell her how amazing her food is (okay . . . that*

one is partly for you, too, because it means you get to keep eating her food).

5. Give her the best sex of her life (also works out pretty well for you).

6. Teach her whatever she wants to know, and learn from her, too. She's a fucking genius.

7. Tell her she's a fucking genius. All the time. When she doubts it and when she doesn't. Just tell her.

8. Never walk away after a fight. Don't. Fucking. Do it.

9. Prove you love her (preferably in bed, but that's optional) once a day. Three times a day. As many times as it takes.

10. Be worthy of her. Not by playing football or pretending to be something you're not. By being the man she makes you feel like you are. Strong and smart and kind and so damn lucky to have her.

I don't know whether to cry or laugh or both as I read his words. And the fist around my heart is shaking, or maybe that's just me. I look up at him, and he has his hand tucked behind his head, watching me from over by the Ping-Pong table. Longing and fear are etched all over his face. He's terrified of what I'll say.

And he didn't play today, and he wrote me a list, and he says he *loves* me. Or he wrote it anyway.

"Well," I say, my voice scratchy with pent-up tears. I take a few steps toward him. "Let's hear number one, then."

He crosses to me in two strides and pulls me up into his arms.

His muscles wind tight around my middle, and he presses his forehead into mine like he can't get close enough. "I love you. I'm so sorry, Nell. You might have reminded me of Lina in the beginning, but what I feel for you is so much bigger than that. So much better. I love you. You're a fucking genius. I love you."

"I love you, too." The words shake coming out of my mouth, so I repeat them. More for me, really, than him. I love him. This is not beyond me. This feeling, the way something in me feels too big for my body, the need to bring him closer and closer . . . that's normal. *I'm* normal.

He turns and sits me right on the edge of the Ping-Pong table beside us, and covers my mouth with his.

Okay, maybe we're not entirely normal. But I like our kind of normal.

His mouth pushes and pulls and dances with mine, and he promises against my lips, "As many times as it takes. You're not gonna doubt me, sweetheart. I'll make sure there's no room for doubt, not when I'm done."

I drag my hands over his back, tracing the muscles, reminding myself that he's here. That this is real. He drops his face into the crook of my neck and groans. His big hands run the length of my thighs, to my knees, and then back to the curve of my behind. He cups me there, squeezing and pulling until I'm right at the very edge of the table, and then he presses his hips into mine.

His hands glide up to grip the bottom of my shirt, and he starts tugging it up.

"Mateo, there are people outside. A lot of people."

He kisses me hard, driving his tongue between my lips a few times before he says, "Don't care."

"Mateo—"

"Keep saying my name. It's only going to make me more determined to have you."

He gives my shirt another tug, and then he's pulling it up and over my head. He groans and bends farther to drag his lips over the swells of my cleavage. I fight to keep him from distracting me, but it's hard, especially when he tugs down one cup on my bra and sucks the tip of my breast into his mouth. My back arches involuntarily, and I clutch the back of his head.

"You kicked all those people out. If we don't open the door soon, everyone is going to know what's happening in here."

"Good. I want them to know." He slides my bra straps down to my elbows and peels both cups down. His fingers dance over the newly revealed skin, stroking softly enough that it tickles and my skin tightens, and oh God, who knew that light, simple touch would go straight to my sex? "I nearly went crazy when I saw that guy holding your ankles outside. If I hadn't been so worried about getting you alone, I would have tackled him."

"That would not have been smart. Your concussion—"

"You can be the smart one in this relationship. I'll settle for being the one that gets to worship these." He cups both of my breasts, lifting and kneading. He replaces one hand with his mouth and skims down my stomach to flick open the button on my jeans. "I'll settle for being the one who gets to peel these off of you. You don't know how badly I want to touch you. I need it."

I want to resist. It's barbaric and embarrassing to do this with everyone outside. But he's not the only one who needs to touch.

"We have to be quiet," I say. "It's bad enough that they know I'm in here. I don't want them to *hear* it, too."

"I'll keep your mouth occupied," he promises.

My pulse is so wild that I can feel it everywhere. And his words make me think of his promise to teach me whatever I want to know, how to use my mouth on him included. I try to clench my legs against the ache, but his position between them stops the impulse.

"Not that," he says, and I frown.

"Why not?"

"I fucked up, Nell. Let me apologize. Tonight is about you. Let me take care of you."

"I should have given you the benefit of the doubt. I should have let you explain. But I was so ready to believe that I'm not made for this kind of thing. That I'm not made for love. I'm just as much at fault here."

"No. You're not."

"I don't just want to let you take care of me. I need to be an active participant in this." I reach a hand down between us and ghost my fingers over the tented front of his sweatpants. "I want to feel like I'm made for this. For you."

I drag my fingers over him a little more surely, and he groans.

"There are probably guys out there who are good enough to turn that kind of offer down." He hooks his hand around the nape of my neck and pulls my mouth up to his. "I'm not one of them."

I push him back, and with his hands on my hips, I slip off the table.

"So this is your room?" I say as we shuffle toward his bed.

"This is it. Get used to it. Because you're not getting out of it until morning. Maybe not even then."

I nudge him backward until he sits on the bed. He leans over to pull off his shoes and socks. Before I can climb up next to him, he hooks his fingers into the open band of my jeans and tugs me forward. My bra is still trapped awkwardly around my waist, and I reach around to unhook it while he lowers my zipper.

I expect him to push my jeans off my hip, but he surprises me by dragging my underwear along at the same time. In seconds, I'm standing before him naked, while, except for his shoes and socks, he's still completely clothed.

I clutch his shirt, and he helps me pull it up over his head. The fabric catches on his broad shoulders, and I suck in a breath at the sight.

He hooks an arm around my waist and pulls until I'm standing between his knees, my belly pressed against his chest. His face is level with my chest, and he drags his cheek over the curve of my breast. "I like the idea of you being made for me."

The short hair on his head tickles my palm as I hold him to me. "You do?"

"I like it so damn much, sweetheart. This . . ." His hands sweep over my backside, then grip tight. "Made for my hands. Makes me feel incredibly lucky."

I laugh and press at his shoulder, and reluctantly he lets go to scoot back on the bed. I climb up on my knees, and he groans before I ever even touch him.

"You don't have a headache?" I ask.

"No."

I crawl a little closer and prop my hands up on either side of his hips.

"Still experiencing blurred vision?"

"No."

I lean down toward the trail of hair that descends from his belly button and place a kiss right beside it.

"Sensitivity?" I ask, not moving away from his abdomen.

He growls, "Not to light and sound, no. Symptoms are gone, Nell. I promise."

"Hmm," I say, and draw a finger along the band on his sweatpants. His ab muscles clench under the touch, and I smile. "This is going to be fun for me."

"You're killing me, you know that?"

"What?"

"That you want to—that you're so fucking eager . . ."

He hisses out a breath when I hook my fingers under his waistband. I take a cue from him and pull his sweats and underwear down in one movement, and his erection springs free, thick and long and dark.

I start with touching him, matching the strength and speed he'd taught me that one time in the shower.

"Ah," he breathes, tilting his hips up toward me.

"Tell me what to do."

He wets his lips and takes a ragged breath before instructing, "Lick the tip."

I do as he says, and I can't even put into words how gratifying his groan is. He directs me through the first couple of movements, telling me where he's sensitive, where to pay special attention, but by the time I take him into my mouth, he's barely getting out one-word replies.

For someone who struggles with thinking too much during sex, this is the perfect way to connect for me. When I can focus on him, on his reactions, I'm free to analyze and catalog my observations, and repeat the moves that get the best reaction. It's a challenge, and even though I don't know what I'm doing, I take pleasure in learning.

And it makes me feel like we're in this together. Like I'm essential, rather than just a convenient replacement. It's the final thing I need to push the thoughts of his ex out of my head, because it's my name he says between groans. It's my cheek he touches, soft and sweet, and at odds with the raw act we're in the middle of.

"Ah, God. Nell . . . God, it's not right that you're so good at this already. Stop. I don't want to come like this. Not tonight."

He guides my head, pulling me away and pushing me back against his bed so he can climb over me. While I settle into the pillows, he reaches into the drawer of his nightstand for a condom.

I watch him put it on, no less fascinated this time than I was the last despite how much better I now know that part of him. He pushes my legs wide and lowers himself onto me. He doesn't enter me, not yet. He just presses his hips into mine and leans down close.

He strokes his thumb over my bottom lip and says, "Fucking made for me."

I lift my hips up into his, and just when he's shifted and is about to push inside, there come three loud knocks on the door.

I panic. "Did you lock the door?" His head drops down to my collarbone, and he groans. "You didn't lock the door. Are you serious?"

Hey says, "I didn't want you to feel like I was trying to trap you in here."

I laugh then, even through my panic. "You caveman-dragged me in here, kicked everyone out, pinned me to the wall a few times, but you didn't want me to feel trapped."

He's about to reply when the knock comes again. "Guys? It's Stella."

I cover my mouth so I don't laugh, and Mateo smothers a curse against my breast.

"I'm not coming in, so don't worry."

"Thank God," he growls.

Stella continues: "Sorry for this weirdness. I just wanted to tell Nell that I'm leaving, and I'm officially passing off the last item on the list into your apparently very capable hands, Torres."

"Bye, Stella," I call out, my voice breathier than I would like. "Thank you for today!"

When we don't hear anything for several long seconds, we assume she's gone, and Mateo climbs off the bed to lock the door. I blush when he walks back toward me, and I can see all of his naked form on display.

He vaults up onto the bed, practically leaping on top of me. He hovers over me on all fours, before leaning down to brush his lips against mine.

"What is this about my very capable hands?"

Oh God, so much blushing.

"You're the one who made me add 'best orgasm of my life' to the list. It's your fault really."

"You told her about that?"

"Not specifics, no. She just asked if it was true."

"And you said yes?"

I lift my arms around him, laying my forearms along his shoulders. I inch up to press a kiss to the middle of his chest. "Best of my life."

"And the last item on the list?"

I grin. "Pull an all-nighter. It's all I've got left. Think you could help me with that?"

He lowers his hard body down on mine, and with excruciating slowness begins to push inside me. "Will that be a first for you? This all-nighter."

I bite my lips against a moan, still entirely too conscious of the people just outside the door. "It is."

He leans down and kisses me, his lips soft as he seats himself all the way inside me. I rock up into him, and swallow his groan.

"I want it. That first. All of them. As many all-nighters as you'll give me."

Then he kisses me, and I love him.

I love him.

I love him.

Mateo

The semester ends quicker than either of us wants it to. Classes end first, then exams, then it's graduation day.

Watching Nell graduate is a strange sensation. I'm happy for her. Fucking impressed with how much she's accomplished already. Terrified of what comes next. But we're making plans.

Nell likes to do that, and I'm just glad that I get to be a part of hers.

I've got her for one more semester for sure. She'll be busy with her job as a research assistant, but not quite as busy as she'd been with all her classes and assignments. And since it'll be the off-season for football, there will be less pressure for me, too.

We're both doing Christmas with our families, but I've got the bowl game (the first for Rusk in over a decade) a few days after that. Then we're holing up together somewhere and not coming out until New Year's.

It's not perfect. Nell still sometimes stresses about the future, but she's excited about her research job. She hasn't mentioned any doubts lately, and I think she's finally settling into the idea of her future.

I like to think I had something to do with that. Because I know she helps calm me. There are things we don't know, things we can't know, about my career and hers, but I believe we can make it work.

She and I, we were *made* to work.

Nell's To-Do List

(With help from Mateo)

✓ -Turn in grad school applications.
✓ -Find grad schools close to Rusk.
✓ -Graduate.
✓ -Celebrate with Mateo.
✓ -Celebrate A LOT with Mateo.
✓ -Book travel for the Rusk bowl game.
    -When they win, celebrate with friends.
    ^^^ But mostly with Mateo.

    -Give Mateo his Christmas present.
        ^^^ I like the sound of this. I hope I get to unwrap
          several things.

    -Get your Christmas present from Mateo.
    ^^^ This sounds interesting.
    ^^^ Oh, it is. VERY interesting.
        ^^^ P.S. I love you.
        ^^^ P.P.S. You're a fucking genius.

Acknowledgments

I thought this would get easier as I wrote more books. But this is the ninth time I've had to find the words to express all my gratitude, and it is still so difficult to do justice to the joy and appreciation I feel.

I would never get a single book finished without the support of my family. It feels like a miracle every time I finish one, but really it's you guys that are the miracle. I am blessed to have you. To love you. To be loved by you.

I've been so honored the last few years to work with some truly amazing professionals in this business. Amanda, Jessie, Molly, Pam, and all the other amazing people at Harper who help get my books into the hands of readers—thank you. Suzie, Kathleen, and all the other New Leaf Ninjas—I adore you all. Thanks for being on my team. KP Simmon—I am so glad to have you in my life. And my career.

Lindsay—you were the hero of this book. You loved it when

I was struggling. You gave me confidence (as you always seem to do). You get me, and there will never be a thank-you big enough for that (or all the hundreds of other things you do for me).

Bethany . . . I adore you. (But no . . . I'm still not naming every character Bethany. Not gonna happen).

To my amazing and incomparable Carmcats: Stephanie Gibson, Kim Baker, Megan Gallt, Amber Noffke, Ethan Gregory, Betsy Gehring, Krista Davis, Kaitlan Heaton, Alana Rock, Yvette Cervera, Christine @IHeartBigBooks, Yesi Cavazos, Andy Estrada, Beth Lattanzi, Momo Xiong, Katie Anderson, Vangelina Osteguin (thanks for lending me your major *hugs*), Brooke DelVecchio, Melody & Betsy @BookCrastinators, Lori Wilt, Ashley Amsbaugh, Whitney B. Swain, Christina Marie, Kristen Chandler, Lenore Mullican, Brittany Berger, Katie Stutz, Kerry-Ann, Wendi Galbreath, and Alyssa Kawata. I am so beyond lucky to have your support. You're all crazy talented and dedicated and compassionate, and you make my day brighter by being in it. I love you guys.

To Antonella in Houston for letting me borrow your name. You were one of the sweetest readers I've ever met, and I was proud to use you as Nell's namesake.

And for every reader who's taken a shot on me and my books—thank you. Thank you so much. I am filled to overflowing with love every time I get a message or an email or a tweet or a review for these books, especially when you fall just as hard for these characters as I do. I never would have thought a series about Texas football could grow to mean so much to me. Like Dallas, it's always been a love/hate relationship for me. But I have loved getting lost in the world of these books and getting to know these characters better. They are so very close to my heart. Thank you for helping me to give them a life outside my head.

ALL BROKE DOWN

A Rusk University Novel

Dylan fights for lost causes. Probably because she used to be one.

Environmental issues, civil rights, education—you name it, she's probably been involved in a protest. When her latest cause lands her in jail for a few hours, she meets Silas Moore. He's in for a different kind of fighting. And though he's arrogant and not at all her type, she can't help being fascinated with him.

Yet another lost cause.

Football and trouble are the only things that have ever come naturally to Silas. And it's trouble that lands him in a cell next to do-gooder Dylan. He's met girls like her before—fixers, he calls them, desperate to heal the damage and make him into their ideal boyfriend. But he doesn't think he's broken, and he definitely doesn't need a girlfriend trying to change him. Until, that is, his anger issues and rash decisions threaten the only thing he really cares about, his spot on the Rusk University football team.

Dylan might just be the perfect girl to help.

Because Silas Moore needs some fixing after all.

Available Now